A SEAL'S DESIRE

By Cora Seton

Print Edition
Published by One Acre Press

Author's Note

A SEAL's Desire is the eighth volume in the SEALs of Chance Creek series, set in the fictional town of Chance Creek, Montana. To find out more about Greg, Renata, Boone, Clay, Jericho, Walker and the other inhabitants of Base Camp, look for the rest of the books in the series, including:

A SEAL's Oath
A SEAL's Vow
A SEAL's Pledge
A SEAL's Consent
A SEAL's Purpose
A SEAL's Resolve
A SEAL's Devotion
A SEAL's Struggle
A SEAL's Triumph

Also, don't miss Cora Seton's other Chance Creek series, the Cowboys of Chance Creek, the Heroes of Chance Creek, and the Brides of Chance Creek

The Cowboys of Chance Creek Series:

The Cowboy Inherits a Bride (Volume 0)
The Cowboy's E-Mail Order Bride (Volume 1)
The Cowboy Wins a Bride (Volume 2)
The Cowboy Imports a Bride (Volume 3)
The Cowgirl Ropes a Billionaire (Volume 4)
The Sheriff Catches a Bride (Volume 5)
The Cowboy Lassos a Bride (Volume 6)

The Cowboy Rescues a Bride (Volume 7)
The Cowboy Earns a Bride (Volume 8)
The Cowboy's Christmas Bride (Volume 9)

The Heroes of Chance Creek Series:

The Navy SEAL's E-Mail Order Bride (Volume 1)
The Soldier's E-Mail Order Bride (Volume 2)
The Marine's E-Mail Order Bride (Volume 3)
The Navy SEAL's Christmas Bride (Volume 4)
The Airman's E-Mail Order Bride (Volume 5)

The Brides of Chance Creek Series:

Issued to the Bride One Navy SEAL
Issued to the Bride One Airman
Issued to the Bride One Sniper
Issued to the Bride One Marine
Issued to the Bride One Soldier

The Turners v. Coopers Series:

The Cowboy's Secret Bride (Volume 1)
The Cowboy's Outlaw Bride (Volume 2)
The Cowboy's Hidden Bride (Volume 3)
The Cowboy's Stolen Bride (Volume 4)
The Cowboy's Forbidden Bride (Volume 5)

Visit Cora's website at www.coraseton.com
Find Cora on Facebook at facebook.com/CoraSeton
Sign up for my newsletter HERE.
www.coraseton.com/sign-up-for-my-newsletter

CHAPTER ONE

Ten years ago, Mayahuay, Peru…

GREG DEVON THOUGHT he'd seen the worst of what the day could offer until a school bus rolled up and parked less than thirty feet away. He'd been struggling to help erect one of the tents meant to house the survivors straggling down from Colina Blanca, a tiny settlement perched high in the Andes Mountains above Lima, Peru. The bus was as covered with mud and grime as everything else in the area, the misty rain not heavy enough to wash it clean. The roads up from the capital, the direction from which it had arrived, had been in rough shape when he'd made the journey before sunrise, and he doubted conditions had improved since then.

In the middle of the night, back when this drizzle had still been a deluge, a mudslide had wiped out most of Colina Blanca. Rescue operations had been set up here in Mayahuay because the roads beyond it were impassible by vehicles. Now it was well past lunch, and everywhere he looked people had gathered in knots and family groups. Babies crying, overburdened mothers swaying and crooning to them tunelessly, more people arriving now and then from outlying hamlets, all of them soaked, exhausted—

Devastated.

Rumor had it other aid groups were on their way, which was good because the one Greg had latched on to wasn't prepared for a disaster like this. He'd been woken in his dorm room in Lima around four in the morning by running footsteps out in the corridor. Never a heavy sleeper, he'd pulled on a pair of pants, stuck his feet into his hiking boots and a minute later was out on the street. He'd recognized another student who'd come here to Peru for the semester. Both of them were a little older than most of the college kids who came to study abroad, and they'd hit it off. Greg was twenty-three, Brandon twenty-four. They hung out frequently, talking about their future plans.

"What's going on?" he'd asked.

"Mudslide. Big one. It's taken out one village at least. We're going to help dig out."

Greg had piled in a truck with him and a bunch of other students, some he recognized, others he didn't. They'd driven straight up into the hills, the rain sluicing off their vehicle's windows until he began to wonder if they'd have to pull over and swim the rest of the way.

They'd stopped in Mayahuay when they found out it was the end of the road—literally—and Greg and the others were put to work setting up tents and shelters, hauling boxes of supplies and stacking bottles of water for the victims when they arrived.

Those victims started straggling in almost at once, and the snippets of conversation he'd heard—and understood—had left Greg chilled. Hundreds must be dead. More than half the village, maybe. As more people arrived, a sound he'd never heard before pervaded the camp, a low, despairing keening that traced up and down his spine. All around him people were grieving loved ones they knew they'd never see again and homes that were buried under tons of debris.

Midmorning, Brandon had tugged his arm, taken him aside, showed him photos forwarded from the village by one or two workers who'd managed to get through, and Greg began to understand the scope of the damage. They showed a moonscape, a flat plain of mud with only rock outcroppings and tufts of greenery sticking out from it here and there—former hills and trees—everything else now buried under the flow. It was a wonder anyone had made it out and walked the miles down to Mayahuay.

Now Greg grabbed a water bottle, took a swig and watched as the school bus idled. He'd come to Peru for the adventure of it, champing at the bit to expand his horizons after a lifetime in Oregon, first at Greenside, the large agricultural commune outside Portland where he'd grown up, then at Lewis & Clark College, where he'd been studying engineering. Nearly five thousand miles away from the farm that once had comprised his world, Lima represented a break from his childhood. Greg had already decided what he'd do next, just as soon as he had his diploma in his hands. Keep traveling around the world and chase more adventures.

He wasn't going to live a settled, small-town life ever again.

The drizzle tapered off, and tepid sunshine tried to break through the clouds. When the bus's door swung open, Greg was surprised to see a young woman exit. Dressed in crisp black slacks and a snowy white blouse, she had raven-dark hair, a slim build. She wasn't soaked like everyone at the camp. Wasn't even damp. A man exited behind her, dressed more casually in cargo shorts and a T-shirt, portable video camera in hand.

A news crew?

He didn't think so. Several of those had arrived from Lima already, and these two didn't quite look the part. When the woman spoke, her clipped British accent surprised him all over again.

"Get all of this, quick. Set up the shot for the reunion," the woman ordered the man holding the camera.

Reunion? Greg stepped closer, nudged Brandon as he passed him. "Who's in the bus?"

Brandon straightened from his task stacking pallets of water bottles, turned and frowned. "I don't know."

"Where is everyone?" the woman was saying. She turned and looked over the camp again. "What's going on here? Is it some kind of fair?"

Dread twisted Greg's gut at her misreading of the situation. This sure as hell wasn't a fair. Who on earth did she expect to meet here? He watched the woman's gaze light on the huddled groups on the far side of the area in their mud-spattered clothes. The crying babies.

He saw the moment she realized something was wrong—the same moment the first of the remaining passengers got off the bus.

The cameraman, who'd been panning the camp and getting a shot of the line of Red Cross vehicles that had just turned up the road, spun around at the woman's oath. He pointed his video camera at her, then at the bus, where a girl—*a girl in a school uniform*—had just stepped down.

"Mama?" the girl said, scanning the area.

Hell, Greg thought.

"Fuck," Brandon echoed beside him. "Are they from—?" He broke off, but Greg knew exactly what he meant to say. Were they from Colina Blanca? Had they arrived back from somewhere else expecting a welcoming committee here in the next larger town? Perhaps when they'd set up the trip, the charter bus operator had refused to make the run all the way up to their hillside village. Greg wouldn't blame him, given the usual state of the roads that far up in the mountains.

Wouldn't the driver have heard the news, though, and turned back?

Maybe not.

The woman was conferring with Diego Alvarez, the man who had organized the convoy of student volunteers from Lima and taken charge of the disaster aid operation so far. Greg had met Diego at a party just last week hosted for all the foreign exchange students at the university and the men and women who helped organize the exchanges. From the way Diego was gesturing up at Colina Blanca, first pointing, then flattening his hand and making it swoop down like the wall of mud had just hours ago, he was informing her of what had happened.

Greg watched her take it in, her face a mask of shock. She stood still a moment. Behind her, girls kept spilling out of the bus, all in pristine uniforms, ranging in age from five or six to teenagers. Suddenly he knew exactly who they were. He'd seen a news story about the girls from the San Pedro School of Excellence who were celebrating the twenty-year anniversary of the founding of their institution with a trip to the capital. The school had been set up to help female students from this rural area achieve an education that would leave them ready to attend a university, serve in government positions and excel in the private sector, too. The idea was that a generation of highly educated women could help bring this entire rural area out of its depressed circumstances. The girls stood alert, maintaining the decorum they'd been taught.

Two more women stepped off the bus after the last of the girls had scrambled out. One was tall with sharp, hawklike features, her dark eyes quickly taking in the scene. The other was shorter, older, her hair going gray and her round face, which Greg somehow knew was normally wreathed in smiles, was grim. These two had seen at a glance that something was horribly wrong. They conferred in rapid Spanish before the tall one clapped her hands twice and barked an order at the girls.

They lined up immediately in front of the bus.

That was when the first woman, the British one with the cameraman, turned around. Her gaze rested on Greg for only a moment before it slid to the girls, but that moment stopped his breath in his chest. The pain in her eyes pierced him. She'd laid a hand over her heart unconsciously, as if trying to hold in a riot of emotions struggling to break free. She was young. His age, he figured, or a year or two older. She'd heard what had happened in Colina Blanca. Knew what the girls standing next to the bus didn't—yet. That most of their families were probably gone—their homes destroyed—

Greg didn't realize he was moving until he found himself by her side. He took her arm. Steadied her. "Tell them fast," he said. "Make it clean."

She swallowed. Opened her mouth. He could feel the tears in her, but she didn't cry, her attention solely on the students. "Girls," she said in Spanish. Her voice wavered, but she steadied it. "Girls, I have something hard to tell you. Last night in the rain a mudslide was loosed. Colina Blanca was in its path. Many people were hurt. Died. You are safe here, and we will do everything we can to reunite you with your families, but you will have to be patient and very, very brave."

Greg kept close to her through all the long hours of that afternoon, evening, night and into the next morning as Renata Ludlow, as he learned she was named, helped Mayra and Gabriela, the tall and broad-faced women, respectively, keep the girls together, feed them, keep them warm and search through the chaos of the camp for their relatives. Renata worked tirelessly, never looking at him, focused single-mindedly on finding the girls' parents, asking aid worker after aid worker if they'd seen any of the missing adults.

As a new day dawned, the truth sank in. The twenty-three girls who made up the student body of the San Pedro School of Excellence were now orphans. Greg, who until twenty-four hours ago had little on his mind except catching a flight home to Oregon at the end of the semester in time for graduation in June, felt as if he'd donned some kind of robotic exoskeleton overnight, leaving him lumbering and unsure in his own body. It took him some time to recognize that the feeling stemmed from a shift inside him: a restructuring of the framework of his mind.

No longer a carefree boy looking for adventure, his aspirations had hardened overnight into something weightier. This was the work he wanted in the future—work that mattered. He wanted to accomplish things. Change things. Help people. Keep them safe.

Something else—he wanted to share his life with a woman like Renata. Someone who could work so stoically and was so trusted by the girls of the San Pedro school that each of them sought her out at one time or another during the long, dark hours of the night to beg her to find their families and cry in her arms.

A new protectiveness had taken hold of him. A desire to patrol the space around Renata and keep her safe while she tended and comforted the students she obviously cared for so much. He'd learned from listening to the people around them that she was from London, a recent film-school graduate here to do a documentary about the San Pedro school and the girls who attended it. He'd learned little else about Renata so far. Nothing at all from the woman herself, who kept moving, kept searching, refused to give up finding the girls' missing parents.

And that was his problem in a nutshell. Greg was falling in love with Renata.

And she hadn't even noticed he was there.

Present Day, Chance Creek, Montana

IT ALWAYS CAME down to money, Renata Ludlow thought as she gazed out the window at the path that led to Base Camp, the sustainable community where she was directing a reality television of the same name. The path cut across a snowy landscape illuminated by moonlight. *At least we aren't having another blizzard,* she thought with a sigh. Chance Creek was the last place she'd ever expected to end up, and reality television didn't interest her in the slightest, but this is where the money was, and she needed money. Martin Fulsom, the billionaire funding the project, paid her well—very well—but every penny she took in went right back out again, winging its way to Peru.

In moments like these, she wondered what her life would be like if the mudslide that had consumed Colina Blanca had held off just a few more days. If she'd been back in London already, editing the reams of footage she and her cameraman had taken of the girls attending the San Pedro School of Excellence, the disaster still would have broken her heart and she would have sent a donation, plus notes of condolence to the teachers and girls. Maybe she would have kept on donating through the years whenever she'd had money to spare.

She doubted she would have single-handedly taken on financial responsibility for twenty-three children and their two teachers, however.

She hadn't left Peru before the mudslide struck, though, and she'd been there to see the horror dawning on the faces of the girls she'd come to know so well as they realized their families were lost forever. She'd held them as they cried, had searched through the night for officials with lists of the confirmed dead, and had stayed there for nearly another month helping Mayra and Gabriela find a new home for the school—one where the girls could live as well as study—fueled by a fierce need to set things right after seeing them go so horribly wrong.

She'd wanted to stay longer. Maybe forever. To become a parent to those motherless girls. To help—

But Mayra had been adamant: She and Gabriela were there to teach and lead the girls. What they all needed desperately was money.

That was Renata's job.

At twenty-six, securing enough money for the girls, even considering the favorable exchange rate and relatively cheap cost of living in the mountains of Peru, would have been impossible without Martin Fulsom's help. When he'd offered her work, she couldn't refuse.

So here she was ten years later on a ranch in Montana, in the manor, a three-story stone farmhouse that now functioned as a Jane Austen–inspired bed-and-breakfast, watching another of the Navy SEALs who'd come here to build a model sustainable community marry the woman of his dreams. It was her job to make sure the viewing public found every episode of the show documenting their progress fascinating.

Not an easy task. Especially since she'd once had different plans.

When she'd gone to film school, she'd meant to direct movies for the big screen. Massive, complicated productions that would make her audiences forget their problems for a few hours.

She'd been only six when her parents died and she was placed in the foster care system. When Mika and Scott Price took her in, their home had seemed like the safe haven she desperately needed. They'd certainly done their best to teach a lost little girl to love again. Bit by bit, she'd trusted Mika and Scott with her heart, and by the time she was eight she had adjusted to her new life, new family, new school and friends.

She still remembered the day the three of them had gone to the bank to open a savings account just for her.

"For university," Scott had said. "We'll put some money in every year, and you'll be all set by the time you go."

Two years later, Scott was gone, felled by a heart attack at thirty-nine.

"I'm so sorry," Mika said the day the social worker

came to take Renata away again. "I just… can't."

In her next placement, Renata made sure not to open her heart. Her new foster parents didn't seem to notice. The following placement was at a group home. In the one after that, the couple's marriage was falling apart. She kept her head down and spent most of her time in the room she shared with their young daughter, Patricia, reassuring her while her parents screamed at each other in their bedroom down the hall. Renata was thirteen when she was placed in her last situation with Mary and Danny Baybrook. It was far from the best, but it wasn't the worst, either. Finally old enough to babysit and make a little money, she opened a new savings account, remembering what Scott had said about school. When she was fifteen, she looked up the price of university tuition and realized she was going to need a lot more money. Reluctantly, she'd given up watching kids and found a proper job waitressing, working every spare hour she had.

"Right, then. We're done," Donny told her one morning as she was making her way out the door two weeks after her sixteenth birthday.

"Done with what?"

"Done with fostering. Had enough. Want the house to ourselves. Expect it's back to the group home with you. Get your stuff packed when you're back from school."

He left for work. Renata didn't bother tracking down his wife, Mary. Didn't bother going to school, either. She tramped back up the stairs, packed her things and walked out.

She didn't need foster care anymore.

After couch surfing at friends' houses for a couple of weeks, she found a live-in nanny position. In exchange for room, board and a modest stipend, she watched three kids after school, cooked and cleaned, and kept her weekend waitressing job. She hustled hard and did what it took to eventually get scholarships to a small but prestigious school. She'd loved Brian, Luke and Amy, and it had been hard to leave them behind when she graduated.

What sustained her all those years were movies. Renata watched everything from kids' videos to epic fantasy sagas. She knew someday she'd create stories that lifted people out of their lives and set them free from the tyranny of the pain of living in the real world.

But first she had to get her girls through school.

There were seven of the original twenty-three left. Paying students, those who matriculated after the Colina Blanca disaster, had steadied the school's finances and would give Mayra and Gabriela long-term security in their jobs, but the seven remaining students who'd lost their families to the Colina Blanca disaster had been left with nothing. Five, six and seven years old when the mudslide wiped out their village, they remembered little else except the school. Mayra and Gabriela were their mothers, Renata a sort of distant aunt.

Renata had promised to cover their costs through graduation. Like her, the girls would need to work and pay their own way through higher education. Many of the older students had done so already. In her emails and texts, she reminded the remaining girls that if she could do it, they could, too.

Three more years. Three more years of paying a monthly stipend for each girl and her pledge to the San Pedro school would be fulfilled. She was proud of what she'd accomplished. Proud of the girls who'd overcome so much sorrow and loss to go on to lead productive lives.

In three years, everything would change. Done with her extra monthly payments to cover the girls' costs, she could tighten her personal budget until it squeaked and finally walk away from Martin Fulsom and his infuriating way of controlling her life. She'd walk away from reality television, too. Who needed reality, anyway?

She'd grab hold of the career she'd always wanted and finally show the world what she could do. Take Hollywood by storm—

Or maybe she'd take a little break first.

Renata inhaled a deep breath, turned around and let the noise and hubbub of the wedding wash over her. The manor was a marvelous old building with hardwood floors and old-fashioned touches. The ballroom where they were celebrating was utterly beautiful. Renata often wished she could come here as a guest, don an old-fashioned gown and while away her hours in some gentle old-timey pursuit, not a care in the world.

Reality television directors didn't have extra hours in which to try old-timey pursuits, though, and right now she was working. No leisurely afternoons for her. She couldn't remember the last time she'd put up her feet and taken it easy. Or hung out with a group of friends. Or anything other than work, really.

She made her way toward a knot of cameramen and crew members filming the celebration, her impractical, old-fashioned bridesmaid's gown swishing around her ankles. She'd been touched when Eve Wright had asked her to be part of the wedding party. Until Eve had arrived at Base Camp, Renata had kept a distance between herself and the cast.

When she reached the crew, she pointed at a couple who were awkwardly dancing: Jericho Cook, one of the four original men who'd come to Westfield ranch to start the community, and his extremely pregnant wife, Savannah. "Make sure you get that," she told Byron, the youngest and most excitable member of the crew.

She slipped through the crowd that thronged the manor. Some of the women in the community ran the Jane Austen–inspired lodging, and all of Base Camp's weddings were held here. There'd been six so far. Seven now.

Three to go, Renata thought. It was late January, and the show would conclude at the end of May, which left her wondering what would happen next. Would Fulsom keep her on three more years to document his work, the way she used to do? Her gaze slipped to the newest member of the *Base Camp* crew. Clem Bailey. He'd joined the show just over a month ago and wanted her job badly. Had almost succeeded in taking it. She'd gotten her revenge—showing Fulsom what a manipulative misogynist he was. Did Fulsom care?

That remained to be seen. No word had come down about who would direct the show from now on. She'd expected Fulsom to kick Clem off the moment he'd learned the man had been let go of his previous job for sexual harassment.

So far Fulsom had kept his opinions to himself.

Sometimes Renata thought no one cared about values or duty anymore. Fulsom certainly didn't, or he wouldn't repay her years of loyalty by foisting a man like Clem on her production. She'd taken Fulsom's ridiculous idea—a television show about ten men building a sustainable community—and his ridiculous rules—they had to build ten sustainable homes powered by green energy, grow enough food to make it through the winter, marry and produce three pregnancies within a year—and made the show a smash hit. Sending Clem to "fix" it was cruel.

That was life, though. Cruel.

"Nice wedding, huh?" a man's voice asked.

Renata hesitated before she nodded. She interacted daily with all the inhabitants of Base Camp, the ten men who'd initially joined the experiment and seven women who'd been recruited along the way as wives—plus Avery Lightfoot, one of the earliest women to join them, who was still single. Greg Devon unsettled her in a way that the other men didn't, though. It wasn't that she caught him looking at her sometimes, or his relative quietness in this group of unruly people, or even the scope of his knowledge—the man was an encyclopedia when it came to information about renewable energy. Something else niggled at her. A feeling that he knew something about her. Or that she knew something about him. Something she couldn't quite remember.

"Saw you looking out the window," he said. "Are you worried this winter will never end?"

"Should be close to over by the time you marry."

Greg's eyes narrowed at the reminder of his upcoming nuptials. "Let's grab a drink."

Normally Renata would decline, but tonight a drink sounded good, and she followed him through the crowd as he fetched her a glass of wine. He chose a beer for himself and shouldered his way back through the throng until they reached one of the tables set up around the outskirts of the room for guests who didn't choose to dance.

Renata sat with him, although she kept her attention on the room at large. She was still nominally the director of *Base Camp*. Co-director. She spotted Clem across the room leering at the daughter of a local rancher. The man was a menace. What was taking Fulsom so long to remove him from the show?

"Do you have any ideas on that front?" she asked Greg to distract herself. "Finding a wife?" The clock was ticking, after all. He'd drawn the short straw this afternoon. Now he had forty days to marry—or lose all of this. Renata had a feeling Greg would do whatever it took to secure Base Camp.

"I know who I want to marry," Greg said darkly. Renata, surprised, turned just as he plucked a seedpod from the floral centerpiece, balanced it on the table and flicked it with his finger. It sailed between two champagne flutes and landed inches from her elbow. "Goal," he added with a sardonic grin. He took a drag of his beer. "If only getting her to the altar was that easy."

Renata picked up the seedpod and turned it in her fingers as she considered this. Greg knew who he wanted to marry? She swallowed against a surge of disappointment. As one of the participants in the show, he had to find a wife. She'd known that for months but hadn't let herself think about it. Now she had to, which meant she had to admit to herself she had the teeniest, tiniest crush on Greg.

Not that she'd ever let him know.

Greg lined up two water glasses on his side of the table, and Renata couldn't help focusing on his hands. They were strong, with square palms and muscular wrists. Over the months she'd interacted with him here at Base Camp, they'd often caught her attention. A man could do a lot with hands like that.

She raised her gaze to Greg's face to distract herself from that thought, trying to ignore the twist of desire low in her body. She'd spent every day of the last eight months in constant contact with ten of the most virile men she'd ever met in her life. It was to be expected that sometimes she would respond to their proximity. That was all this was—a bodily response.

Or so she'd told herself many a time. It wasn't true, though. Not even a little bit.

She hoped like hell Greg couldn't read her mind.

"Take your shot." He indicated the glasses.

Why not? She balanced the seedpod on end on the tablecloth and flicked her finger. It sailed through the glasses as easily as his had. She'd always been good at contests, with a natural dexterity and athleticism she might have had more opportunities to nurture if her life had turned out different.

Greg raised an eyebrow. "Impressive."

She shrugged.

"Two out of three?" he challenged.

She gestured to the champagne flutes. "Be my guest."

He took a shot. Scored.

She took a shot and scored as well.

"Shoot-out," he said. "First unanswered goal wins."

She nodded, getting into the game. He scored again.

So did she.

Greg grinned. "Folks, I think we have a contender."

"Wrong sport."

"What do you know about sports?" He scored again.

"A lot." She took the seedpod back, balanced it. Flicked.

Greg took a swig of his beer as the seedpod cruised straight between the water glasses.

"With that posh English accent of yours, I figured maybe you'd know a little about polo, but…" He made his shot.

"My *British* accent isn't that posh." Americans had no idea when it came to accents. Greg's was hard to place, but Renata knew from the show's records he came from a small town near Portland. A rural town. What had it been like to grow up in a commune?

He never talked about it.

Greg set down his beer and leaned forward, his elbows braced on the table, looming over the water glasses that made up the goal she was aiming for. "You won't make this one," he said menacingly.

Renata flicked the seedpod.

Made the goal.

Then leaned over the table just as he had and tried to adopt his menacing expression and tone. "You, my friend, are the one who won't make this one."

Greg's lips twitched. "I'm frightened."

"You should be."

His shot cruised right through the flutes and hit the bodice of her gown with a soft thwack. Renata glanced down at the iron-gray fabric. Turned back to Greg. Picked up the seedpod, balanced it on the white tablecloth, flicked it and hit him square on the chin—after it sailed between the water glasses.

"Goal."

Greg didn't move—until he did. His right hand gripped her wrist so fast she didn't have time to pull back. They leaned over the table like arm-wrestling contestants. Renata's heart beat a fast tattoo as a swoop of sensation washed through her, a fast rush of lust followed by a long, slow burn that left her much too aware of him. It wasn't the first time today such a thing had happened. Greg had taken her hand earlier—before the wedding—and left her just as breathless.

She had to make it stop.

"Don't you know you're playing with fire when you come at me like that?" he asked.

"You don't scare me." He hadn't until now. She'd never expected her body to react so strongly to him, and it unnerved her to think he could penetrate her defenses so easily. She was used to being in control, but she couldn't pretend she hadn't kept an eye on him during her time here. Greg was handsome. A man with a thick shock of dark hair, deep brown eyes and a way of sitting back and watching what went on around him with a ghost of a smile that implied he was enjoying some inside joke. He was rarely the center of attention in this group. Boone Rudman tended to take charge. Curtis Lloyd was the jokester. Jericho Cook the poster-child whose model-level good looks fooled people into overlooking his intelligence. Greg hung back, but he was an intriguing man. He reminded Renata of someone, but she'd never quite been able to put her finger on who.

He was capable. Accomplished. Sure of himself. Dedicated to his work and to Base Camp. He was the kind of man she'd want to be with if she wanted to be with any man. He'd be a good husband. A good father—

She didn't have time for that now, though. Romance was for some distant future when she'd gotten her girls through school and made her mark on the film industry. As for children—

"Good. I don't want to *scare* you." Greg's fingertips brushed her palm as he let go, and Renata's breath caught. She missed his touch as soon as it was gone.

She needed to lay off the wine.

Greg was watching her again. "What?" she demanded, thoroughly flustered and angry at herself for it.

He shrugged. "Nothing. Just enjoying the view. You're a beautiful woman, Renata."

Renata snorted. This kind of flirtation she knew how to handle. "Don't think I've forgotten my question." She was back in director mode, her voice sharp, brooking no evasions. "Who are you going to marry?"

Greg grinned again, and something inside her fluttered. She wasn't the fluttering type, damn him.

"You sure you want the answer to that?"

Renata swallowed. No. Come to think of it, she really didn't want the answer. But it was her job to ask the question.

"Renata?"

She nearly blessed Byron for the interruption, but she'd never let him know how much she appreciated it. The only way to keep an unruly crew in line was with iron control. "Yes?"

"They're cutting the cake. I can't find Clem anywhere. Do you want to come and—"

"I'll be right there." She stood up as Byron darted off. "Remember, we're tied," she told Greg. No way was she going to let him think she was conceding their contest.

He stood, too. She was tall, but he was taller, and

the frank pleasure he seemed to take in that fact unnerved her all over again. He moved around the table to place a hand on her back and guided her through the crowd. Another tingle ran through the network of her nerves.

"We'll get our rematch another time," he promised. When they reached the table where the happy couple was prepared to slice into an enormous frosted confection, his hand dropped to hers, and he squeezed it, then slipped away.

Renata watched him go.

The next forty days were going to be hell.

CHAPTER TWO

WHEN A COMMOTION woke Greg just after one in the morning, he thought a prowler must have been caught on Base Camp land. After their root cellar had been broken into and most of their food stolen some months back, they'd set up patrols through the night, but Westfield was a large ranch, and there were only so many men. They couldn't all stay up every night.

The bunkhouse door swung open, and Jericho stuck his head inside. "Savannah's in labor. We're heading to the hospital now. Clay, Nora and Riley are riding with us." All around Greg, the single members of Base Camp, who slept on mats on the floor here, sat up, fully alert.

Greg stumbled out of his sleeping bag. Angus was already on his feet, jeans half-on. Walker was rising silently. Avery sat half in, half out of her bag, blinking sleep from her eyes. Walker touched her shoulder as he passed, heading to stow his bedroll away. Avery got to her feet and padded to the bathroom, stopping to grab some clothes.

In one corner of the large room, Byron the cameraman was talking quietly on his phone. He'd been sleeping at Base Camp recently on Clem's orders. When he was in town last, the director had become convinced they got up to all kinds of shenanigans at night. Byron was his spy. He wasn't supposed to film after lights out, but Greg had no doubt if anything unusual happened, he'd been told to get his camera rolling.

"Yeah, they're already on their way to the hospital. No, I wasn't filming, I was asleep. I know. I know, all right. I'll get there as soon as I can." Byron hung up. Caught Greg watching him. "Clem," he confirmed. "I'm supposed to call him right away when anything exciting happens."

"What about Renata? Did you call her, too?"

Byron shook his head warily. "She'd skin me alive if I woke her up."

Greg assessed the situation. Clem was probably on his way to the hospital right now, crew in tow. He'd get the footage of Savannah checking in. Renata would be skunked. After the way she'd showed Clem up in the weeks since he'd come on board, Greg had a feeling Clem was eager for revenge.

Greg made up his mind what to do.

Fifteen minutes later, he was driving into town in one of Base Camp's communal trucks, with Avery, Walker, Angus and Addison Green joining in the convoy. Addison was married to Kai, Base Camp's cook, who was one of the men on patrol tonight. He and Anders would stay at Base Camp to keep watch.

Everyone else was packed into the trucks winging their way to the hospital.

Renata met them in the hospital intake room and took Greg aside. "Thanks for calling," she said brusquely. "I'm going to kill Byron."

"Clem is the one you should be pissed at."

"I'm always pissed at him."

As the hours passed, Greg wondered why they'd all been in such a hurry to get to the hospital. It was clear this wasn't going to be a fast delivery. They practically filled the whole waiting room. Boone and Riley held hands and whispered in one corner; Nora and Clay Picket slumped in a pair of chairs, her head resting on his shoulder; Avery, Walker, Angus and Addison stood with Curtis and Hope Lloyd, talking quietly. Everyone else was asleep in awkward positions in the plastic chairs.

Except Renata.

She looked far more approachable than she had at the wedding in that gunmetal-gray gown. He'd rarely seen her dressed so informally. In fact—Greg flipped through his memories. No, he'd never seen Renata in jeans before. Paired with a deep-blue sweater, her feet stuffed into winter boots, she looked human. Vulnerable. Far from the polished, ultra-serious persona she wore to deal with *Base Camp*'s cast and crew. She was watching the corridor down which Savannah was presumably now laboring with her husband, Jericho, to help—

And Clem to film.

The ultimate coup, Greg realized. Whoever got footage of Base Camp's first birth would be the star, at least for a little while.

"Byron doesn't look too happy," Greg said when he took a seat next to Renata, hoping to distract her.

"He filmed the whole ride to the hospital and Jericho carrying Savannah inside—then Clem got here and took over. He chose Adrienne to do the filming." She was referring to one of the crew's female members, a mousy woman who'd barely said a word in the months Greg had been here. "Byron's pissed, as well he should be."

Clem had shown a little tact for once, though, Greg thought. Choosing a woman to film the birth—

All of them jumped when a door down the hall swung open and banged into the wall, and two figures lurched out, one of them holding a video camera. A loud string of curses preceded Clem and Adrienne down the hall.

"—doing my goddamn job, that's all. How the hell am I expected to put together a winning show if—"

"Sir, you'll have to lower your voice if you want to stay here. No filming," a stern nurse snapped from behind a desk. Clem glared at her and stalked into the waiting room. Adrienne followed quietly, her shoulders high, her face pink. She didn't enter the waiting room, though. Instead, she positioned herself against a wall near the front entrance, as if hoping it might offer some camouflage.

Clem ignored her, making a beeline to Renata.

"You can take yourself right back to the motel," he snarled at her. "If I can't get footage, you don't stand a chance in hell."

Greg surged to his feet, fists balled, ready to do battle with the man, but Boone intervened and corralled Clem into a seat across the room, peppering him with questions about Savannah and Jericho.

"She's fine." Clem was annoyed. "Doctor says it'll be hours."

Greg sat down again.

The time crawled by, broken only by coffee runs, desultory conversation and the silent flickering of the waiting room TV with its sound on mute. When Clem and Renata nearly got into blows over one of the three outdated magazines available in a room that held seating for more than twenty, Greg took her hand and tugged her outside into the crisp dawn.

"At least we'll see the sun today," he said when they were safely outside.

"For a few hours," Renata added dryly.

"Don't knock Montana. Britain isn't known for its blue skies," he pointed out. "If you grew up there, you must be used to this."

"Why do you think I left?"

"Did you spend a long time in California with Fulsom before you came here?"

"I spent time everywhere with Fulsom. He's hardly in one place for three days strung together. The man can't stop moving."

"Which do you prefer—moving all the time or being here?"

Renata frowned as if she'd never pondered the question before. Maybe she hadn't. "I'd prefer to get to choose for myself," she said quietly.

Greg supposed he could understand that. "You could quit."

An expression he couldn't pinpoint flashed over her features and was gone. "That wouldn't be my best move," she finally said. She pulled her jacket's zipper up the last few inches and shoved her fists in her pockets. "Cold."

He nodded. The comment didn't require an answer. It had been cold for months. He was ready for spring, too—they all were. He didn't want to go back inside, though.

"At least Clem isn't getting any footage, either," he remarked. The man was visible through the glass doors into the hospital, pacing and holding a phone to his ear.

He turned when a snowball thwacked into his arm. "Hey!"

"Don't even mention his name. That jerk is after my job." Renata stood with her hands on her hips.

Greg scooped up a handful of snow, considered tossing it back at her but decided that was a bad idea. He threw it at the side of a nearby bus kiosk instead and hit the shoulder of the businessman pictured in the advertisement that ran the length of the kiosk's side. Renata's eyebrows raised.

"Beat that," Greg said.

"Ten points for a body shot, twenty points if you hit

his face. First one to a hundred wins," Renata rattled off. She scooped up some snow and took her shot. Tied with Greg when she hit the man square in the chest.

The game went fast after that, each of them taking their shots and calling out their score. Greg got two more body shots and finally hit the man's face. "Fifty!"

Renata hit the face on her second shot but then missed the kiosk altogether before getting another body shot. "Forty." Her frustration was clear.

"Seventy," Greg gloated when his next shot hit the man's face.

"Sixty." Renata's confidence returned.

"Eighty." Damn it. That shot had nearly missed altogether. He was letting Renata get to him.

"Eighty!" Renata crowed after her shot hit the man square on the jaw. "I'm going to take you down, Devon!"

"Not likely." This time Greg knew his shot would land the moment it left his hand. It hit the kiosk with a satisfying smack, dead center in the businessman's face.

Greg didn't think. He simply reached out, caught hold of Renata's jacket and tugged her closer at the same time he stepped toward her. He saw surprise widen her eyes just before his mouth met hers. Their kiss was brief—over almost before it began.

But he knew it would change everything.

"RENATA! GREG! THE baby's here!"

Avery's voice cut through the silence, jolting Renata out of her shock. Still facing Greg—staring at him—

Renata shook herself back into the present. Took a step back. She didn't think Avery had seen what they were doing—thank goodness.

"Renata." Greg's low, rich baritone stopped her. "We should talk about this."

"Come on!" Avery cried. "They're letting us in a few at a time. You have to cover this, Renata. Don't let Clem win."

That snapped her out of her shock. She was never going to let Clem win.

"Renata," Greg called after her as she strode toward the hospital.

"Later. I've got work to do." She was tingling all over, though, and Renata wasn't sure she'd ever get over the shock of that kiss. She supposed it made sense he'd make a pass at her—the way he'd been watching her—but it had still taken her by surprise. Somehow she'd supposed that her absolute unavailability would be as clear to the men of Base Camp as it was to her. She'd never given a single one of them so much as a flirtatious glance, least of all Greg, because he was the one to whom she was the most attracted.

Inside, she made her way down the corridor to where the members of Base Camp had clustered around Savannah's room. She'd have to sort out Greg later. Right now she had a job to do—one that would keep paying for the girls of Colina Blanca.

"Out of my way," she ordered, marching through the gathered people, grabbing Byron's arm as she went. She'd need a cameraman.

"Three at a time," Riley said apologetically.

"That doesn't apply to me."

"Or me," Greg said, hurrying after her.

"Like hell it doesn't," Clem said. "If I have to wait, so do you!"

Renata barged past him into the hospital room, still dragging Byron along, followed by Greg, who shut the door behind him. Hope and Curtis Lloyd, spotting them, straightened from where they'd been bent over mother and child.

"We'll see you again tomorrow when you've gotten some rest," Hope told Savannah. "You have a beautiful baby."

"I'll go, too," Nora Pickett said. "I'm so happy for you, Savannah."

"You next," Savannah told her.

Nora patted her slightly rounded belly. "Can't wait."

As they left, Renata edged closer to the bed upon which Savannah lay, supported by pillows, her baby in her arms. Jericho sat close by, beaming at wife and child as if he couldn't be prouder.

"It's a boy?" Renata asked, hardly daring to breathe. The baby was asleep, a tiny bundle with a sweet, puckered face. What she would give to have a baby like that. The thought should have surprised her, career woman as she was, but she felt the same longing every time she saw a little one. It was just part of being a woman, she supposed. Or maybe her history was to blame. She'd grown up around other lost, lonely children in the foster care system, all of them craving care and love. She'd done her best to give it to them—while she was there. It seemed to her the foster care system was simply a series of goodbyes.

"Yes. Jacob Boone Cook."

"That must have made Boone happy." Renata drew nearer, taken by the baby's tiny hands among the nest of blankets Savannah held him in. This baby would never know the kind of sorrow and loneliness she'd felt and seen during her childhood years. He would grow up surrounded by love—as a baby should.

"I think he cried a little when we told him," Savannah admitted.

"Boone was bawling like a newborn himself," Jericho put in. "But he's been a good friend for a long time."

"Jacob is so sweet." Renata bent even closer. "What a perfect baby."

"Do you want to hold him?"

Renata nodded. Her arms were aching to hold him. How had Savannah known?

She sat down on the edge of the bed, and Savannah transferred the little mite, swathed in his blankets, into her arms. "There."

The small weight felt wonderful, and Renata drew in a shaking breath. She couldn't even place the feeling filling her heart. It went so far beyond longing—eclipsed even her commitment to the girls she was supporting in Peru, something she'd dedicated her whole life to these past ten years. When she allowed herself to think of the future, she focused on work—on the films she'd promised herself she'd one day produce. She wanted to provide an escape from reality to all the people who had suffered like she had.

But—

Jacob shifted, his tiny fingers straightening, then curling into fists again.

A baby. She wanted a baby, too. A house. A real home. Somewhere she never had to leave again. Roots. A family. One that would last forever. Maybe a husband—

A noise escaped her, and shame washed through Renata at having exposed herself like that. It was a noise someone like Savannah would recognize. And maybe Greg might, too. Not to mention Clem if he were in the room.

Renata's back stiffened even as Savannah reached out to pat her arm.

"It's all right," Savannah said. "Everyone loves new babies."

Renata blinked back the tears that were threatening to slip down her cheeks.

"It's that they're so new," Savannah said. "It reminds us we were new once, too. Innocent. Before the world got to us."

In a flash, Renata was back in England—the small town outside London where she was born. She had a sense of a living room. A soft couch. A fireplace. Snow falling.

Hot chocolate.

Her mother singing. Her father in the easy chair

with a book.

Another sound escaped her, and she swayed forward to deposit Jacob back into his mother's arms. She stood up and scraped a hand across her cheek. What was wrong with her?

Greg caught her when she stumbled over her own feet and put his arm around her waist to steady her, but when she moved toward the door, it swung open, and Clem stepped in her way. He looked her up and down scornfully. "What's wrong with you, Ludlow? Are you crying?" He glanced at Savannah in the bed, baby Jacob in her arms, and sneered. "No wonder Fulsom gave me your job. You're on the mommy track. Not a serious director at all. Just killing time until a husband comes along, huh?"

Renata didn't know what she'd have done if the door hadn't swung open a second time—and ushered in Fulsom.

She sucked in a breath, completely taken aback. Dashed her hand quickly over her cheeks again, grateful she hadn't had time to put on makeup before rushing to the hospital. She didn't think she could face her boss with mascara running everywhere.

"How'd you get here?" Greg asked him.

"The same way I always get here," Fulsom said calmly. He brushed past them to pay homage at Savannah's bedside. "Beautiful as ever, my dear," he told Savannah. "I don't know how you always manage to look like a painting by Raphael, but you do. And look at this little man. Jacob Boone, right? He'll be the spitting image of his father. Good job, you two." He turned to Clem. "You getting the footage you need?"

Fury filled Renata. What about her? She wasn't getting any of the footage she needed. And she'd exposed Clem days ago for the criminal he was. This situation was intolerable. Two directors were one too many—

"I'm getting everything," Clem assured him. "Unlike some people, I don't have anything to distract me."

"Good. As for you, Renata…"

Here it came. Renata swallowed in a dry throat, her pulse tripping along like a toddler on hot sand. Fulsom was going to fire her. She was going to let everyone down. Her students—

"I'm not sure you're needed at Base Camp anymore," he began, confirming her worst suspicions.

"Yes, she is!" Greg blurted behind her. "She damn well is!"

"Clem here is perfectly capable of directing—"

"She's the one." Greg cut off Fulsom again. "She's the woman I'm going to marry. She has to stay because she's going to be my wife!"

Clem's laughter filled the room.

CHAPTER THREE

"...AUDIENCE WILL LOVE it. They'll eat it up. It'll be great for ratings," Fulsom was telling a furious Renata when Jericho pulled Greg aside.

Greg hadn't even noticed him skirt around the bed and cross the room. He'd been too busy watching the blood drain from Renata's face as she realized Fulsom was going to force her to remain on the show—as a participant, not a director.

"What the hell are you doing?" Jericho hissed at him. "You have to marry in forty days. You can't mess around trying to save Renata's job."

"I'm not. I'm telling the truth—she's the one. She's always been the one."

"Renata? How?"

Greg knew what he meant. As director, she'd been a sharp-tongued battle-ax of a woman, but that was what the job required. She was bossing around ten men who'd spent years with the Navy SEALs. Did Jericho expect her to be a soft-spoken schoolgirl?

He knew another side to Renata. He'd been there in

Peru—

Even if she didn't remember him.

"Sleep on it," Fulsom told Renata. "You'll still get paid, so don't worry about that," he added. Behind him, Clem smirked.

"Pay me double." Renata's voice was tight with rage.

Fulsom shrugged. "Sure, I'll pay you double. It's worth it."

She whirled and strode to the door, her cold gaze slicing through Greg like a knife as she passed.

"Renata—"

She lifted a hand to stop him and kept going. The door closed behind her a moment later.

"Let her simmer down." Fulsom came to stop Greg from following her. "She needs sleep. Time to think it over. She'll see the value of playing along."

"I don't want her to play along, and I don't want her to lose her job," Greg told him. "I don't know what game *you're* playing—"

"The same game I've always been playing. The one that makes this show so damn watchable to our national audience. They've seen Renata grilling you people. They know who she is. Now that the table is turned on her, they won't be able to take their eyes off the show. And what you want doesn't signify," he reminded Greg. "You signed a contract. This is out of your hands now." Fulsom kept going, leaving him with a mouthful of unspoken protests.

A sound reminded him there were others in the room, and one of them had just given birth.

Greg turned back to Savannah. "Sorry about all that. I'll let the next people in. You've got a beautiful baby there."

Savannah smiled. Jericho walked him to the door.

"Renata? Are you sure?" he asked again.

"Doesn't matter, does it? She'll never want me now," Greg said.

It was hard to believe it was only ten o'clock when Greg finally got back to Base Camp, late for getting started on his chores but far too early considering how long he'd been awake. It was going to be a long day, he decided as he made the rounds of the solar panels, wind turbines and other power installations, checking all was well. He was approaching the barn when he ran into Walker and his grandmother, Sue Norton.

"Morning." He touched the brim of his hat and nodded at Sue. It was easy to see where Walker had gotten his impassive personality. As many times as Greg had spoken to Sue, who came to consult with Nora each week on the curriculum they were developing for the local schools, he never felt like he got to know her any better.

"Morning," Sue said. She was older than Greg's grandmother, but only a few silver strands lined her straight, dark hair.

"Here to see Nora?" Greg asked as the sun slid out from between the clouds and then disappeared again.

"Here to talk to my grandson."

"I won't hold you up."

Walker seemed about to say something but shook

his head instead. "I'll find you later." He walked on with his grandmother, leaving Greg to wonder what that had been about. Trouble, he figured. As if they needed any more of that.

He tramped back up the snowy path to the bunkhouse, ready for the late breakfast Kai had promised to rustle up for them. Renata, who'd hung back at the hospital to confer with Fulsom, was just walking over from where she'd parked one of the crew's big black SUVs.

She didn't look any happier than when he'd last seen her. Greg braced himself for another confrontation. "Hey. You all right?"

She stopped in her tracks. Considered him. "Do you always mess things up this badly?"

"No." He wasn't the type to screw up a mission, if that's what she meant. He'd served with honor, and he'd put in nearly eight months of hard work here. He could be depended on, and he was proud of that fact. "You moving in?" he asked, spotting the heavy-looking bag she carried. Looked like she'd failed to change Fulsom's mind. If the billionaire had ordered her to move to Base Camp from the motel where the crew stayed in town, that meant she would be on the show.

"Not for long. I'll find you a replacement bride in a day or two, don't worry—"

"I don't want a replacement." Greg moved closer. "If I did, I'd get one myself."

"You can't have me."

That was direct. Greg searched for a way to salvage

this conversation. "Why not?" was all he managed.

"Because…" She cast about. "Because you don't know anything about me!"

"I know a hell of a lot more than you think I do." It was true. Not only did Renata not seem to remember the hellish night they'd spent together in Peru, she had no idea how aware he was of all her movements around Base Camp.

She gathered herself together and marched onward with an audible, "Hmph." Greg followed her, but she ignored him, and once inside the bunkhouse, Avery came to meet her, spoiling his chance for further conversation.

"Come store your belongings over here." Avery led Renata to a set of shelves built along the far wall of the room, leaving Greg by the door, uncertain whether to stay and wait for breakfast to be served or get far, far away from here before he made things worse.

Angus came in behind him, and Greg shifted so the man could get his jacket off and hang it up.

"Heard you're marrying Renata," he said as he came to stand beside Greg. Both of them watched Avery chat animatedly to the director, while Renata simply nodded once in a while.

"Don't think she plans to have me," Greg said. "And it's all Clem's fault. His and Fulsom's. Always interfering—"

"At least your woman's in the same state as you," Angus said glumly. "Don't know what the hell I'm going to do when it's my time."

It hadn't occurred to Greg before that his own wedding wasn't going to be the last of his problems. If by some miracle he managed to convince Renata to marry him—or Fulsom forced her to—there was still Angus and Walker to go. Walker had some mystery arrangement with another woman he had to clear up before he was free to pursue Avery. Not that Avery seemed to need a lot of pursuing. Her feelings for Walker had been clear almost from the start. And Angus—

Well, Win Lisle had already broken his heart. She'd spent several months at Base Camp early on before disappearing one morning after her mother sent her an ultimatum—return home to her family in California until the show ended or give up her substantial inheritance.

Greg clapped him on the back consolingly but had no wisdom to offer his friend.

Or himself.

"COME ON, IT'S fun to ride in a sleigh," Avery said later that afternoon as Renata stared at their neighbor, James Russell, perched in the front seat, the better to control the horses that were pulling the old-fashioned contraption. "What better way to get to the Reed place so Alice can fix you up with some proper clothes? I called the Russells and Alice this morning. I figured you'd need to escape for a while, and you know James is always dying to get his horses out and drive someone around, and Alice already had a hunch we were coming. She said to tell you she has four gowns ready to alter for you."

"I don't want to wear a Regency gown!" Renata lied. The women of Base Camp had started the tradition of wearing Jane Austen–era clothing when they'd first arrived—before they'd known Boone and his friends had bought the place out from under them or that Fulsom was planning to film them all. Wearing the gowns was supposed to remind them of the path they'd chosen: to eschew their modern, busy lives for slower ones that allowed them to pursue creative endeavors.

Look at where that has gotten them, Renata thought wryly. No one took you seriously when you dressed like that—

"Fulsom said to tell you if you want your money, you need to follow orders." Clem's grating voice announced his arrival behind her. Renata moved forward automatically in her desire to avoid him, but the only way out of here was up into the sleigh.

"Fulsom's gone," she told him.

"I'm supposed to call the minute you start acting up."

Had the billionaire actually used that phrase? she wondered. *Acting up?*

"Lovely day for a ride!" James called out. Renata swore the man would be cheerful at the end of the world as long as there were horses present. The Russells had attached themselves to the inhabitants of Base Camp almost from the start. The wealthy older couple were devotees of the Regency period themselves and spent much of the year traveling to reenactments. In between they thought of every reason they could to entertain the members of Base Camp at their large, lovely home.

"Fine," Renata growled. She wouldn't admit to James, or Avery—or Clem—that secretly she loved traveling in the sleighs and carriages. As director she didn't get much chance to savor these rides. Usually she was crammed into a corner with a cameraman who was trying to capture the action for the show.

She allowed Walker to hand her up. He'd been standing with his grandmother by her car when James directed his horses down their lane. Walker's grandmother had nodded to them before driving off, and Walker had joined the group around the horses and sleigh.

He handed Avery up next.

"What's wrong?" Avery asked, peering into his face. Renata wondered how she knew anything was wrong. Walker looked as impassive as ever. Those two spent a lot of time together, though, so if anyone could interpret his moods, Avery was the one to do it.

"Missing something." Walker didn't elaborate. Renata didn't know how to interpret the look that flashed over Avery's face, but she had her suspicions. She'd never pointed it out to anyone else, but she was sure she wasn't the only crew member who'd caught Avery in places she didn't belong.

"Hope you find it soon."

Walker stepped back, and Clem and a cameraman climbed into the sleigh. "Shove over," Clem said to

Renata. She didn't budge—and paid for it when Clem sat on one side of her and William, an older cameraman, plunked down on the other side on the bench seat. Avery, getting into the front seat with James, bit back a smile.

James got the horses going, and soon they left Base Camp behind. The sleigh took a circuitous back route since the main road wouldn't be snowy enough. Unlike the jouncing carriage rides, the sleigh glided smoothly over the snow, and despite being squashed between two men, Renata's heart lifted a little. Traveling like this was magical, and she wanted to remember the sensation in the future when she left Base Camp—and Greg—behind.

Renata ignored the pang that thought elicited. Despite herself, she'd grown kind of attached to this place. And to Greg. Just a little, but still—

Okay, more than a little.

"Looking forward to your wedding night?" Clem leered at her. Avery looked back at them.

"Leave Renata alone."

"Not likely. This one's the star of the show for the next thirty-eight days, right darling?" He nudged Renata. She elbowed him back. William tried to film it all, leaning forward and twisting awkwardly to get them in his frame.

"I guess since you'll never have a wedding night, you have to feed off other people's dreams," Renata said.

Clem's brow furrowed. "What's that supposed to

mean? I could marry any time I want to! I just don't want to."

"Prove it."

"I don't have to prove anything to you. You're the one who's going to ruin Base Camp. Thirty-eight days from now that bulldozer will be trundling on in. You're not going to marry Greg, and he's not going to marry anyone else."

Renata met Avery's disconcerted gaze. Did she look just as flummoxed? Did Clem know something she didn't?

"He'll marry someone else," she said.

Clem just chuckled.

After that it was hard to enjoy the ride, and Renata was relieved when they pulled into the drive at Two Willows and parked behind the old white farmhouse. Alice Reed, a lovely woman with long, light-brown hair, met them with a welcoming smile at the back door and led them across to the carriage house in which her studio was situated on the second floor.

It was a big open space with tall windows that would have let in the sun on a brighter day. Overhead lights made up for the gloom outside, however, and Renata was as struck as she'd ever been by the hundreds of period costumes hanging on racks around the room, the large tables in the center. This was the studio of an expert seamstress.

Alice surprised Renata with a hug. "So glad you're here. Look at you." She held both of Renata's hands out and looked her up and down. "You'll make a beautiful bride."

"I'm not going to be a bride." Renata felt like she'd said it a million times already today.

Alice bit her lip but couldn't hold back a smile. "Of course you're not," she said in the placating tone one usually reserved for children. She was an awful liar, which somehow made it all worse.

"Alice has hunches," Avery reminded her. "If she says you'll be a beautiful bride, then you'll be a beautiful bride. Relax and let Greg woo you."

"I don't want him to woo me!" Not exactly true, but given the circumstances a relationship between her and the handsome man wasn't in the cards. She had girls to get through school and a job to win back if she wanted any kind of future in the film industry.

"You have to." Avery lowered her voice to a stage whisper and pointed dramatically at Clem. "You don't want *him* to win, do you? He can't wait to bring in that developer and destroy everything we've built."

"Of course I don't." Renata didn't like talking about it with Clem listening, but she wasn't going to let that happen, for her own sake as well as everyone else's. She needed *Base Camp* to end on a good note if she wanted this directing credit to mean something. How on earth was she supposed to spin the fact that she'd been forced to stop directing and start participating on this show? She needed to get Clem out of here and take control again, or she was going to struggle to get work when it was all over.

Just thinking about trying to break into directing a

major film made Renata tense. She knew she should be reaching out and developing more contacts, but she hadn't been able to convince herself to do so for months. She found herself dreaming of a different life these days. A slower one that included a home of her own, time for good friends, sunsets, meals and lazy Sundays.

Had she ever had a lazy Sunday since her teenage years?

She didn't think so.

Those were dreams for someone else. She had ambitions. If Fulsom—and *Base Camp*—had worn her out, surely that would change when she'd finished the television show, discharged her promise to the girls of the San Pedro School of Excellence, and was free to choose what to do next. Maybe she'd take a vacation for a week or two before storming Hollywood. Refill the creative well.

Maybe she'd take a month.

"If you follow your heart, you'll be fine," Alice assured her, leading her to a little changing room at the back of the studio where several gowns hung. Clem and the cameraman followed.

Her heart? It hadn't done a very good job of keeping her out of trouble so far. It was her heart that had gotten her into the predicament of paying for her girls' schooling.

Still… Renata had to admit she wouldn't do anything different if she had to do it all over again. The girls were wonderful young women, and she'd have given anything to keep them together with Mayra and Gabriela so they could have a stable, loving home as they grew up.

The real problem was she wasn't part of that loving home. At first, Renata had been able to pretend she was. She'd talked and texted with the girls as much as she was able. Had flown down to visit. Tried to keep up with their hobbies and hopes. As time passed, however, work took over her life. Fulsom was a demanding boss, and she'd never found another job that paid enough to cover the girls' costs.

Without that constant contact, her relationship with them faltered. She'd be forever proud of them. She'd forever love them and wish them well, and she was sure they would remember her fondly, too. None of them had seen her in years, though. The oldest ones were already busy with careers and families. To the younger ones she was simply a far-away benefactor to whom they owed respect and gratitude. Nothing more, nothing less.

Renata was proud to be their helper and friend, but she still longed for a real family.

Maybe she'd never have one.

She shook the maudlin thoughts from her mind. What she needed now wasn't more attachments—it was independence. The freedom to chase her dream job for all she was worth. She had no idea why the idea didn't excite her the way it used to. Was she getting old? Worn out chasing a bunch of men and women around this sustainable community, trying to film them when they didn't want to be filmed?

Now it was her turn to see what that felt like, she thought with distaste. "Get that camera away from me," she said, stepping into the changing room.

"Spoilsport," Clem said.

"Let me show you something you'll want to get on film," Alice told him. Renata was grateful when she heard their voices moving away.

"I'm guarding the door," Avery said through the curtain. "Clem's a pervert. I won't let him get any footage of you."

"Thanks."

"Can't wait to see what Alice has picked out for you. Do you need any help?"

"I've got it."

In the end, however, she did need Avery's help to get the old-fashioned undergarments on correctly. She'd seen the women help each other dress plenty of times, and now she understood. It wasn't that she couldn't do it herself; it was simply much easier to have a second pair of hands, especially with her corset, which needed to be adjusted to fit her figure.

"Oh, Renata—it's beautiful," Avery breathed when she had the first gown on. Renata supposed this was meant to be for fancy occasions. It looked far more elaborate than the ones the women usually wore. The wine-red fabric set off her dark hair and eyes and creamy skin. The bodice was cut very low, the better to display her décolletage.

It was beautiful. She was beautiful. Renata felt her

carefully constructed armor crack just a little bit. That was dangerous. She'd long ago learned people would exploit any weakness they could find, and Clem would be quick to pick up on any enjoyment she might get from her present circumstances. He'd ram it down her throat at every turn.

"Let's try on the next one."

"Alice needs to see this one first." Avery didn't wait for her answer. "Alice—come look. Does this need any alterations?"

Alice hurried back to them, and Clem and William followed just as quickly. Clem slowed to a stop when he drew near, however, and a look crossed his face that made Renata wish she was back in the changing room. A hungry look.

It was gone in an instant, making her wonder if she'd interpreted it right. Now he merely looked bored. "Dresses," he said scathingly. "You women make such a fuss."

"That fits you to a T," Alice said, ignoring him. "Renata, you were made for the Regency. What a figure!"

Renata had long ago learned to use her figure in an aggressive way to put men back on their heels, pairing mannish tailored shirts and lacy scarlet bras. Pencil skirts and knife-edged stilettos. The kind of clothes that told a man that yes, she was a woman, but he'd better not mess with her. She was the one in charge.

This gown threw all of that on its head.

"You could lose your wallet down that cleavage,"

Clem drawled.

"Why the hell would you have your wallet anywhere near a woman's breasts?" Avery challenged him.

Clem shrugged. "Some women like money."

"I bet any woman you're with demands it."

Avery's snappy comeback was exactly what Renata needed to regain her equilibrium. Even though Clem had gotten the better of her once or twice since he'd arrived, and currently had the winning hand, she had never felt vulnerable around him until she'd put on this gown. She knew how to take care of herself, and Clem was an idiot, but that look—that hungry look—put her off balance. She shouldn't underestimate him.

Alice fussed about her, pinching and pinning the fabric in various places until the gown met her specifications. Then she shooed Renata back into the changing room. "Come on, Clem."

"Coming." Clem kept his gaze on Renata until she firmly tugged the fabric of the change room curtain into place. She swore she could still feel his gaze as Avery ducked around the curtain and joined her, beginning to undo the fastenings of her gown.

"He's gone," Avery said.

"Good." But Renata's skin still crawled when she thought of what she'd seen in his eyes.

An hour and a half later, they were safely back at the bunkhouse, Renata clad in the gown that had fit her best, topped with a long spencer—an old-fashioned, ankle-length jacket—that somehow already fit her perfectly. She kept the jacket done up even when she entered the building, too aware of Clem's proximity for comfort. He'd insisted on sitting next to her in the sleigh again on the way home, his thigh pressed against hers too firmly for comfort. Avery wasn't laughing at them this time. Her lips had pinched together as she took in Clem's encroachment on Renata's personal space, and as the trip home continued, storm clouds had brewed in her eyes.

Renata had shaken her head, telling her silently not to comment on the situation. Clem fed on comments. Loved riling everyone up. He was trying to throw her. To make sure he was the one in control of the situation. She wouldn't give him the satisfaction of protesting. With the jacket closed to her neckline, he couldn't see any of the cleavage that had caught his attention earlier, and this forest-green dress wasn't nearly as low-cut as the wine red one, anyhow.

Still, as soon as she entered the bunkhouse, the other women present—most of them, it seemed—crowded around.

"Let's see what Alice made for you," Riley said happily.

Reluctantly, Renata undid the fastenings of her outer garment. Greg appeared from the kitchen and strode over to take it from her and hang it up.

"Wow," he breathed when she turned. "That's… stunning."

"It is stunning," Riley said.

"I know, right?" Avery put in. "Alice outdid herself, but you should see Renata's ball gown. Alice plans to send it tomorrow with the rest of her things."

Greg's gaze slid over Renata like a caress, far different from her experience with Clem back at Alice's workshop.

"You always look beautiful, Renata, but that takes the cake," he said.

Renata prayed she wouldn't blush. Usually she could control that, another trick she'd learned early on, but something about Greg got under her skin. Made her skittish as a schoolgirl.

"Makes you think maybe she's not so frigid after all," Clem brayed.

"Fuck off," Greg told him evenly. He kept his eyes on Renata, his gaze letting her know how much he liked what he saw.

Did her gaze reveal she liked what she saw, too? A solid man who'd done a day's work in worn jeans and a long-sleeve T-shirt that stretched across a muscled chest. She'd never admit it to anyone, but from time to time she imagined his arms around her, and it felt—familiar. He was the kind of man you wanted next to you in a crisis, guiding your steps, whispering encouragement, steadying you when you thought you couldn't make it through another moment.

Renata had a flash of the night she spent in Peru when she'd combed through the woebegone refugees who'd made it down the mountain from where the slide had wiped out most of Colina Blanca. Again and again she'd asked for news of her young charges' parents. Again and again she'd gotten the same answer—gone—

until she wondered if anyone was left alive in the whole world.

Someone had walked with her. Steadied her. Kept close through the night.

She'd forgotten all about that until now.

Who—?

"You'd be fun to fuck in that gown—Hey!" Clem protested as Greg twisted his hands in the fabric of the man's shirt at the back of his neck and his waist and half dragged, half carried Clem across the room, turned the door's handle, shoved it open and threw the director out into the snow. When he shut the door—and locked it—a cheer went up in the room.

"As I was saying," Greg said, back a moment later, "that's some dress. Kai's got dinner just about ready. Can I get you a chair?"

"I guess." She was still angry at him, but she couldn't help the smile curling her mouth. Clem was such an ass, and it was rare in her life that someone stood up for her.

That didn't change anything, though. Greg had put her in an awkward position. She had to reclaim her job and hold on to it for three more years.

The last thing she could do was fall for him.

CHAPTER FOUR

HE WAS GOING to regret tossing Clem into a snowbank, Greg thought the following morning, when he'd finished an early round of checking the energy systems and entered the bunkhouse looking for breakfast. He didn't know where or when Clem would take his revenge, but he was sure it was coming. It had still been worth it. When he'd shut the door on the man last night, he'd turned back in time to catch Renata smiling, even if she'd been short with him for the rest of the evening.

"I'm not marrying you," she'd told him before they turned in for the night.

"We'll see" was all he'd said.

He caught sight of her now across the room and went to fetch each of them a folding chair after divesting himself of his outerwear. The bunkhouse filled up, the noise level increasing as people grouped in knots of two or three and chatted, waiting for Kai to ring the cowbell that announced it was time to eat.

"Savannah's back!" Nora exclaimed as the door

opened again and Jericho ushered his wife into the bunkhouse solicitously. She was holding baby Jacob in her arms.

"We just popped in to say hello," he called out as everyone circled around them. "I'm going to get Savannah and Jacob settled in our house, and then I'll be back to fetch some breakfast for us."

"I'm doing just fine and so is Jacob," Savannah added. "But Jericho insists we take it easy for a day or two, and I don't mind being spoiled."

Greg gathered close like everyone else and caught sight of the tiny baby in her arms, but when he turned to make sure Renata could see as well, the expression on her face arrested him. Pure longing had softened the sharpness of her features, and Greg's chest tightened. That was the second time he'd seen her look like this. Did Renata want a family?

He did.

Anders cleared his throat. "Hold up a second, if you don't mind. While you're here, Eve and I have an announcement to make. An important one. We're hoping to finish what you and Jericho started. The baby requirement," he clarified when no one seemed to get it. "It's early days yet. Really early. But Eve's pregnant. That's baby number three for Base Camp."

A cheer went up, and Savannah moved forward to embrace Eve while others shook Anders's hand. Greg clapped Anders on the back when he got the chance. "Congratulations!"

But he was looking at Renata, who was looking at

Eve, biting her lip and blinking just a little too fast.

Was Renata—jealous?

That strange feeling washed through Greg again. Did the director want a family so badly she'd envy another woman who was starting her own? If so, why was she resisting marrying him? Aside from the rushed forty-day aspect of it all. And the fact she was being filmed. And Clem taking her job—

Things weren't auspicious now, but maybe that would change in time. He knew he hadn't imagined the spark between them when he kissed her at the hospital. Renata liked him—at least a little. And despite her hard-bitten determination to excel at her job, she had a softer side, too. He remembered how she'd been in Peru. A natural with children. Her arms open to any and all of them that terrible night.

Did she want a child of her own? A rush of desire washed through him at the thought of making a family with her, and he took a step closer to Renata, wanting to take her hand in his and make a connection. He suppressed a grin. Stake a claim, more like. He wanted Renata to be his and his alone.

Renata was backing away, though, heading for the kitchen. He followed, slipped out of the crowd without anyone noticing and found Renata leaning against a counter in the smaller room.

"What are you doing?" she challenged him when he entered.

"Just keeping you company."

"I don't need company." But she didn't send him

away.

"You seem… tired. It must be hard directing this show—having to keep everyone in line."

She met his gaze with suspicion but nodded.

"I wish I could make it easier for you."

She shifted uncomfortably, and Greg decided he'd said enough to let her know he cared what was happening to her. "Looks like it's going to be a few more minutes before breakfast. Come on." He gestured her to precede him back into the main room.

Just in time.

Kai hurried into the kitchen and seemed surprised to find them there together. Addison came, too. Greg ushered Renata out of there before there was time for them to ask questions and found Savannah, Jericho and Jacob gone and everyone else back to hanging around and chatting.

Renata still looked pale, and Avery was eyeing her as if she'd guessed something was wrong. Greg knew Renata wouldn't want to be questioned, so he thought fast. A competition would change the energy between them. She seemed to thrive on competitions. Searching in his pocket, he pulled out a handful of change, counted out two nickels and handed one to Renata. "First one to ten." He gestured toward the wall and used his toe to point to the crack between two floorboards. "Here's the foul line."

"You want to pitch pennies?"

Her British accent made it sound positively Dickensian.

"I want to play nickels." That's what they'd called it at the commune. He'd thought he'd have to explain the game to her, but it seemed like she knew it already. "It'll pass the time until we eat."

"Fine." Renata took her place behind the foul line and tossed the coin toward the wall. It landed about four inches away. She stepped back so Greg could have his turn. His landed three inches away, and he strode forward to collect them. When he handed one back to her, she shook her head. "You're supposed to keep it when you win."

"Do you have change hidden in that dress somewhere?" he asked.

Renata looked down as if surprised to see the old-fashioned gown. "No," she admitted.

"We'll just play for the glory of it," he told her and put the nickel into her palm.

Clem snorted. "No one plays for the glory." Greg hadn't seen him come in. "Make a bet," he goaded Renata. "That's what real players do."

"Don't let him get to you," Greg said. "I'll go first this time." He stepped up to the line.

"Twenty dollars," she said flatly before he could toss his coin. "First one to ten wins twenty dollars."

"Okay." Greg knew if he refused she'd be angry since Clem was watching. He had a feeling if he won the twenty dollars, she'd be angry as well. He couldn't *let* her win, though. She'd hate that worst of all.

He was going to lose no matter what, he realized. Clem's grin told him that was exactly the point.

Greg tossed his coin and bounced it off the wall hard enough it landed a foot away.

"Don't let him get to you." Renata parroted back his earlier advice, tossed her coin and won handily. "We're tied up at one."

They took their turns, a small crowd gathering around them as people realized what they were doing. By the time Kai came out to announce lunch, Renata had seven, and he had eight.

"Don't let the food get cold," Kai called out when no one moved to come get it.

"Hurry up," Boone told Greg.

Greg took his shot. Landed the coin within an inch of the wall.

Renata frowned. Took hers.

"Oh, lucky shot!" Hope exclaimed. The coin had landed only a millimeter or so away from the wall.

"Eight–eight," Riley called out.

Renata went first. This toss wasn't nearly so accurate. A good six inches separated it from the wall, and Greg was confident he could beat that.

He did. But Renata took the next one.

"Nine–nine," Riley said. "This is it!"

Renata tossed her coin and landed it a fraction of an inch from the wall.

How was she doing that?

Greg slid a look her way. Caught a tiny, satisfied smile on her lips that threw him for a loop and did distracting things to him low in his anatomy. That was the look of someone who knew exactly what she was doing. Renata had played this game before, hadn't she? A lot, if he wasn't mistaken.

"Take the shot. Let's eat!" Boone exhorted him.

Greg took the shot, realizing only after the coin had left his hand he'd barely stopped to aim. He swore, knowing before the coin landed how badly he'd miscalculated.

"Renata wins! That's twenty bucks for the lady," Avery crowed.

Greg took out his wallet and handed over the bill, shaking his head. He leaned in close to Renata, keeping his voice low so no one else would hear. "I think I've been played."

"Spend enough time in the foster care system, and you learn all sorts of things." She snapped her mouth shut, and Greg realized she hadn't meant to say that.

Foster care system? Renata?

He let it go for now but promised himself he'd ask about it later. "Come on," he said instead. "Let's eat."

"I COULD BEAT you. Easy," Clem sneered when the meal was over and people were trickling out the door to their morning pursuits.

Renata, waiting for Greg to come back after dropping their dishes in the kitchen, stood with a hand in a pocket she blessed Alice for putting in the gown, her fingers curled around the twenty-dollar bill she'd won. Twenty dollars closer to the amount she'd pledged to send the girls' school in Peru over the next three years. Twenty dollars closer to the day when she could explore other work options.

Or have a baby of her own.

Stop that, she told herself. Her mind was out of control these days, and she needed to focus on her goals.

In the beginning, when she'd first taken on responsibility for the girls, she, Mayra and Gabriela had set a budget to cover their expenses—a certain amount per girl per month that Renata had assured them she could pay. Over the years, that number had diminished as the older students graduated and went on to support themselves. Seven students left with twenty-nine months until they all graduated still added up to a substantial number—but a finite one. Renata hated to focus so much on the money when she'd always loved helping the girls, but she was looking forward to a time when she'd have more options.

"Baloney," she told Clem. "You couldn't beat me if my hands were tied behind my back and I had to toss the coin with my teeth." Too late she realized how he'd take her words.

He leered at her. "I'll beat you any way you like."

"Ick," Avery said, passing by. "Clem, why can't you say anything normal?"

Clem ignored her. "First to ten. Right now."

"And let me guess. You want to bet twenty dollars," Renata said tiredly.

"Not twenty. One hundred. I'm a man, not a weasel."

Avery snorted. "Debatable."

"Fine," Renata said. "Let's bet." Why not? She'd barely unleashed her potential in her game with Greg. It had been fun seeing the moment Greg had realized she'd been playing him. She couldn't count the number of games she'd participated in as a kid in one group home or another between placements in families. She'd practiced all the time when she was alone back then, a way to stave off the fear of what might come next. She wasn't just good at pitching pennies—or nickels; she was an expert.

She stepped up to the foul line she and Greg had used before, took out the same nickel Greg had given her and tossed it, deliberately making a creditable, but not very good, shot.

Clem stepped up next, tossed and won, of course, his triumphant smugness laughable as he retrieved the coins. Her skin crawled when he deliberately stroked a finger over her palm as he handed her coin back, but Renata didn't let it get to her: she'd faced plenty of that, too, back in the group homes.

She let Clem win four out of the five first shots.

"Four to one," Avery announced. The bunkhouse wasn't nearly as full as it had been, but those who were there began to gather around.

"Pathetic," Clem said to Renata. "See? I can beat you any time."

Renata took the next round. And the next. And the next.

Clem began to sweat.

She won the next round. And kept winning, mercilessly landing every coin within an inch of the wall.

Clem swore when the score reached eight–four. Swore again when it became nine–four.

And kicked a folding chair when Renata won the game handily.

"Give one hundred bucks to the lady," Avery crowed, getting in Clem's face.

Clem pulled out his wallet and tossed a hundred-dollar bill onto the floor. "You cheated," he snarled at Renata.

"How could she possibly cheat?" Avery demanded. "We all watched her toss her coins."

He gave Avery the finger and flounced out of the bunkhouse. Avery picked up the money and handed it to Renata. "Good job."

"Thanks."

"What did I miss? What was all the cheering out here?" Greg asked, coming back from the kitchen.

"Renata just handed Clem his ass on a platter," Avery said.

Greg frowned.

"Pitching pennies," Renata explained.

"Got it." He hesitated. "Boone suggested you help me today since Clem's taking charge as director. I'm working on the design for extending our energy system when the community grows in the future."

"Is that really something I can help with?" she asked skeptically. "Sounds pretty specialized."

"I'd still enjoy the company."

"Maybe I should help Avery with the animals," she suggested. "You can update me on your progress later this morning," she added diplomatically when it looked like he'd protest. The truth was, she wasn't ready to spend time alone with Greg, and this was the perfect excuse to hold him at arm's length. It was hard enough to keep her head around him when they were with everyone else.

"I guess energy systems are pretty boring."

"It's not that." Now she'd gotten herself into a corner, Renata realized. She couldn't very well say she didn't want to spend time with him because she was afraid he'd wear her down into agreeing to marry him. "I'm interested in your work—just not enough to take it on myself."

"What would you want to work on if you stayed—"

"Avery, we'd better go," Renata cut across him. She wasn't going to indulge in any fantasies about staying—especially not as his wife. The maternal pangs that kept overwhelming her meant nothing. Just her internal clock ticking. She had another clock to worry about—her career clock. If she wanted to tackle Hollywood, the time was now. In any case, she couldn't have a baby until all the girls in Peru graduated. And she'd be thirty-nine by then.

She swallowed against an upwelling of panic. It wouldn't be the end of the world if she didn't have kids. Success was the important thing.

"We'll catch you later, Greg," Avery said decisively and took Renata's arm, leading her toward the door.

"Byron, William, come on. You'll want to film this," Renata ordered. "Adrienne, you keep an eye on things here."

"Will do," Adrienne said.

"Hey, I'm the director here," Clem said.

"Did you hear someone talking?" Renata asked Avery as they headed outside.

"Nope, didn't hear a thing."

"See you later," Greg called after them.

CHAPTER FIVE

"FIGURED YOU COULD use this," Clay said later that evening, setting a folding table down by the chair Greg occupied by a window in the bunkhouse. Greg was glad to be back inside after his evening chores—it was cold out there.

"What for?"

"Your scale model." Clay gestured to the little buildings lined up on the bunkhouse windowsill. "That's what you're doing, right? Building a model?"

Greg nodded, trying to hide his surprise. He hadn't said anything to anyone, had just started whittling replica copies of the structures here at Base Camp. Clay was right: he didn't have anywhere to put them yet.

Clay unfolded the table's legs and set it upright. He reached over and picked up the model of the bunkhouse. "If we start with this..." He put it down in the middle of the table. "Then the barn goes here." He picked up another model and plunked it down. "And the tiny houses go here." He spaced them out and frowned. "You need a base that's topographically correct or you won't be able to tell much."

Greg had thought of that, too. "Near as I can figure, I'll have to do with a flat map with the topography indicated on it."

Curtis drifted over. "Why not build a base?"

Greg held up his carving tools. "That would take a long time with these."

"I could do it," Curtis told him. "Wouldn't take long. I'll build a table for it, too. A sturdy table."

"That would be great." The folding table wobbled a bit.

"What's going on? Why isn't someone filming this?" Renata demanded. Greg hadn't seen her come in, although now that he had, he couldn't take his eyes off her. Her hair, usually wound into a tight updo, was loose around her shoulders. Her old-fashioned gown rustled when she moved, as she did now, coming to bend over the tiny buildings Clay had placed on the table. "You made these?" she asked.

He flicked his gaze up from where it had rested on her cleavage and met hers. "Yes." He hoped like hell she hadn't caught him staring. When she lifted a hand to smooth it over the neckline of her dress, he knew she had.

"And you're going to build a proper base for them?" she asked Curtis, not acknowledging what she'd seen.

"That's right," Curtis said.

Renata scanned the room impatiently. "Byron, get over here," she snapped. "Why aren't you filming this?"

Byron hurried over. "I don't know." He spent a

moment fiddling with his equipment and waved at them to keep talking.

"Who taught you to carve, Greg?"

Renata had slipped into interviewer mode. Greg supposed it was better than nothing, although he'd prefer a real conversation with her.

"Jason Wheeler. One of the men who lived at Greenfield. He told me the best cities—and towns, for that matter—grow up around the needs of the people who live in them. 'People will walk where it makes sense to walk,' he used to say, and he'd show me parks and other places like that where there were paved pathways—and then dirt shortcuts where people stepped off them to get where they needed to go. 'Whenever you see a dirt path, some planner valued his own vision above the needs of the people he built it for.'"

"Guess that makes sense."

Greg rearranged the little carved buildings on the folding table. "I figure if we make a model now, we can talk about it before Base Camp grows. We can think about the whole, not just the separate parts. Try things out and adjust them before we commit to everything."

"That's a really good idea."

"Are you surprised?"

"No." Renata seemed flustered. "It just shows how much you care about Base Camp."

"Of course I care about Base Camp." She had to know that. This was his life now—the life he wanted her to share.

"Enough to marry a stranger when the time

comes?" she probed as if she wasn't the woman in the equation. That burned him.

"Are you really going to make me marry a stranger?" he countered.

She rolled her eyes. "Cut."

"I don't think you should cut. I think you should answer the question," Clay interjected. "Are you going to marry Greg? Because if you're not, I don't get why you even stay here, the way Fulsom and Clem are treating you."

Greg restrained himself from telling Clay to shut his mouth. Was he trying to sabotage his chances with Renata?

"I'm staying for the money," Renata snapped. "I get paid well—very well—to be here, despite what Clem says. I'm going to collect that paycheck as long as I can. Byron, film!"

"I'm filming," Byron assured her.

Greg thought she was going to snatch the camera right out of the young man's hands. "Film the *model,*" she said between clenched teeth.

"Right. Okay." Byron swiveled the camera to pan over the models set up on the table. It looked like Renata was counting to ten.

"What do you need the money for?" Clay asked. Even though Greg had wondered that, too, he wished Clay hadn't asked. The other man caught Greg looking and shrugged. "If she's getting paid so well, and she's been working for Fulsom for years, she must have a bundle squirreled away," he said. He turned back to

Renata. "Far as I can tell, he pays all your expenses, too, right? Don't you have enough already?"

"I have responsibilities."

"Responsibilities? Like what?" Clay asked.

"You know what, Byron?" Renata turned to the cameraman. "Let's go find something interesting to film."

"No, stay." Greg reached for her. "Film the model. Clay was just leaving."

"But—"

"Leav-ing." Greg was firm.

Clay looked from him to Renata. Seemed to get it suddenly. Shook himself. "Yeah, I was just leaving," he said. "Sorry, Renata. Curiosity got the better of me."

Greg let out a breath of relief when he left. Renata plucked at the neckline of her gown, as if making it less revealing could somehow shield her from being exposed on the show.

"This sucks," she said finally.

"Being filmed?"

"All of it." She must have caught his expression. "I mean—" But she didn't finish what she was going to say, and why should she?

"You didn't ask to be put in this position," he said stiffly, letting his arm drop again.

"No." Her gaze lit on Byron, still filming, and then the table. "Byron, come on. Focus in on these buildings. Look at the detail."

Greg understood why she'd changed the subject. He was glad she hadn't simply left, like Clay had, and he supposed if he wanted her to stay, he'd better give her a reason. He knew the kind of footage needed for the show, so he turned to Byron's camera and waved at the table. "I'm building a scale model of Base Camp to better understand how we can maximize efficiency."

"In powering it?" She moved closer.

"Efficiency of the power grid, yes, but also other systems. Look, right now we live here, the barns and outbuildings are here, the gardens and greenhouses are there…" He set it all up, then traced a finger over the table. "And the manor is here. Nearly all the women travel up to the manor on a daily basis, right?"

"Right."

"So what do you notice about the layout?"

Renata looked it over. "All the men's chores take them in one direction, and although some of the women join them, most of the women's chores take them in a different direction. Is that a problem?"

Greg shrugged. "Not necessarily, if that's what people choose after thinking about it. None of us thought about it, though, did we? Spreading out over the property in this way means if we hadn't decided to take our meals together communally, and if the women hadn't been assigned certain chores because of Fulsom's rules, the men and women wouldn't see each other much, especially those not paired up in couples."

"I hadn't thought about that."

"Sometimes it takes an eagle-eye view of a place to really see it." He shifted one of the tiny houses. "Angus is right. We need a sturdier base. One that shows the topography of the place." He caught her pensive expression. "What are you thinking?"

"About an eagle-eye view of my life. I grew up in Britain. Traveled to South America before I came to the United States to work for Fulsom, and then zigzagged all over the world."

"Peru," Greg said, then realized his mistake.

Renata frowned.

"You traveled to Peru after film school," he blustered on, cursing himself for the slip.

"How did you know that?"

"I… looked it up," Greg hedged. He had looked her up when he'd discovered she was directing *Base Camp*. "When I applied to join this place, I checked out who was going to direct the show. I was curious," he explained. "I saw you did a documentary there."

He wondered if he should simply tell her he'd been there that awful, rainy day and night after the mudslide and helped her search for information about the girls' families. He didn't blame her for not recognizing him. Back then he was thinner. Far less muscular. His hair had been long and shaggy, always falling into his eyes. He'd worn a scruffy college-boy beard, and he'd been covered in mud from erecting tents and hauling supplies in the pouring rain. She'd been in shock, too busy searching for news of the girls' families to even notice him dogging her steps, trying to help.

Some stubborn part of him wanted her to remember him for herself. Wanted his presence there to have meant something. Besides, if he told her now she'd think he was some kind of stalker, and he hadn't joined Base Camp to stalk Renata. He'd come—

Hell, he'd been interested in joining the group because of the chance to show people how sophisticated green energy systems had become, but the truth was he'd never have joined another… commune… if Renata hadn't been the director. Some part of him had always been convinced she was the one who got away. Now he was here and so was she—why wouldn't she make the connection?

Renata shrugged. "My first film. Outside school, that is."

"I wonder what ever happened to those girls."

Something flashed in her eyes. Of course, Greg realized. She would have kept in touch with them—or at the very least followed their progress from afar. It pained him now to realize he hadn't. As much as he'd tried to help, he hadn't connected to anyone involved in the disaster—not even Renata. When the other women with her had finally convinced her to get a little rest in the bus the following morning, he'd returned with the others in his contingent to Lima. In all the chaos, there'd been no chance to hit up Renata for her phone number, and later he'd rejected the idea of trying to hunt her down. That twenty-four hours had been a sort of adventure to him, but he'd known it was devastating to Renata. He'd returned to the whirlwind of finishing school and graduating. By then, it felt like the moment had passed.

"They're doing all right," she said softly. "Most have

graduated from high school and are getting on with life."

"I don't suppose you ever get over losing your parents, though," Greg said.

"No," Renata said shortly. "You don't."

Too late he remembered what she'd said about foster homes. "How old were you when you lost your folks?" he asked softly, knowing most likely she'd tell him to mind his own business.

"Six," she said. "Car accident. I was at school. First grade. The headmistress came to tell me. Everything changed like that." She snapped her fingers.

Guilt suffused Greg as he thought about his own childhood. Always surrounded by family—and the extended circle that made up the commune. One hundred eighty acres of agrarian paradise. A loving adult everywhere you went. That was what had driven him crazy—all those adults in his business. Every decision made as a group. The slow process that accompanied implementing any new idea—

"You lived in foster homes," he said.

"Until I was sixteen. I had a job by then. Supported myself. Put myself through school."

"You must have busted your ass."

"I suppose you broke a sweat once in a while yourself in the Navy," she countered.

"Once in a while," he agreed.

He was rewarded with a grudging but genuine smile. "What made you join up?"

He gave a quick and what he hoped was humorous

description of his childhood, knowing Byron was filming it all. He didn't intend to get into the desperate restlessness he'd felt during his high school years. His craving for the anonymity of a wider world. "My parents hoped my sister and I would settle at Greenside, like they had. We both got the hell out of there." He realized how that would sound on television. "Don't get me wrong," he hastened to say. "Greenside isn't a bad place. We just wanted something different."

"A different kind of commune," Renata said dryly.

"Yeah." He acknowledged the irony of ending up here. "A different kind of commune. But one with the distinct advantage of being filmed," he ended.

They grinned at each other.

Greg didn't realize he was edging closer to her until Renata glanced at Byron and broke the spell. He'd have to try another time, he decided. When they were alone.

If they were ever alone.

TWO DAYS LATER, Renata was beginning to feel like she'd always been in front of the cameras instead of behind them. As director, it had been her job to keep her subjects under constant surveillance. As a participant on the show, she found being surveilled exhausting.

Clem was making her his personal victim and made sure to follow her everywhere she went, Byron or one of the other cameramen in tow. Her only consolation was that he was making it impossible for Greg to make a move on her. She knew he wanted to, and his impatience was a kind of an aphrodisiac, if she was being honest, but she knew that if Greg tried anything, she'd have a hard time resisting him.

He'd nearly kissed her when she'd talked about her parents. She'd wanted him to, she admitted to herself now. Thank goodness for Byron and his snooping camera. Greg had understood she couldn't let herself be filmed like that and had backed off.

They'd had several close calls since then, and a constant ache of wanting accompanied her everywhere, letting her know that even though she'd long told herself she'd shut down the part of her that wanted a connection with a man, it wasn't true—

Not one bit.

In off minutes, when there was nothing to do, Greg tended to pick up a bit of wood and pull out his pocket knife and start whittling, which always caught her attention. She found herself watching his hands, imagining them doing other things—to her. She'd experienced kissing him already. Now she wanted more.

Clem made that impossible, which made it easier to tell herself she'd get through these forty days, watch Greg marry someone else and keep on with her life—

But she didn't believe it. Watching Greg marry someone else was going to be harder than she'd ever expected now that her lazy daydreams about him had turned into something far more real.

For the first time in years she wasn't sure how to proceed. She knew she had to finish what she'd started and earn the money to get the remainder of the girls through school. If she had a normal job, getting married wouldn't affect her earning power, but working for Fulsom was far from normal. He demanded total loyalty—and paid enough to make it hard to say no. In all the years she'd been on his payroll, he'd expected her to be available morning, noon and night. He'd allowed her those first couple of early vacations to visit Peru but had made it clear he resented her absence, and she'd stopped asking for time off. Fulsom might not know why she needed the money he paid her, but he knew she needed it and took full advantage of his power over her.

If she married Greg—

She'd lose her job—the job that was already nearly gone. It was that simple. By keeping Clem on after she'd shown the world exactly what kind of man he was, and forcing her to become a participant of the show she was supposed to be directing, Fulsom had made it clear he was nearly done with her. No one else would pay her so well, and being fired by such a famous man would leave her in no position to pursue a career in Hollywood.

Did she want that career, though?

Of course she did, she told herself furiously. That's what she'd worked for all these years—

No, that wasn't true. Renata's shoulders slumped. That was what she'd put herself through school for in her late teens and early twenties, but it wasn't why she'd worked with Fulsom for the last decade.

That had been for Lorena, Noelia, Elena and the rest of the girls in Peru. The same ones who were growing up and leaving her sphere of influence one by one. She could no longer even pretend to be a surrogate mother to any of them. Not that she ever really had been.

Every time she got a glimpse of Savannah and Jacob, a different kind of ache filled her, followed by a surge of frustration. This was the worst possible moment for the baby bug to bite her. She'd decided to give Savannah a wide berth for now. For good measure, she'd started to avoid Nora, too, whose belly was getting round. Nora wouldn't give birth until spring, but every time she caught sight of the woman—a dozen times a day despite her best intentions—Renata thought about what pregnancy would feel like, and another blast of hormones would suffuse her, leaving her looking for Greg and then angry at herself for doing so.

"There," Avery said, finishing doing up the fastenings of Renata's gown. "Breakfast?"

"Breakfast," Renata agreed, eager to get away from such uncomfortable thoughts, but when they stepped out of the bunkhouse bathroom, they encountered pandemonium.

"Boone was the one who noticed. They were all like that, though," Riley was saying indignantly.

"Every inch of our solar panels was covered in snow. Packed down—on purpose," Hope added.

"All of the panels were the same," Boone said. "Where were the patrols? Why didn't anyone see anything?"

"We can't be everywhere at once—you know that," a rather disgruntled Curtis answered. He and Anders had the sleepy look of men who'd been awake for far too long. "Whoever did it must have snuck around while we were out checking on the herd."

"Maybe we need more patrols," Boone said.

"Covering up the solar panels with snow is sort of a dumb prank," Curtis pointed out. "Sounds like something the crew might get up to rather than malicious intruders. Especially since it's January in Montana and we're not expecting much out of the panels right now. If they go after the geothermal or wind—"

"Pipe down," Boone ordered. "If it's the crew, you don't need to give them ideas." He spotted Renata and clamped his mouth shut.

Renata hesitated, knowing she was still far more crew than Base Camp participant. She wasn't going to waste her breath trying to convince them otherwise. Clem might very well have instigated something like this.

Her phone chimed just as Kai announced that breakfast was ready, and she moved to the far side of the room to evade the crush of hungry people. Mayra was calling.

"Hello?"

"Renata, it's Mayra." Neither Renata nor anyone else could convince the woman that her name came up on screen when she called.

"Good to hear from you. How is everyone?"

"Everyone is fine, but our bus—not so much." She got down to business in her usual fashion. Mayra never minced words. "The engine is done for. It's an expensive bill."

Renata's heart sank. She knew exactly what the woman was asking for. "How much?"

The sum she named made Renata grit her teeth. Thank God Fulsom had doubled her pay. That didn't mean he'd keep her on once the show's season was done, however. She'd hoped to bank that extra pay for future months—

She tallied the amount she'd pledged to pay per month over the next twenty-nine months until all the girls graduated from high school, a calculation she performed several times a day.

"I'll cover it," she said, mentally adding the new sum to the old tally. What else could she do? As far as Mayra and Gabriela knew, she was a wealthy woman with unlimited access to funds. She'd cultivated their belief in her since the day she accepted Fulsom's offer of employment. Those women had enough to worry about mothering so many orphaned girls. She'd resolved from the start they would never have to worry about money.

"Everything okay?" Greg asked when she joined him in line a minute later.

"It's fine." She couldn't keep the frustration out of her voice, though, and she had the feeling he wasn't fooled. When he followed her and Avery outside after their meal, she knew she was right.

"Don't you have solar panels to fix?" Renata asked him as they all trudged toward the animal pens.

"The panels weren't damaged, only covered with snow to try to hamper their effectiveness. Like Curtis said, it's the dead of winter; they're only one small part of our energy scheme. I'll get to them, but first I'll help you and Avery."

"The more the merrier," Avery said when Renata didn't answer. She was wondering what Clem was up to this time. He must have ordered the panels to be covered. Had Fulsom told him to do it to shake up the show? Was the billionaire talking to Clem more than her now?

Probably.

As they made the rounds, caring for the animals, bumping into Walker on his way to check the bison herd, Renata wondered how she should fill the rest of her days at Base Camp. Obviously, they were numbered, and if she wanted to change that without marrying Greg and letting down everyone in Peru, she needed to think of a way to prove to Fulsom he still needed her.

She remembered the question Greg had tried to ask her. What would she do if she stayed at Base Camp for good? She wouldn't work on solar panels or wind turbines. She didn't think designing or maintaining the energy grid was for her. She wasn't big on animals, either. Gardening?

Not really her thing.

She was a director. Had always been a director.

"Chickens next," Avery said.

They trudged on to the chicken coop. Avery took the lead. Behind her back, but well within sight of the camera crew that had tracked them since they left the bunkhouse, Greg took Renata's hand.

She knew she should shake him off, but the little thrill that zipped through her body at his touch—even through their gloves—made her hesitate. Everything else in her life right now made her feel so hopeless—at least this was positive.

Renata nearly snorted. Falling for Greg was hardly positive. It meant failing to fulfill her promise to her girls and failing to fulfill her dream of a Hollywood career, too.

"You've got the energy grid. Avery has her animals. What am I supposed to do here?" she made herself ask, dreading the long hours she had to fill before bedtime.

Avery cast her a strange look over her shoulder, and Renata knew why. The other woman wasn't here for the animals; she had hoped to be an actress and spent all her free time messing around with filmmaking.

"I always pictured you, Avery and Eve starting a movie production company when I thought of our future," Greg said.

Renata stopped dead, flummoxed equally by his suggestion and by the idea he'd been thinking about their future. How much time had he spent on that?

Avery whirled around to face them. "A production company? In Chance Creek?"

"Why not?" Greg asked.

"Because films are made in California. New York. Vancouver. Atlanta." Avery ticked them off on her fingers.

"That doesn't mean you can't start a new trend. Hell, you've even got a star actress in town. Ella Hall.

Isn't she working on a screenplay or something?"

"That's true," Avery admitted.

"That's the whole point of Base Camp, right? Doing what you love in a sustainable fashion. So start a sustainable film company."

"No one wants sustainable movies. Could you get more boring?" Clem brayed from behind them. Renata had nearly forgotten the crew was there. When she was directing, she was more formal about inserting herself into the show, doing so only during planned interviews. Clem had always been front and center on *Tracking the Stars*. He must hate playing second fiddle to ten Navy SEALs.

Greg ignored him. "Wouldn't you like to build something from the ground up?" he asked Renata.

Renata didn't know how to answer that. She'd never even considered such a thing.

"Give us some action, would you?" Clem complained. "Talk, talk, talk—that's all you ever do."

Greg rolled his eyes, but instead of telling Clem to shove it, he said, "Fine, I'll give you some action." For a moment, Renata thought he'd kiss her, but he seemed to change his mind. Instead, he grabbed a shovel leaning against the coop.

In a matter of minutes, he'd dug two long, parallel trenches through the snow and placed a scattering of feed at the end of each of them.

He opened the door to the chicken coop. "Come on, Renata. Let's have a chicken race."

"You've got to be kidding," Renata said, but still

buzzing from his suggestion and grateful for the distraction, she joined him in the coop, caught a chicken—a black-and-white-speckled one—and carried it carefully to the start of one of the trenches. "Won't it fly away as soon as I put it down?"

"Their wings are clipped. It won't get far," Avery reassured her. "I think a chicken race is just what we need. I'll call the start."

Greg took his place with a red chicken in his hands.

"On your mark. Get set. Go!" Avery called.

Renata and Greg let their chickens go. Renata's ran in a quick circle and nearly took off for the bunkhouse before she managed to shoo it back into the trench. Greg's headed straight for the feed at the far end.

Byron signaled from behind his camera, a gesture that plainly said, *Hype this up or it'll be too boring to use.*

"Go, chicken," Renata called half-heartedly after hers.

"Go, chicken. Go!" Greg hollered, getting into the swing of it.

The film crew raced to keep up, but after the initial flurry of movement, the chickens seemed to decide they weren't in that much of a hurry to get to the feed at the end of the trenches after all. Greg's got distracted by something in the snow, a discolored patch surrounding a dead leaf. Renata's seemed inclined to turn back.

Five minutes later, Renata's finally made it to the finish line.

"Well, that was exciting," Clem drawled.

"What do I win?" Clem's disgust made Renata happy. To her surprise, the chicken race had been kind of fun. Silly, but sometimes silly was just what you needed.

"A kiss. What else?" Greg came to stand in front of her, put his hands on her hips and tugged her closer. He gave her time to pull away, but Renata didn't. She was too busy anticipating the feel of him—

She sighed when their mouths met. No one kissed like Greg. No one made her feel so melty inside. She couldn't help slide her hands over his shoulders to wrap them around his neck.

"Am I the only one who cares that the chickens are still loose?" Avery demanded.

Renata chuckled but didn't pull away, and neither did Greg. She could hear Avery racing through the snow, swearing now and then. Greg's kisses were far too delicious to forgo, even if she should be helping.

"Guess we'd better go chase chickens," Greg said finally.

"Guess so," she agreed. She tried not to notice the cameras focused on them or Clem's sneering expression as they helped Avery round up the escapee hens.

"Who gives a crap about a lousy kiss?" Clem said. "You need to start betting for some real stakes."

"Like what?" Renata snatched up the black-and-white-speckled hen.

"Like five hundred bucks." Clem pointed to the chicken in her arms. "You and me. Let's go—right now."

"You don't need to do that," Greg said when Renata moved automatically to the starting line again.

She did if she wanted to earn some extra cash. Her chicken had already proved it knew how to win this race.

"Let's do this," she called to Clem.

Avery, who'd just managed to catch the red hen, handed it over to the director reluctantly. "Don't hurt Sammy."

"Sammy?" Clem took the hen with distaste, holding it out from his body as if afraid it might soil him. Which it easily could, Renata knew. The hens didn't discriminate about where they pooped.

"It's named for Samantha," Avery explained. "That one is Nora," she told Renata.

Renata considered the bird. She could see the resemblance and decided not to ask if one was named for her.

"On your mark. Get set. Go!"

The birds were off. As before, Sammy dashed off toward the feed at the end of the trench like she might make it there in moments but got distracted along the way by the same patch of snow that had waylaid her the first time.

Nora ran in a circle and then made her way very deliberately toward the feed in her trench.

The race continued in fits and starts, neither chicken in a very big hurry to get anywhere.

In the end, however, Nora proved the winner again.

"Five hundred bucks." Renata held a hand out toward Clem.

Clem pulled out his wallet and counted bills. His

face was grim, but he laughed off his defeat. "Should have known better than to use a bird this loser chose." He nodded at Greg as he placed the final bill in her hand. "Besides, five hundred bucks is nothing when you earn what I do. I bet Fulsom pays me double what he pays you."

"I doubt it."

But Renata wondered if she knew as much about Fulsom as she thought she did.

CHAPTER SIX

GREG WATCHED RENATA pocket her winnings with a heavy heart. All Clem had to do was suggest a contest and she'd jump in with both feet. He wasn't against placing a friendly bet or two now and then, but whatever she had going on with the other director wasn't healthy.

She kept her hand in the pocket of her spencer a moment or two longer than necessary, as if assuring herself the money was there. An odd thing for a woman to do who had to earn a decent living working for a billionaire like Fulsom.

Was she short on cash? Did she have a gambling problem? What else didn't he know about Renata?

They needed to start spending a lot more time together.

"Let's get those hens back in their pen," he said shortly and went after Nora. Renata managed to catch Sammy, and they finished the chores with Avery, neither of them talking much. Greg wasn't sure if Renata had noticed his mood or if she was still savoring her victory.

He was glad when Harris Wentworth came along and asked them to return to the bunkhouse for an announcement. Anything to get his mind off his dark thoughts.

Greg had always appreciated Harris. He was a tall, thoughtful man who had a knack for knowing the right thing to do in a situation. He'd been studying metalsmithing with a local rancher and had set up a makeshift forge in back of the barn.

"What's this about?" Renata asked Greg as they neared the bunkhouse.

"I don't know."

They filed in with the others, and when everyone was grouped inside, Harris led Samantha to the front of the room. Greg couldn't help think of the chicken named after her. Renata caught him smiling and smiled back. He leaned companionably closer to her and put an arm around her waist. It felt so natural he was grateful Renata didn't shrug her way out from under it.

"Thanks for giving us a minute of your time," Harris said. "I guess we could have waited for lunch or dinner, but we just found out—and hell, we couldn't wait a minute to share our news."

Samantha nodded in agreement, a smile spreading over her face. "I'm pregnant!" she cried. "Eve, you and I are going to be pregnant together!"

A chorus of happy cries greeted her announcement, and everyone pressed forward to congratulate the happy couple. Greg couldn't help himself. He squeezed Renata and gestured at them. "That could be us one of these days."

Renata snapped her head around to look at him. "Putting the cart before the horse a little bit, aren't you?"

"Maybe. Maybe not. We're good together, don't you think?" He tried to brazen it out, but it was clear he'd crossed a line.

"We've barely kissed. Now you're talking children?" Renata had her no-nonsense director face on. In a minute she'd cross her arms and tap her toe.

He leaned closer and whispered into her ear, "I'm up for anything you want. Anytime you want." He meant it to be funny, but he'd surprised her again, and he saw the moment she thought about it—really thought about being with him. The flash of desire in her eyes fired up an answering surge of longing within him. Hell, knowing she wanted him—even a little bit—made him want her more.

He bent lower. "We can find someplace to be alone right now if you—"

"Popping the question?" Clem blared in his ear. The director was standing as close to him as he was to Renata. "Is there going to be another happy announcement? What do you say, Renata? Ready for wedding bells and baby booties?"

Renata ducked out from under Greg's arm and flounced off to congratulate Harris and Samantha. Greg faced Clem. "You've got lousy timing."

"I've got impeccable timing," Clem informed him.

"The last thing the world needs is you and Renata getting together making a bunch of little Renatas." He shivered dramatically.

And Greg knew what was really going on. "You've got the hots for her."

"Do not." Clem backpedaled.

"Sure you do. But she's mine, got it?" Greg went to join Renata and tried to put his arm around her again. She evaded him.

"Stop that."

"Renata—"

"Greg." Curtis came over to their group. "I've got something for you. Want to see? It'll just take a minute."

"Sure. Be right back." Greg left Renata reluctantly, but it seemed like courting trouble to stay.

Curtis led the way to one of the outbuildings where a grimy cloth covered something on a workbench. When he whipped the cloth away with a "Ta-da!" Greg had to smile.

"That's awesome! When did you make this?" It was a 3-D topographical map made in such a way that his little carved buildings could sit on its contours.

"Last night," Curtis said. "Wasn't hard."

"It's great. Let's take it back to the bunkhouse."

Once there, he cleared all the buildings he'd carved off the side table so Curtis could put it down, then rearranged the buildings where they went. This was ten times better than what he had before.

"It still needs a better table," Curtis said.

"This will more than do for now."

Everyone clustered around to check out the model, and soon they began making suggestions for changes.

"That last house is too far over," Jericho said and nudged it into position.

"You need to carve the manor now," Addison said.

"And you need trees. All of this part is forested," Avery pointed out.

"This is so cool; we can use it to try things out, too," Riley said, leaning over the model. "Like, if we wanted more greenhouses or a pagoda or something, we could try it out on the map first."

"You want a pagoda?" Boone asked her.

"I kind of always have," she told him.

"Someday we'll need more tiny houses," Clay said. "Where are we going to put them?"

Clem, who was making sure his camera crew was documenting the scene, snorted. "Expanding is the last thing you lot need to worry about. Packing is more like it. Pretty soon you'll all have to clear out of here and the bulldozers will flatten the place." He swept a hand forward, knocking over most of the buildings. Greg caught his wrist before he could knock them to the floor.

"Hey," Clem said, trying to pull free.

"Don't. Touch. My. Stuff," Greg said. He let Clem go, and the director stumbled back a few paces. Clem noticed the cameras filming and straightened up.

"You're pretty cocky," he said. "We'll see how you feel when this is all over."

"Right back at you, pal," Greg said.

"Come on," Clem said to his crew members. "There's nothing interesting going on here."

RENATA WAS STILL thinking about Harris and Samantha's announcement after dinner after a long day of shadowing Avery and Walker, doing her best to help them with the animals and other chores, then following Avery to the manor, where Avery was working on a film project. She'd brought along her own laptop and tried to answer emails and other small tasks, but she'd found it hard to concentrate. Clem was working hard to keep her out of the loop, and he made sure to keep all the camera crews busy.

Two women were pregnant now—plus Nora, who was already several months along. That more than satisfied the baby requirement for them to win permanent ownership of the ranch. It took the pressure off everyone else, too. If she married Greg, there'd be no necessity to try to conceive quickly.

She wasn't going to marry Greg, she kept telling herself.

It would be fun to try to conceive quickly with him, though, some insurrectionist part of her brain kept answering back.

Despite her best efforts not to, she kept imagining the two of them in various scenarios—trying for a baby. They'd have to be together morning, noon and night, she supposed, sighing at the longing that curled deep within her, such a crazy desire given her circumstances. She figured Greg would be just as dexterous with her body as he was with everything else he did if she ever gave him the chance.

Was she being dumb holding herself aloof from him? What if she just—

Married him?

They'd have their wedding at the manor, Renata knew. A wedding night together. Sheer bliss, probably, she admitted.

Then the day after, when Fulsom relieved her of her place on his payroll, she'd have to tell Mayra and Gabriela she had no more money to send them. Too bad, so sad.

She didn't think she could do that.

Renata huffed out a breath. Why had none of the magazines and newspapers that loved to write about Fulsom's every last exploit never noticed the extraordinary number of singletons in his employ? She wondered if his HR people ever brought it up. Surely it was a lawsuit in the making, but she wasn't going to try to take on one of the richest men in the world in court. She wasn't dumb.

If this was a normal situation and she and Greg were dating, she'd tell him she wanted to take it slow, really get to know him, and would stretch out their courtship for as long as possible. Then, if he proposed, she'd tell him about her promise to the girls in Peru and work that much harder to pay off her obligation so they could marry.

She tallied up the amount in her head again—the new, larger amount with the cost of the bus's motor added to it.

Renata shook her head at herself. Look at her, ready to upend her life for Greg—

"What are you thinking about?" Greg asked.

She hadn't even heard him approach. Renata took a sip from the cold cup of tea she held in her hand. She'd been at a bit of loose ends after dinner, without a task at hand, whereas everyone else knew exactly what to do, and she had poured herself the cup just to have something to fiddle with.

She didn't have a ready answer to Greg's question, not without exposing the risqué places her mind had wandered—or her financial difficulties. He must have showered recently. He smelled clean, and his short, dark hair was still damp.

"Uh… nickels. I was thinking about our game. Figuring I could beat you again."

"You were thinking of *beating* me?"

He made it sound so overly suggestive, Renata laughed. "What else is there to think about?"

"I suppose this is where I say I want a rematch?"

"Do you?"

He hesitated, then shrugged. "Sure. Why not."

Renata glanced over her shoulder and caught Clem looking their way. What a perfect setup for making money, she decided. Not from Greg—from Clem. But only if she played this right.

"All right, then," she said loud enough for everyone in the bunkhouse to hear. "I can beat you again if you like." She went up on tiptoe and kissed Greg's cheek, mostly to capture Clem's attention but a little bit to make up for what was going to happen next. Greg was a good guy. He didn't deserve to be used to swindle Clem.

For a moment, she was caught up wishing she and Greg had met somewhere else. They'd have gotten on well together, considering the way they were able to find the humor in situations when they were alone. When she found him poring over information about his energy systems or staring off into space thinking about how to improve them, she liked the way this strong, capable man wanted to use his brain to make others' lives better. She couldn't pretend it wasn't a turn-on that he'd set his sights so firmly on her. How did he know he wanted to marry her? She wished she could ask.

Greg's shoulders relaxed a fraction. He caught her around the waist, surprising her, and kissed her back. Renata wished his kisses didn't affect her so strongly, but she felt them all the way through her body. Found herself leaning into him, spreading her hands wide against his chest. It was all she could do not to twist her fingers in the fabric of his shirt and cling to him.

Renata was sure she was flushed when she pulled back, but Greg's kiss was a good thing, she told herself, noticing Clem and one of the cameramen drawing near to film the action. She'd accomplished her goal. That was what mattered. Not the zing of desire lighting up every nerve in her body.

They set up the game quickly, clearing chairs away from the wall and marking a foul line. Renata forced her thoughts into calmer waters. She needed to play this well or she wouldn't get more money out of Clem.

"Ladies first," Greg said.

Renata obliged him and tossed her coin. She pretended Greg wasn't anyone special. That he didn't make her want to throw all caution to the wind and get him alone. She knew how to focus when things got tough. She could focus when they got… interesting.

Despite how flustered she'd been a minute ago, the game played out exactly as she'd planned. She made a couple of wild tosses and let Greg take the lead, Clem's comments on her lack of skill getting more and more derisive as they went. She made up some of the gap between their scores in the middle of the game until it was a contest again. Lost a couple of tosses, then tied the game at nine–nine. If Greg recognized her pattern from their last game, he didn't comment.

"Last shot" was all he said and waved her forward.

Renata took the shot and landed her nickel about seven inches from the wall. It was still possible she could win if Greg really blew his toss, but she'd left him enough margin to easily take it.

He did and landed his coin less than two inches from the wall.

"Go, Greg!" Avery cheered.

"You suck," Clem said to Renata. "You throw like a girl! And you two didn't even bet. Both of you suck."

"I could beat you," Renata said.

Something flashed in Greg's eyes, warning her he might be on to her little game, but Clem took the bait instantly.

"Like hell you could."

"Name your bet."

"A thousand dollars." Clem's chin lifted, his grin making her skin crawl. He thought he was so hot, didn't he?

"Renata," Greg warned.

"Game on," Renata cut across him.

"Ladies first," Clem parroted and gestured the way Greg had at the start of their game.

"Fine." Renata tossed her coin and landed it nearly a foot from the wall. Clem hooted, tossed his and won the round—

And they were off.

Renata wondered several minutes later how Clem could be so oblivious to the way she was playing him, especially since she'd done this to him before. She kept letting him win a few rounds, then nearly catching up to him again. Clem alternated between glee and fury depending on the score. She let him keep the lead until they tied with seven each.

Then she was merciless.

"Seven–eight," Avery intoned when Renata made her shot. "Seven–nine. Seven–ten! Renata wins!"

"That's a thousand dollars, if you please," Renata said.

Clem swore as he pulled out his wallet. "Beginner's luck."

"You're probably right," she said innocently. Behind Clem, Greg rolled his eyes. She pocketed the cash. If he kept doubling his bets, she could earn everything she needed in a matter of weeks.

Renata stilled. Was that true?

She thought about the new number she'd memorized after tallying it a half-dozen times throughout the day. That depended on how much Clem was willing to bet. He was easy to throw off his game. Wild to prove himself against her. Reckless.

Possibly hot for her.

What if she could raise the rest of the funds she needed in the next couple of weeks—before Greg's deadline to marry? What if Clem was the answer to all her problems?

"Whatever you're thinking, it's a bad idea," Greg said in a low voice, moving close to her.

"I want a rematch," Clem said.

"Hell, no. You've taken enough of my girlfriend's time. We're going for a walk."

Renata didn't protest either the girlfriend part or the walk. She had to play this out carefully with Clem. Making him wait for his next shot at revenging himself would make him all that much more eager to place a higher bet next time. Double their last bet would be two thousand dollars. Then four thousand, then eight, then…

Could she make bets that big?

She followed Greg to the door and let him help her on with her spencer.

"You're playing with fire," he said as he opened the door and stepped outside. When she joined him, the cold night air felt good on her flushed cheeks. She let him take her hand and left the bunkhouse—and Clem—behind. Pumped with the possibility she could earn the money she needed quickly, she went up on tiptoe and kissed Greg again. Really kissed him, showing him how much she enjoyed the taste of him, the feel of being in his arms.

"I sure hope so," she breathed when they parted again.

Reality crashed in a moment later. It wasn't just the money standing in the way of her being with Greg. She had her career to think about.

No matter what Greg said, no one was going to make Hollywood movies in Chance Creek, Montana.

CHAPTER SEVEN

HE WAS THE one who was playing with fire, Greg decided as he took Renata's hand again and led her down the track to Pittance Creek. It was dark out here. Cold. But a moon shone down through ragged clouds, and here and there stars were in view. No snow tonight, at least.

He cast about for something to talk about as they walked. Not Clem, or her seeming need to provoke the other director at every turn. Not her penchant for gambling, either. Something that would pull them together rather than causing them to fight.

"What do you think about Eve and Samantha being pregnant?"

Renata was quiet a moment. "I think they're lucky. They've found their life partners and work that's important to them. They have a community of friends. Now they're starting their families."

"You have work that's important to you," Greg said. He waved a hand to encompass Base Camp. "You're a natural as a director."

She shrugged.

"Someone told me when Base Camp is over you want to do bigger and better things." He hated even bringing it up, but he had to know Renata's state of mind.

"That was the plan."

"Was?"

"Is," she said quickly. "I mean, I think… I mean, of course it is."

She didn't sound so sure.

Renata sighed. "It's just—I don't know. I want…"

"Something different?" he suggested.

She looked startled. At first he thought she would deny it. "I'm just a little burnt out," she said finally. "I know what I want, but somehow it doesn't feel like I want it anymore."

He chose his next words carefully. "What does it feel like you want?"

"Something totally different. Has that ever happened to you? Wanting to clear the slate and try again?"

Greg thought about the way he'd felt leaving Oregon. "Hell, yeah."

She looked up at him curiously. "Did it work?"

"It did, although not the way I expected. I was young then. I wanted to see the world. Have a lot of adventures. I was totally wrapped up in myself. Then something happened, and I realized I wanted something more than that selfish kind of life. It changed everything."

"You became a Navy SEAL."

"That's right. Is that what's happening for you? Are you redefining your goals?"

She thought about it. "Maybe."

"If you stay and marry me, you can do anything you want to," he said, needing her to know he'd support any decision she made. "Like I said, Eve and Sam have the whole baby thing wrapped up. No reason we have to rush to have kids."

"What if I want kids?"

Don't answer that, Greg told himself. This was the crux of her dilemma, even if she was pretending it was no big thing. He tried to put himself in Renata's shoes. She'd worked for Fulsom for years. Pretended to be hard as nails, always focused on her career.

He'd seen the way she'd looked at Savannah and Jacob, though. That longing…

Why hadn't she spoken of it before?

Probably because of Fulsom, he realized. The billionaire was nothing if not selfish. He demanded a lot from the people he employed, and when Greg tried to picture Fulsom working with a new mother, he could imagine the man's impatience. Renata had already said she needed money. Needed her job, in other words.

As Renata bit her lip and turned away, Greg guessed she hadn't meant to express her desire for a child out loud. If he wasn't careful, she'd become angry she'd exposed something she meant to keep to herself. Time to lighten the mood.

"Baby, if you want kids," he proclaimed theatrically, "we'll have them. Lots of them. As many as you want.

Give me the word, and we'll start right now. I mean it, Renata. I'd give the world to be your man."

He thought she'd push him away, laugh it off and move on to a different topic, but when he leaned in to capture her mouth with his, she didn't resist. Want and need reared up strong inside him, leaving him struggling to keep his body under control.

The crunch of boots stepping through snow alerted him they weren't alone.

"Hell," he whispered against her cheek. "A camera crew."

A sound escaped Renata, a moan of thwarted frustration that echoed his feelings exactly. They drew apart, and by the time the crew caught up with them they were strolling hand and hand again, even if his gait was a little uneven.

"What happened to change you?" Renata asked after a moment. It took Greg a moment to catch up, but he remembered their earlier conversation.

"I left home."

Renata cocked her head. "Most people leave home," she observed.

"Most people don't grow up on a commune."

A smile twitched her lips, and he relaxed a little, although walking was still uncomfortable. Damn the camera crew. If they hadn't shown up, who knew what he and Renata might be doing right now? Best not to think about that too much.

"Tell me about the commune. Was it like people picture them to be?" she asked.

"Damn straight." Greg remembered this was Renata he was speaking to. She'd have researched him back when she came to Base Camp. She was asking these questions for the cameras. "A certifiable Oregon commune. It was a big farm."

"Kind of like Base Camp," Renata pointed out.

"Base Camp is situated on a ranch," he corrected her. "Greenside is a lot different."

"How many people lived on this commune?"

"About eighty-five. Roughly nineteen families."

Renata whistled. "And this was an egalitarian commune? Or was there some kind of guru running it?"

"No guru," Greg told her, knowing all of this would end up on the show. "Just a few savvy leaders who made sure everyone involved knew all about consensus building and the democratic process." Those lessons had been drummed into him and every other kid on the place. That didn't mean they all acted like saints, though.

Far from it.

"Each year various committees set mission statements and goals, and everyone talked them over, hashed out their differences and voted on them. We did our best to come up with a consensus. Didn't always work out."

"If it was so idyllic, why did you want to leave?"

"Because it was too idyllic. Too boring for a kid who was raring for some adventures."

"But now you're back in a commune," Renata pointed out.

"Ironic, huh?" Greg shoved his gloved hands into

his jacket pockets, wishing they were alone rather than talking about this stuff. The crew trailed after them, spoiling the romance of the intermittently moonlit night.

"What made you decide to join Base Camp?" Renata sounded genuinely curious. She wouldn't have been able to discover the answer to that in her research. Greg had never told anyone.

"A girl."

"A GIRL?" RENATA wasn't sure how to take that, and her surprise made her gruff. Had Greg come here chasing some other woman? Or had he been running from one? Somehow she'd thought she was the only one he'd been interested in since coming here. Right from the start she'd noticed the way he watched her—

But she could have mistaken necessity for something more.

The way he'd been kissing her when the crew arrived, though—

"It's more complicated than it sounds," Greg went on. "But the girl shows up a couple of times in my story. In my senior year of college, I took a semester abroad. That's when I met her. It was during a kind of crisis."

He was watching her now, making sure she was following the story. He shouldn't have worried; she couldn't help but hang on every word.

"We were thrown together. I knew her for only one night, and then I had to leave. I didn't think I'd ever see her again."

Renata nodded. She knew what crises were like. So intense you focused on one thing at a time. If you met someone in those conditions, you'd remember them for a lifetime—if you noticed them at all. After the crisis in Peru was over, she'd realized she could hardly remember anything about it except the girls in her care. She must have talked to a hundred people that first night, trying to find word about their families, but she didn't remember a single face.

"Anyway," Greg continued after a moment, "after that, I decided I wanted to do something meaningful. I wanted to be a man who knew what to do in a crisis. I joined the Navy."

She nodded. That made sense. A young man would think that becoming strong and powerful would make a difference.

"After a number of years, I was ready for a change, and I'd realized that the kind of natural disaster that inspired my decision so many years ago was only going to get more common if we didn't do something about climate change. I heard about Base Camp—"

"And you didn't think twice about the communal aspects?" Renata pushed.

"Oh, I thought twice, believe me. But I figured I could handle it."

"Where does the girl come in? You said she figured in your story a few times." It hurt to ask the question, but she did it anyway. If there was someone else in the picture, it would make it easier to stay away from Greg.

Greg's gaze held hers for a moment. He shook his head, a half smile tugging at his mouth. "Heard she was in the neighborhood" was all he said.

"And yet you keep kissing me." She didn't mean to sound so bitter. Hell, this would end up on the show, too.

"And yet I keep kissing you," Greg agreed. "Funny how life works, isn't it?"

He drew her close and kissed her again.

"You look like a fish when you're kissing, Renata. Can't you be sexier?"

Clem's voice cut through the night air like a buzz saw, and Renata nearly leaped out of Greg's arms. She drew a shaking hand over her mouth as if she could wipe away the evidence of the kiss, sure she was flushing. Thank goodness it was dark.

"Ignore him," Greg murmured, stepping closer again. "He's jealous."

She hated the way Clem kept getting under her guard, the epitome of every bully she'd faced in her years in foster care.

"It's late." She wriggled out of Greg's arms, threaded through the crew and walked swiftly back the way they'd come, moonlight illuminating the track well enough, although the snow made the footing treacherous. She heard the huff and puff of the crew working to keep up, mild swearing behind her probably meaning someone had slipped.

"Renata, wait."

She hurried on, and they were nearly to the bunkhouse by the time Greg caught up to her, took her arm and walked with her. "You can't let him get to you."

"He does get to me, though," she admitted almost in a whisper.

"I know. He's an annoying ass, but don't let Clem ruin… us."

Before she could answer, Avery stepped out of the bunkhouse.

"Renata, Greg, there you are. Come in—there's an announcement."

"Another one?" Greg asked.

They picked up their pace and followed Avery inside to find the rest of the members of Base Camp already gathered.

"Thanks for interrupting your evening for this," Kai said. "There will be snacks in order to make it up to you!"

A little cheer went up from the gathered crowd. Late-night snacks weren't the norm.

"We have some special news to share," Addison said, clinging to Kai's hand. "Of course a few other people beat us to the punch. I'm looking at you, Eve and Samantha!"

"If you haven't already guessed," Kai said. "We're…"

"Pregnant!" Addison blurted. "Come and eat!"

The two of them picked up platters of canapes and began to pass them around, even as the others thronged around them to give them their congratulations. Renata spotted homemade smoked bison topped with homemade cheese, among other things.

"That looks good," Greg took a couple of the appetizers from the tray as Kai passed. Renata took one, too, but she wasn't really hungry.

Another baby.

Another happy couple.

"Things are looking up around here," Greg said.

They were—for everyone else.

"WHAT ARE YOU looking for?" Greg asked Walker the next morning when he found the man going through shelves and cupboards in the bunkhouse. He'd finished his daily check in of the energy systems and ducked inside to warm up before his next task.

"A ceremonial fan," Walker said. "Need it in a couple of weeks. Can't find it anywhere."

"Is it valuable?" He hated to ask. Of course something like that would have all kinds of significance to Walker and his family. He had no idea what the protocol was when something like that went missing.

"Passed down in my family for eight generations."

"Hell." Greg got to work helping him look, figuring he'd know a ceremonial fan when he saw one, even if he'd never seen one before. "Where's the last place you saw it?"

"My bag. With my other things."

All of the men had large duffel bags they used for storage until they married and got their own tiny houses. It was a drag living out of your luggage for months, but as SEALs they had been through far worse. Life at Base

Camp was downright cushy compared to that.

"Who would go through your bag?" Another dumb question. Their food had been raided. Their energy systems messed with.

Walker didn't bother to answer. When they'd searched every corner of the bunkhouse and kitchen, Greg walked him to the door. "Sorry, man. I'll keep an eye out for it."

"Grandmother's going to freak out."

Greg pictured the taciturn woman in his mind. That would be something to see. He'd heard about the time Sue laid into Walker at the grocery store early on during their time at Base Camp. She hadn't been happy about him spending time with Avery.

"You ever straighten things out with the woman she wanted you to marry?" He'd never asked Walker such a personal question. Wasn't sure the man would answer it.

Angus, who'd just walked into the main room from the kitchen, raised his eyebrows, obviously listening in to their conversation.

Walker shook his head. "Soon."

"You'd better get on that," Angus said testily. "After Greg marries Renata, it's just you and me, and I'm not going next, so you'd better be ready to marry Avery."

Something like pain flashed over Walker's face, and Greg's gut tightened. Surely the man wasn't going to ditch Avery after stringing her along for months?

"Get it sorted out," Angus repeated.

Walker nodded again and headed outside. Off to search somewhere else, Greg figured. He didn't know if he should follow and offer to help.

"What a damn mess," Angus said, watching the door shut. "Him and me both. Hell of a way to end this thing."

"You'll marry, though, right? When the time comes?" Greg pressed him. They were all screwed if he didn't.

"I will if you will. What if Renata says no?"

"I'll marry," Greg assured him through gritted teeth. It might kill him, but he'd do it. He'd never let the others down.

"I'll marry, too," Angus said darkly. "But I bloody well won't like it, will I?"

He stormed out of the bunkhouse before Greg could answer.

Clem's chuckle made Greg's fingers flex. He hadn't noticed the director in the kitchen doorway, but he kept his anger under control and headed out to his own chores.

At lunchtime, they were all back at the bunkhouse again, and Greg was sitting with Avery and Renata.

"This is really good," Avery said, swallowing a bite of homemade pizza.

"It is," Renata agreed.

Greg had no idea how Kai had managed to make the crust without flour. If he wasn't mistaken, there was a lot of cheese in it, but he couldn't place the rest of the ingredients.

Avery leaned closer to Renata and asked in a low voice, "Do you think every woman on this ranch is pregnant except me?"

"I'm not," Renata assured her. She refused to meet Greg's gaze when he tried to catch hers, but he'd seen her frown when Kai and Addison had made their announcement, and he was sure she wanted a family of her own. Did she simply not want to start one with him, or was there something else keeping her from going after it?

"If this pizza wasn't so damn good I'd lose my appetite," Avery said darkly. "I'm going to be the only one at the end of this show unmarried, childless and alone."

"A lot of women spent their lives fighting for the right to be that very thing," Renata told her tartly.

"They spent their lives fighting for the choice," Avery corrected her. "I'm choosing to want to settle down and be with—" She broke off, and her shoulders slumped. "Maybe I do need to ask Boone to find me a backup husband."

"Walker will come around," Greg assured her. "He's just distracted right now. He can't find that ceremonial fan of his."

Renata frowned. Avery nodded. "I know. It's killing him." She toyed with her food. "Do you think Clem took it?"

Renata's frown deepened, and Greg wondered if she knew anything about the theft. He didn't like to think of her participating in anything like that, but the crew had messed with them before. Maybe Renata needed some encouragement to put a stop to it. "I don't know, but if he did, he's messing with the wrong man. Walker seems all mild-mannered—until he isn't," Greg said. "And once he's mad, you don't want to be anywhere near him."

"You served with him?" Avery asked.

"For a while," Greg said. "We didn't get to know each other too well, but there was a real troublemaker serving with us. The guy was messed up. Stole cash from all of us. Had a habit he couldn't kick. He took this little statue thing Walker had. Something a relative had sent him—didn't look like it was worth anything, but this guy must have thought it was. Walker caught him. One minute the guy was standing there holding it. Next he was on the ground, and Walker had it back. None of us even saw Walker move—and I'm talking a room full of highly trained men." Navy SEALs, in other words. "Kid was transferred asap after that. I doubt Walker made the complaint—someone else did, but Walker was a guy you wanted happy. Worth five of anyone else, and everybody knew it. You don't want to be on the wrong side of him."

"That sounds like a threat," Renata commented dryly. She was watching Avery, Greg realized. Was she trying to send the young woman a message? Hinting that Walker wasn't an ideal partner? Or trying to cover her own tracks?

Greg didn't want to be the one who got between Avery and Walker. No matter what obligations the man was trying to sort through, it was obvious Walker cared for Avery. "All I'm saying is he'll forgive just about anything, help just about anyone, unless you cross that line. His family comes first. His heritage. You mess with that, and all bets are off."

Renata was still watching Avery, who had twisted her hands together, but as Kai walked past, Avery straightened her shoulders and turned to him. "Terrific pizza."

"Wanted to keep celebrating our good news." He clapped Greg on the shoulder. "You'd better hurry up if you want to be part of the babypalooza around here."

He kept going, leaving an awkward silence behind him. "Hear that?" Greg drawled, trying to make a joke of it. "We need to hurry up."

Renata was focused on Avery again, who was watching Walker across the room.

"Walker will come around," Greg assured Avery. "He's crazy about you."

That got her attention. "You think?"

"I'm sure of it."

"But will that be enough?"

"THEY KICKED IT over?" Renata asked early the following morning. She'd just gotten dressed and found Byron gathering his camera equipment to film something outdoors.

"It's on its side," Byron confirmed. "All of them are."

"Maybe it was the wind," Addison said, pulling on her spencer. She'd arrived at the bunkhouse only moments ago, but apparently she meant to go back outside and assess the damage. An icy breeze was whipping in fits and starts around the building, rattling the windows.

"Who even uses the composting toilets anymore?" Avery asked, joining them. "The outside ones, I mean."

"The guys do sometimes when there's a line in here and the outside ones are closer than their tiny houses."

Renata pulled on her spencer, too, and headed outside with the others. Byron was right; the closest composting toilet stall had been knocked over. Presumably the composting toilet itself was on its side in there as well.

She shivered in the cold breeze. The tiny houses the married couples lived in had their own composting toilets. The bunkhouse and the manor had flush toilets and presumably septic fields. In the beginning, before the tiny houses had been built, several other composting toilets had been placed around the property in outhouse-style stalls. Avery was right, though; she doubted they saw much use these days.

"Someone's getting desperate for our attention," Renata said.

"It wasn't you?" Byron asked.

"Why on earth would I knock over composting toilets?"

"For attention, like you said!" Clem boomed behind her.

Renata jumped but didn't turn around. The ass had snuck up on her.

"I don't need attention. I'm getting plenty of it," she said. A crowd was gathering around them, including

Greg, who ran a hand over a stubble-covered jawline as he took in the overturned stall.

"I think it's strange the way everything started going wrong when you began to spend your nights here," Clem went on, loudly enough for everyone to hear. "You'd think you'd find something more interesting to do than slip outside and knock over toilets, but maybe Greg's not man enough to keep you occupied at night."

"Fuck off," Greg said cordially. He threaded through the onlookers to Renata's side. "You been tipping toilets?"

"No." Her teeth were chattering in the cold, but she refused to stand down.

He chuckled at her frustrated tone. "It was probably Clem."

"Probably," she agreed, although she couldn't imagine Clem being willing to do physical work. "This is getting out of control. I'm calling Fulsom." She moved away before placing the call, and as soon as Fulsom's secretary, Julie, patched her through, she said, "Your boy Clem is making a real nuisance of himself. He's damaging property now. Did you know that?"

"Good morning to you, too, Renata."

She wasn't wasting her time with niceties, gripping her phone to her ear and turning her back on the wind. "He's a menace. You know it's only a matter of time before he steps over a line. You know what he did on *Tracking the Stars*. You saw our video." Clem had been fired from his last job for assaulting a female crew member.

"What happened this time?" Fulsom asked. She could hear him tapping on a keyboard in the background. She only had half his attention, if that. Meanwhile Clem had sidled up next to her, listening in blatantly.

"He knocked over all the outdoor composting toilets. Before that he covered all the solar panels with snow."

"Solar panels can't be generating much energy in the dead of a Montana winter," Fulsom pointed out. "And you still have the inside bathrooms, right?"

"That's not the point! The point is—" She cut off. She couldn't finish her sentence with Clem standing right there. The point was that Fulsom already had her to direct the show. Why wasn't she enough? She'd given up everything she'd wanted to do for him—and for the girls back in Peru.

"The point is we're entertaining the masses. And teaching them a few things, right?" Fulsom asked.

"About what? Harassment? Hooliganism?" Renata pressed.

"About not kowtowing to bullies, I hope," Fulsom countered. "Come on, Renata, you can handle Clem. If not, you aren't the woman I thought you were. Gotta go."

He cut the call before she could think of a proper retort, leaving Renata fuming. Clem's sardonic smile didn't help.

"You're going to lose," she told him. The wind whipped a tendril of her hair into her eyes, and she tossed her head.

"Not if you lose first. Your boy's not going to marry anyone else. We'll wrap this show in less than thirty days with a big ol' bulldozer flourish."

"Boone's lining up backup brides, you know. He's got a whole list. Pretty soon they'll start arriving for interviews." She was making it up, but she couldn't be too far wrong, could she? Boone always had backup brides waiting to go.

"Leave her alone." Greg approached and stepped in between them. "Come on," he told Renata. "I have an errand in town. Let's go."

She let him lead her away before she really embarrassed herself. Had Greg heard their conversation? Had he talked to Boone about backup brides?

"What about these toilets?" Clem called after them.

"Better get them upright again," Greg called back.

"HE REALLY KNOWS how to push your buttons, doesn't he?" Greg said when he turned the truck onto the highway at the end of the lane.

"You don't know the half of it." Renata kept her head turned away, her gaze on the snow-covered fields they passed, where the wind whipped along the ground, lifting sprays of snow into the air. Greg searched for a way to distract her. He didn't know what Clem had said right before he'd caught up to them, but it had hurt her, that was clear.

"If you could be anywhere right now—anywhere in the world—where would you go?" Could he distract her? He'd give anything to take away her pain.

She didn't answer for a long moment, her face still turned away. Then, to Greg's surprise, she reached a hand out toward him.

He took it, not saying a word, afraid to ruin the moment. Was she saying she wanted to be with him?

He'd follow her just about anywhere. Already had.

When the silence stretched out too long, she wriggled her hand in his, and he let go reluctantly.

"I know how to deal with guys like Clem." She shifted in her seat. "I ran into a lot of them growing up."

"In foster care?"

She nodded. "The trick is to figure out what they're afraid of. They're always afraid of something."

"What do you think Clem is afraid of?"

"Losing the spotlight altogether. He might be director, but he wants time in front of the camera, and he can't compete with all of you. He was front and center on *Tracking the Stars.*"

"Which means he'll fight hard to keep on top here. You'll have to fight harder if you want your old job back."

Renata sighed. "What if I don't want it?"

Greg kept driving, unsure what to think of her question. All the months he'd been at Base Camp so far, Renata had kept up a solid facade that had left him thinking there were no chinks in her armor. She'd been professional, punctual, driven—

What had happened to change that?

Landing on the show as his potential wife?

If anything, he'd have thought that would propel her into being even more driven, more hard-bitten, more determined than ever to stay on top. Instead, she was… falling apart.

Greg gripped the steering wheel harder. He hadn't meant to make her fall apart. Certainly hadn't meant to ruin her career.

"Renata, you know how I feel about you—"

"Do I?" she challenged him.

"Don't you?" Coming to a decision, he pulled off the highway and parked on the shoulder. "I fell for you the minute I saw you—" He cut off. They still hadn't talked about Peru. "I love you," he said instead of opening that can of worms. "I have for a long time. I want you to be my wife."

"I can't be your wife and direct *Base Camp* at the same time, and I can't just… fade away. I have to get Fulsom to give me my job back, or no one will hire me to direct anything again." Her frustration was palpable, and understandable, too, but he wasn't clear if she meant she was giving his proposition any real consideration. She felt… *something*… for him, that was clear, but what?

"I know your work is important to you." He hesitated, not really wanting to ask the next question but knowing he had to. "And I know you want more than to direct television shows. You want to do movies. And you probably don't want to do them in Chance Creek." He remembered how surprised she'd been when he suggested it.

It had been a stupid idea.

She shook her head.

Just like he'd thought. "What would you do if you could do anything?"

Renata lifted her shoulders in a delicate shrug. "What does it matter? When have I ever gotten to do what I want?"

"What about Peru?" He'd gotten the sense back then of a woman entirely dedicated to her goals.

"Peru?" she echoed and finally looked at him. After a moment she nodded. Half smiled. "Going there was the last time I made a choice that actually felt like a choice."

"You didn't want to work for Fulsom?" He would have thought landing work with a billionaire would make any aspiring filmmaker happy, but maybe he had it all wrong, Greg thought. If choosing to document the lives of a group of poor but aspiring young Peruvian girls was Renata's idea of happiness, then working with a billionaire as self-centered as Fulsom had probably been frustrating from the get-go.

Directing a reality TV show must be her idea of hell.

A gust of wind rattled the truck. It had been blowing all day, but it was getting worse. Did Renata think she needed to get away from Fulsom—and Base Camp—to be happy? If so, what was keeping her here?

Something else occurred to him. Something so obvious he didn't know why he hadn't thought of it before. She'd been in foster care for years. Had traveled endlessly working for Fulsom.

"Are you looking for a home?"

RENATA CLOSED HER eyes, immediately picturing the small, tidy home in which she'd lived her first six years. Sometimes she thought she must be making up her memories, but one image was clear as anything in her mind. She and her father sitting at a kitchen table with a red tablecloth. Red had always been her favorite color, and it was her birthday. Her father sat across from her. Her mother had just lit the candles on her cake. Her favorite: Devil's food. Both of them were singing.

"Make a wish," her mother said, setting the cake down in front of her with a flourish. Renata didn't remember the wish, but she remembered this moment. The cake. The candles. The tablecloth. The small, homey kitchen.

Her parents, beaming at her.

Two months later, they were gone.

No one had ever looked at her like that again.

Was she looking for a home? Renata struggled to swallow the pain swelling her throat. How could there ever be a home with her parents gone from the world? She was on her own. She knew that. She simply couldn't depend on anyone else—for love or money.

Renata turned to Greg to tell him so.

Saw the way he was looking at her.

She must have made a sound, or Greg must have seen something in her face.

Suddenly he was gone, out of the truck, the door

slamming shut behind him, a chill blast of air in his wake. Renata straightened. Where was he going?

When her door opened, she nearly fell out of it into his arms. Instead Greg bent inside, undid her seat belt, lifted her up and climbed into the passenger seat underneath her. Perched precariously on his lap while he shut the door again, her head nearly brushing the ceiling, Renata cried, "What are you doing?"

"Holding you."

His strong arms came around her, and he eased her down until her cheek rested against his shoulder.

"But—"

Renata didn't know when she'd been ensconced in such a circle of warmth. Greg's jacket was open, and she could hear his heartbeat. He'd gathered her against him and was holding on as if he wanted to protect her from anything that might do her harm.

"I'd make a home for you," he said. "Forever, if you'll let me."

"But—"

"You could do whatever you wanted. You could do nothing at all—or everything. I would be your family."

She had to tell him no. She had a job. Goals. Responsibilities. The money—

"We could have babies. As many as you want."

She already had children to raise. Seven of them still needing her support. Sixteen who'd moved on to bigger and better things. They were her responsibility, and she wasn't going to let them down for anything.

"I have savings, Renata. If you need a break, I can

cover the bills."

And that was when the tears came. Because she'd worked so hard and so long to get this far, always alone with the fear that she'd let everyone down. She knew what it was like to trust someone—and have it all taken away.

She would never, ever do that to her girls.

Even if it meant she'd miss this chance with Greg. Even if they grew up one by one and moved on, leaving her alone.

Like always—

Greg's arms tightened around her, and new tears slipped silently down her cheeks.

"It's okay," Greg kept murmuring, but it wasn't okay. It never had been, and it never would be.

She didn't want to be alone.

"I'm here," Greg told her. "I'm not going anywhere."

But he would, in roughly thirty days when he had to marry or lose Base Camp forever.

For now she clung to him like she'd never let go.

CHAPTER EIGHT

"THANK GOD FOR Riley," Greg said sometime later when he'd fished a package of tissues out of glove compartment of the truck and handed it to Renata. "I swear she's stashed these in every vehicle Base Camp owns."

He was rewarded by a small smile as Renata wiped the tears from her face. She was still sitting in his lap, a minor miracle, and she was calmer now, although every now and then another tear streaked down her cheek.

Greg wondered if she'd held in those tears since Peru, or maybe even longer. Maybe since she'd been a girl. He tried to fathom losing his family as a boy and living with strangers. He couldn't. He'd grown up in a community so tightly knit every member felt like family. Renata hadn't mentioned keeping in contact with anyone she'd been placed with. That spoke volumes about the quality of care she'd received. From what Greg had read, the foster system was full of people who genuinely meant well, but the system was overburdened and understaffed, so oversight wasn't always what one might wish.

Renata clutched the damp tissues in her lap, her shoulders slumped. "I can't believe I did that," she said dully.

"Cried?"

She nodded.

"Everyone cries sometime. It's healthy."

"Like *you* ever cry."

"Not too often," he admitted. "It's not a big tradition in the SEALs, but I grew up in Oregon on a commune," he pointed out. "Manly tears are completely acceptable there. Besides, seems like those were building for a long time."

"I guess."

"Renata, it's okay to change your mind, you know that, right? Just because you wanted to be a movie director in the past doesn't mean you always have to. You can do more than one thing in your life. More than one thing at a time, if that's what you want."

"Directing movies doesn't work as a side gig," she countered.

"And if that's what you want to do, that's great," he told her. "All I'm saying is there's nothing keeping you trapped in that concept of yourself if you want to do something else."

Renata wouldn't look him in the eye. There was something she wasn't telling him. Did Fulsom have some kind of hold over her? Was that what was keeping her at Base Camp? Or was she the kind of person who simply couldn't leave a job half-done?

"You don't want to break your contract?" he hazarded. She must have some kind of agreement with Fulsom.

"Something like that."

"Renata—" Greg didn't have anything else to add; he just liked the sound of her name. Liked saying it. Liked holding her, too. He didn't want to let her go.

When he bent to kiss her, she didn't pull back. Instead she met his kiss as naturally as if they'd done it hundreds of times before. Greg shifted beneath her, and she leaned into him, her arms twining more tightly around his neck. No matter what obligation was holding her back from being with him or changing her life, she was attracted to him. When they broke apart, he dropped a kiss along the neckline of her old-fashioned gown. Her jacket had come unbuttoned along the way, affording him access, and he couldn't resist the temptation.

He thought she'd put an end to things then, but she didn't. Instead she leaned closer, and he brushed another kiss over the softness of her skin.

Renata sighed, and he wondered what she was thinking. He let the silence extend, hoping she'd speak up.

She finally did. "I don't suppose…"

"What?" Greg held still. Did she want him as much as he wanted her? He was hard, having difficulty keeping himself in check with her in his lap, her every move shifting her weight against his crotch.

"We could be together—without it meaning anything."

He chuckled. "We can be together any time you want, but it'll sure mean something to me." At the pleading look in her eyes, he brushed a kiss at the base of her neck. "How about this? We can be together, and I won't think you're making me any promises. Does that work?"

After a moment she nodded.

"That works."

"Are we talking about some specific time?"

In answer to his question, Renata kissed him again, moving her mouth over his lightly at first but then leaning in and asking for more.

"Here?" As surprised as he was, Greg was all for it, but they were in a truck on the side of the highway. Someone might stop to check on them.

"I can't take you back to my motel room. Fulsom made me give it up."

Greg wished she could. A real bed and a room with a locked door sounded perfect right about now. "Let's at least get farther off this road."

Untangling themselves wasn't easy. Nor was finding a place to turn far enough off the road that they wouldn't be visible from the highway or some ranch house. By the time he found a turnoff that took him around a bend behind a copse of trees, he was worried Renata would change her mind. He parked and turned to her, ready to offer her an easy out if she needed one. He wasn't going to push her and ruin his chances for the future he wanted.

"In back?" she asked, cocking her head toward the bench seat.

"Hell, yeah." Greg was out of the truck and into the back seat in a matter of moments. Renata followed a little more slowly, taking care for her gown, but when he pulled her into his lap and growled, "Where were we?" she smiled, a wry twist of her lips.

"Oh yeah, you were about to rock my world."

He'd do his best.

Renata shimmied out of her jacket, and Greg was thankful the cab of the truck had heated as they'd driven. He knew the warmth wouldn't last and was happy to find a couple of blankets half shoved under the seat. He shrugged out of his own jacket, shook one out and wrapped it around them. "How's that?"

"Perfect. Warmth and protection from prying eyes." Renata was fiddling with something behind her back. "Gathered neckline," she told him. Greg had no idea what that meant, but when she moved her hands to the front of her gown and loosened the neckline, he was intrigued.

When she lifted her breasts out over the top of her corset, he groaned with approbation.

Renata kicked off her boots, shimmied out of the yoga pants she was wearing under her Regency dress and shifted to straddle him, her knees braced on the bench seat to either side of his legs. Pressed up against him like that, her skirts hitched up around her bare legs, she had to be able to feel every inch of his hardness. His hands fell to her hips, and he snugged her in tight against him, wanting more of her warmth. She leaned forward, and Greg grazed his lips over her breasts, then teased one perfect nipple with his tongue. It hardened beneath his touch. Renata rocked against him, and Greg knew this wasn't going to be the most sophisticated bout of lovemaking. He wanted her too badly. Needed to bury himself inside her and prove their connection was real.

"Can't we get all this off?" He plucked at her gown. Underneath it, the hard frame of her corset blocked his hands from getting to know her body better.

"It takes time." She hesitated. "It'll be a pain to get back on again."

"I'll help," he promised.

After a second, she nodded. Then she turned on his lap, an exercise in agility in itself, keeping the blanket covering them mostly. Presented with the fastenings of her gown, Greg surveyed them and got to it, Renata issuing instructions as he went.

A minute later, he lifted her gown up and over her head, then tackled her corset. Soon he had that off, too. Renata was left wearing a thin cotton undergown—a chemise, he thought it was called. She turned again, bringing the blanket with her, and straddled his lap. When she lifted his hands to cover her breasts, they both groaned. Renata shut her eyes, but Greg kept his open, watching her as he caressed her, so turned on by the naked desire on her face, he found it hard to resist tugging up her chemise and taking her right then.

Soon, he promised himself. For now he took the

time to explore her body. Under all those tailored, severe suits she used to wear, she had curves to die for. Greg had imagined those curves endlessly in the last seven and a half months, but the reality was far better. She was warm under his touch. Soft.

When Renata arched back, Greg lifted one of her breasts to his mouth, suckling it through the thin material of her chemise until her breath sped up. It was Renata who finally tugged the chemise over her head. When she did an interesting maneuver, leaning sideways, shifting her legs and sliding out of her tiny panties, Greg was struck dumb with admiration.

"Why are you still dressed?" she demanded.

He had no idea why and commenced to fixing the situation asap. Once naked, the blanket back around them, Renata straddled his lap one more time, but then she shivered.

Greg took stock of the situation. Body heat would soon fix that problem, but that blanket was going to slide off the minute things got interesting. He lifted Renata, laid her out on the bench seat, covered her with his own body and flicked the blanket over himself.

"I'll get you real warm in about thirty seconds," he promised.

Renata chuckled. "It's kind of neat how you do that," she said.

"Do what?" Greg began to explore her with kisses, trailing his mouth over the smooth skin of her cheek, jaw, neck and breasts.

"Move me around."

He paused. "Was afraid you wouldn't like that. You're pretty independent."

"I am," she said happily. "I just feel so solid all the time. The rock that everyone else braces themselves against."

"Maybe I'm a bigger rock. You can brace yourself against me." Greg wondered who was dependent on her like that. Was she talking about the crew? Fulsom's constant needs?

She stilled underneath his touch, and Greg lifted his head to look into her eyes.

"Really?" Renata asked. "Are you saying I can depend on you?"

"Haven't I made that clear?" He kissed her mouth. "That's what I'm here for. That's what I was put on this earth to do." He kept on kissing her, but Renata didn't move, and when he looked up again, she was watching him.

"You're just saying that."

"I'm promising you that." God, she felt good underneath him. He worried he might be crushing her, but feeling every inch of her pressed against every inch of him felt so right he couldn't bear to think of moving away from her.

"People aren't dependable." But she lifted her hips and moved with him, arched her back so her breasts were in easy reach of his mouth.

"I am." He wanted to spend the rest of his life being Renata's man. If only she'd let him.

He braced himself with a hand beneath her. Let the

other one run the length of her body and back again. This was the shape of the woman he loved. He wished he could show her what was in his heart.

Greg decided to do his best.

He took his time with her body, getting to know every inch of it, lavishing attention everywhere until Renata was clinging to him, her fingertips digging into his skin.

"Greg—" she whispered finally, and he understood what she meant. He shifted between her legs, nudged against her.

"You sure?" He didn't know what he'd do if she called things off now. Accede to her wishes, of course—and then die of want.

In answer, she tugged him closer. Inside her. Greg surged forward and filled her in one long thrust. A ragged breath tore from Renata's mouth, and he stopped. Her fingers dug into his skin again, their message clear.

Keep going.

He'd keep going as long as he could.

The heat of her was sweet torture as he began to rock against her. With her legs wrapped around his hips, she offered him everything he'd only dreamed of up until now. Greg set about discovering what made her moan and found that Renata responded to him so naturally it was hard to believe they'd never done this together before. Of course, they'd done it a thousand times in his dreams.

Renata urged him onward, moving with him, pulling

him tighter, clinging to him as his pace increased. He was right; they were warm now, and he shrugged the blanket down around his waist.

When he slowed a little, worried he'd set too fast a pace, Renata gave a frustrated moan that told him all he needed to know. He plunged deeper inside her, and she threw her head back.

Greg held on, waiting to see if she trusted him enough to fall apart in his arms. She'd cried there, but that was easy compared to taking pleasure. He had a feeling Renata put everyone else first and denied herself most things.

He'd hang in there as long as he could to make sure that wasn't how things went this time.

NO MAN HAD ever made love to her like this.

Scratch that. She'd never let any man make love to her like this. Renata's skin flamed, her heart pounded, she was panting for breath—

And she never wanted this to end.

Every touch of Greg's hands on her body left trails of fire tingling along her skin. If only they could stay like this forever. If only he could be hers.

I could marry him.

But she couldn't. If you loved people, you lost them. If you depended on people, they let you down. Better to keep a distance. Help where you could. Be a force for good in the world. Love was too dangerous. That meant taking a chance that it all got ripped away from you—

But how could she stop loving Greg now?

She'd granted him permission to explore her thoroughly, and he was doing just that, breaking down every defense she'd ever erected, his hands and mouth stirring her to increasing desire. Not just for this kind of pleasure—but for the connection it represented.

When he plunged into her, she'd let out a cry that expressed years of pent-up longing. He fit her perfectly, and every shift of him inside her elicited so much sensation Renata realized how flat her life had been until this moment.

Greg electrified her, letting loose a whirlwind of feelings she hadn't known she'd been holding back. And now he was building a want in her that threatened to consume everything. She couldn't help moving with him, couldn't help lifting her hips and inviting him farther inside. Couldn't help wanting it all—

But if she let go—truly let go—

She'd be taking the chance that her heart might be broken all over again.

Renata decided she didn't care. She wanted this, even if it was momentary. Wanted to feel Greg—become part of him. Wanted to show him everything. Wanted to bare herself—her soul—to him, just for a moment.

When she cried out the beginning of her release, Greg cried out, too, joining her. Bucking against her. Crushing her to him, their bodies spasming together, their breath catching and letting go, Renata gave into the sensations completely, letting them run their course. Letting Greg know her utterly.

Afterward, fighting to regain control of her breathing, Greg still sheathed inside her, Renata braced herself for the return of reality. Soon they'd draw apart, and she'd be alone again. At least she'd have the memory of this encounter. For a few minutes at least, she'd forgotten everything else.

"I love you," Greg breathed into her ear. "I will always love you."

Renata kept silent. She loved him, too, but what did love mean in this world? Love was a prelude to loss. Dependence the prelude to disappointment. She didn't think she could bear waiting and dreading either outcome with Greg.

"Renata? Did you hear me?" he asked.

She nodded. She'd heard.

Still, she said nothing.

CHAPTER NINE

HE'D RUSHED HER. Acted like a schoolboy confronting his first crush. *Did you hear me?* His skin crawled just thinking about the way he'd practically begged Renata to tell him she loved him back.

It was far too soon. She obviously didn't remember him from Peru. Hadn't spent a single moment daydreaming about him the way he'd always dreamed of her. He should have let their time together speak for itself.

It had sure told him a lot.

Being with Renata was even better than he'd hoped. She was responsive. At home in her body. She'd given it to him freely, reveling in their closeness. Shattering before him as if she was only too pleased to give him everything.

And then she'd closed right down again.

Had he scared her? Did she think he was going to force her to the altar today?

Hardly.

Although, time was ticking by.

Was Renata against marriage?

Greg drove to Base Camp, neither of them pretending anymore that there'd ever been a real errand in town. Getting Renata back into her gown had been a difficult task with both of them stiff and formal with each other. *One step forward, two steps back*, Greg thought. He hoped he could still salvage this.

Renata's phone buzzed, and she checked in, frowning at something she read on the screen.

"Problem?" he asked.

"The usual. Everything's going wrong."

"At Base Camp?"

She shook her head. "Personal stuff."

He waited for her to explain, but she didn't, and he wasn't sure it was smart to pry. Besides, they'd reached the turnoff for the long lane that led to the bunkhouse.

"Renata—"

"I wanted everything that happened back there to happen," she cut him off. "That doesn't mean my life is easy, or that we have a future."

She could have sliced him with cold steel, and he would have been less shocked. She'd told him as much before they'd made love. That didn't make it easier to hear. "Of course we have a future—if you want one."

She faced him. "You don't know me. You don't know my situation. I think you should get a backup bride. Boone must have found you one by now."

Greg swung the truck into the lane and then stopped it. "I don't want Boone's backup brides. I want to know why you won't marry me."

"I—I can't make any promises right now. There's… something I need to do. To finish. I'm not free until I do."

Suspicion filled him. "Are you married?"

She stared at him. "Married? No, of course not." She stopped. "I guess in a way I am."

Greg's heart plunged. *Hell.*

"Not married to a man. Married to… a promise. I owe somebody something. I have to make good on it. Greg, I'm not ready for this."

Her last sentence was so anguished it had to be true. "You're not ready for marriage."

"No. I'm sorry."

So was he. More than she could ever know. He didn't think he could marry someone else after an experience like the one they'd just had.

"Is there… any chance you could be ready before the month is up?"

She sighed. "It would take a miracle."

"I believe in miracles." He reached out and took her hand. "I believe in us."

She held his gaze a long moment. "I can't make any promises. You need a backup bride—or two or three."

To hell with the backup brides. As far as Greg was concerned, he'd marry Renata or no one—

Strike that, he realized with a twist of his gut. He couldn't let everyone else down, so he'd have to marry no matter what.

He just didn't want to think about it. Greg started the truck again and drove them down the lane. He wanted to keep trying to change Renata's mind, but he didn't want her stubborn streak to kick in. He'd take up his campaign again later.

"Something is going on," Renata said, nodding toward a cluster of people at the door to the bunkhouse.

Greg sighed, parked and got out.

"Greg, there you are," Boone called. "There's a problem with turbine three. It hasn't shut down like the other ones, and it's way too windy for it to be running. Jericho's gone to take a look."

"He shouldn't be doing that." It was cold. Icy. Windy as hell. Climbing the turbines could be treacherous. There were protective railings, but still, in weather like this…

Jericho was a new father.

"Let's talk more later," he added to Renata, who had just pulled out her phone.

"I'll find you a bride if you don't like the ones Boone's got," she told him.

"Renata—" Greg gave up. One emergency at a time, he told himself.

"IT'S JUST ONE thing after another," Mayra said when Renata took her call. With everyone else, including the camera crews, distracted by the problem with the wind turbine, she had been able to slip inside the bunkhouse and answer it without a camera crew following her.

"What happened?" She braced herself. With each call she was getting further in the hole financially.

"Philomena's scholarship fell through. The company that sponsored it has declared bankruptcy. I know this isn't your responsibility. You aren't supposed to pay for them after they graduate, but she's worked so hard, and there's no guarantee she can find another one quickly enough to keep her spot in the program."

"Of course I'll pay," Renata said. She wasn't about to deny Philomena her chance at a very prestigious business program in the capital. "How much?"

The sum wasn't large compared to the cost of getting a similar degree in the States, but Renata cringed just the same. It was all adding up. All making it impossible for her to marry Greg—

And she might… just might… want to marry him, she admitted.

"Renata? If it's too much, just say so. There must be a limit even to your wealth," Mayra said.

If only she knew. "It's not too much," she forced herself to say. "I'll send the money as soon as I can."

"Soon, if you don't mind. The payment is due."

"I'll get it to you." And that would be the last of her cash. She had no idea what she would do next.

Best not to overthink it. Renata slipped outside and joined the rest of the group, which had moved to the back of the bunkhouse, the better to see Jericho and Greg's progress with the wind turbine, one of three they'd installed months ago to help power their community. Their turbines weren't nearly as huge as the big ones you saw on windfarms, but they were tall enough she had to tilt her head back to see the top.

"I don't think either of them should be anywhere

near that thing," Riley murmured when Renata approached. "This wind is crazy. They could get hurt."

"They've got to get it turned off," Avery said. "Otherwise it could break."

"We can replace a turbine. We can't replace a person," Riley countered.

Renata's breath caught when she looked up and took in Greg high on the turbine's ladder. Jericho was on the ground beneath him. Greg seemed to be fiddling with a panel at the top, trying to open it and get at whatever was inside. Renata supposed she should know more about turbines by now, but the truth was mechanical things had never interested her. She was far more fascinated by people and relationships.

"They're all programmed to stop when it gets crazy like this," Riley said. "You aren't supposed to have to go near them in a storm."

"I should be up there," Jericho said, coming over to them, his hands on his hips. "I'm in charge of the energy system."

"Think of Savannah and baby Jacob!"

"It's just as dangerous for Greg as it is for me."

Renata had to agree with Jericho. Greg was much too high. The wind was gusting much too hard. In the truck the gusts had added to the excitement of making love to him. Now her heart was in her mouth.

"He's coming down!" Avery cried.

Renata held her breath until his feet were on the ground, but her relief was short-lived when he approached Jericho. "Something's overridden the system.

I can't get the failsafe to kick in. Any ideas?"

The two men conferred surrounded by a camera crew. Clem hung back, his arms folded over his chest, wrapped in a heavy winter coat and a ridiculous knit cap that he probably thought made him hip but instead made him look old.

He had something to do with this, Renata realized. He wouldn't look half so satisfied if he didn't.

"Greg!" Renata shouted through the wind as he turned to head back to the turbine. She hurried to catch up to him. "It's another attack. It's Clem; it has to be."

"I know." Greg bent down and brushed a kiss over her lips. "I'll be fine. Don't worry."

Easy for him to say.

Renata couldn't bear to watch. Instead, she hurried into the bunkhouse and called Fulsom. This had to stop.

"Martin Fulsom's office. May I help you?"

"Patch me through to him, please, Julie. Now." She didn't have time to play games.

She breathed a thank-you to the powers that controlled such things when Fulsom came on the line. Greg's kiss still tingled on her lips. Maybe she wasn't going to get to marry him, but she loved him. She couldn't let Clem put people in danger like this.

"What's the problem, Ludlow?"

"Clem's the problem. He's trying to get someone killed." She ran down the facts, knowing Fulsom wouldn't want to hear any editorializing.

"He told you he messed with the turbine?"

"He didn't have to. It's obvious. The man's a menace, and he won't stop until someone dies. Do you want that on your conscience?"

"Bailey doesn't want to kill anyone."

Renata wasn't having it. "He hates me, and he'll do anything he can to keep that job—"

"Is that what this is about? Your job?"

"I don't want Greg killed!" Renata exploded. Why wouldn't he listen?

"Greg, huh? So things are going well between you?"

She sputtered helplessly until Fulsom took pity on her and kept going. "Look, send me proof that Bailey jiggered with the wind turbine, and I'll can his ass. I can't do that without proof, though."

"Yes, you can. You just don't want to."

"I have to take the long view. You of all people should understand—"

Renata hung up on him. He wasn't going to help her stop Clem.

She was on her own.

"RENATA WENT UP to the manor with Avery," Riley told Greg when he finally made his way down off the wind turbine again and went looking for her. He was cold to the bone, his fingers frozen, but he'd gotten it to stop spinning. Whether or not he could start it again remained to be seen.

"Why?"

"Seeing you up there was making her nervous. Avery distracted her by saying the manor needed cleaning for our next guests." Riley sighed. "It probably does. I'll head up there now, too."

Greg would have followed her, but his phone buzzed, and when he saw his parents' number, he answered it.

"Greg, you haven't called in ages," his mother, Phoebe, said.

"Hi, Mom. Sorry, it's been a little crazy."

"You drew the short straw," she guessed. The episode showing it hadn't aired yet, but it would be soon.

"I did."

"Have you found a bride?"

"I'm not giving you any spoilers." He wasn't sure he was ready to tell her about Renata.

"Fine. Call your sister, though."

Her quick switch of topic threw him off guard. "What's wrong with Eileen?"

"Nothing's wrong, except the two of you hardly talk. And neither of you ever come home."

"We're just busy, that's all." He swallowed against a surge of guilt. She was right; he did avoid Greenside.

His mother was quiet. "I get that you two needed to sow your wild oats, but I hoped you'd return sometime to settle down. This is your home, after all."

Your home, he wanted to tell her. His parents loved Greenside, but he'd felt hemmed in there, and Eileen had, too. She loved traveling as much as he once did, and she was rarely in her Santa Monica apartment. Back when he'd been a Navy SEAL, they'd played endless rounds of phone tag trying to connect with their erratic schedules until they'd gotten out of the habit of talking to each other at all.

If she was anything like him, she'd been afraid that if she spent too much time at Greenside, somehow the place would swallow her whole again, like it had when they were children. That had been their parents' mistake—thinking Greenside could be their whole world.

"I'll call her," he promised, although he didn't say when.

"Do it now," his mother urged him. "Call me back tomorrow." Before he could protest, she'd hung up.

What could he do but put the call through to Eileen? He tapped at his phone, lifted it to his ear and began walking slowly up the hill toward the manor, ready to leave a message on voice mail as usual, so when she answered after two rings, he was almost too surprised to say hello. "H-hey," he managed finally. "Eileen. It's me."

"I saw your number. Is something wrong with Mom and Dad?"

His whole family was hopeless, he thought. "Nothing's wrong. Just wanted to see how you're doing."

"I'm… fine."

"Really? You don't sound fine."

There was a long pause. "It's just… I lost my job. I got downsized," she corrected herself. "I don't think it's going to be too long until my company folds altogether, actually. There are too many people doing what we do. Did." She sighed. "I haven't been without a job in years. I can't wrap my head around it."

He understood why the job loss was hitting her so

hard. Eileen worked for one of the major travel guide companies and was sent around the world to research up-and-coming destinations. As internet influencers swarmed the globe and made the same type of information available for free, smaller companies had given up the ghost, but hers had kept chugging along. She must have hoped it would continue to beat the odds.

"What does a thirty-something-year-old washed-up travel writer do to make a living?" she joked, but there was real fear underlying that question.

"Have you looked around for something local?"

"That pays enough to keep an apartment here?" She sighed again. "I'm going to have to move. Reinvent myself. God, it's so depressing. You want to know the worst of it?"

"Sure."

"I've spent the last two weeks here in Santa Monica, in the condo I've owned for over fourteen years, and three separate people in my complex have stopped me to ask who I'm visiting. One of them practically forced me to show her my ID. I guess people have been sneaking into the complex to use the pool, but really, Greg. Fourteen years—and no one knows me."

"You never built up a community there."

"I never built a community anywhere. My community is the people I work with—over the internet. We're never in the same place at the same time. Now that I've lost my job, they've disappeared."

"You said you needed to reinvent yourself. Maybe that's where you should start. By identifying a community you actually want to be a part of."

Eileen laughed. "The really sad part is the only one that comes to mind is…"

"Greenside?"

"Yeah."

"You could come here."

"Not sure I'm ready for some Navy SEAL to find me as his bride."

It was Greg's turn to laugh. "The show is over in just a few months. No one will be forced to marry after that. Think about it."

"I will. But first… I think I'm ready to go home for a while."

"Mom will be over the moon to hear that."

"Speaking of marriage," Eileen went on. "Who drew the short straw? I can't wait to watch the episode. Was it you?"

"Yes," he admitted.

"Who's the lucky girl?"

"You know the director? The British one who narrates the show sometimes?"

"You're marrying Renata?"

"I sure hope so. Haven't convinced her yet. Don't tell Mom and Dad. I don't want to get their hopes up if it doesn't work out."

"You'll get her hooked. You always could charm the girls. Make sure you bring her home to meet all of us."

It sounded right when she talked about Greenside that way, and Greg realized he no longer felt like the place was something to run from, either. He wasn't a kid anymore. He'd seen the world. Chosen a home of his own. Now he could visit as an independent adult and enjoy it for all its good qualities.

"I'll do that," he said.

"YOU'RE AVOIDING ME," Clem accused when Renata entered the manor's kitchen to get a drink of water. She'd thought Avery had been making an excuse when she said they needed to clean the B and B for their next set of guests, but she'd been wrong. They'd spent several hours giving the large home a thorough cleaning, and oddly enough, it was just what she'd needed. If only she could put her life in order as easily as they had the manor.

"Just doing my work, like any other cast member," she said dryly and moved past him to fetch a glass out of a cupboard. One more thing she'd need to clean.

"You're afraid of me."

"God, you're self-absorbed." She moved to the sink and let the water run until it was cold.

"It doesn't have to be like this, you know." He moved closer. "You and I have a lot in common."

She didn't like the silky-smooth tone of his voice or the insinuation in his words, but it was his body language that spooked her the most.

"Rematch," she said loudly, hoping to head off whatever nasty proposition he was about to make.

"What?"

At least she'd confused him. "Nickels. I want a rematch. With a *real* bet." She needed money, after all.

Clem eyed her suspiciously, but in the end his need to best her apparently won over whatever twisted fantasy had him thinking she might agree to be with him.

"You're on." He dug a handful of coins out of his pocket and gave her one. "Where?"

Renata looked around the large country kitchen. There weren't any suitable walls in here. "The ballroom." That was all bare floors and large expanses without furniture.

She led the way without looking back, bringing her glass of water with her, setting it on a windowsill when they entered the ballroom. The room was overly quiet with just the two of them occupying it. She hoped Avery was still somewhere upstairs.

"Ladies first."

"You always say that like you doubt I'm a lady." Renata regretted her quip almost immediately. She'd set him up for another innuendo.

"Maybe I'd like confirmation that you are. Personal confirmation," he said, right on cue.

"Ick." Renata took her shot and landed her coin expertly. No fooling around this game.

"We didn't say what the bet was."

"Five thousand dollars."

"You're on." Clem took his shot and beat her.

Surprised, Renata hesitated before going to retrieve her coin.

"Why are you always trying to steal my money?" Clem strode to the wall, scooped up both coins and handed hers to her. "Desperate for cash for some reason? Coke habit? Secret baby?"

"I'm not desperate for cash. And I don't have a baby." She had seven teenagers and a college student who needed help, though.

Clem studied her before taking his next shot. "You *are* desperate for cash, aren't you?"

"I just said I wasn't."

Clem's shot landed far from the wall. "Hell."

Renata beat his shot easily. She beat him the next three shots as well. Still, he recovered and tied her at seven.

"How much cash do you need?"

"None," she lied. Enough that five thousand dollars would barely make a dent.

He took his shot, and it landed wildly again. Maybe talking to him was the key to winning, Renata thought. Overall, his aim was certainly better than it had been last time, though. She took her shot and won the round. Took the next one and landed the coin a fraction of an inch from the wall.

"Have you been practicing?" she asked as he flicked his wrist to toss his coin. The nickel landed a good six inches from the wall.

"No."

She laughed and easily won the next round, as well. "Yes, you have. Five thousand dollars, please."

"I'll have to do an e-transfer."

The both took out their phones and completed the transaction. Renata was tickled to see her balance, such as it was, increase by so much.

Clem didn't seem all that put out to have lost.

"What are you smirking about?" she challenged him.

He tapped at his phone. Hers buzzed.

Renata realized her mistake in giving him her email address to complete the transfer.

"Want to get laid?" the subject line of his email read.

"What are you two doing?" a male voice said.

Greg.

Renata felt herself flush as she deleted the email as quickly as she could.

"Just getting to know each other a little better," Clem said.

"Just taking his money." She went and scooped up the nickels. Handed them to Clem. "We had a rematch."

Greg looked grim. "A rematch."

Why should she feel guilty about taking Clem's money? She did, though. Not about winning but about playing the game with Clem at all. From Greg's point of view, it might look like she was choosing to spend time with the director. Clem certainly wasn't doing anything to dispel that impression.

"It's almost dinnertime," Greg said. "Is Avery still here?"

"I think so. She was upstairs last I saw her." With every word, she was digging herself a deeper hole. Now Greg might think she'd deliberately tried to be alone with Clem. Did Greg think she wanted to flirt with him—or worse?

She shivered.

"Cold?" Clem asked, moving closer.

"Disgusted," she countered. "And ready to get back to the bunkhouse. Any idea what's for dinner?" she asked Greg. She led the way to the hall.

"No."

"Avery?" Renata called up the stairs. "Time to eat!"

"Coming," Avery called down.

They collected their jackets from where they'd left them in the kitchen, and the four of them tramped silently down the path to the bunkhouse.

CHAPTER TEN

WELL, THIS WAS awkward, Greg thought, leading the way down the snowy path. He was angry at himself for not hiding his suspicions better when he came upon Clem and Renata in the ballroom. His first thought was that Clem had been making a pass at her. His second, that maybe Renata and Clem had planned some elaborate scheme together to upend things at Base Camp, and he'd been a fool to think she really cared for him.

That was paranoid, though. Probably the easiest answer was the right one: Renata had wanted to bet money again, and Clem had gone along with it.

"Has Walker found that fan he's looking for?" he asked Avery when the group's silence became too unbearable.

Avery stumbled. "Fan? Uh… I don't know."

"He's been looking all over."

"I'm keeping an eye out for it, too. Do you think someone sabotaged the wind turbine?"

Her rapid change of topic made it difficult to keep

up. "Possibly, although it could simply have been a mechanical failure." The attacks on his energy systems were getting to be worrisome, and he feared they might get worse before the show ended.

"We should set up security cameras to monitor your equipment," Renata said.

Hell. Why hadn't he thought of that?

"Security cameras?" Avery stumbled again. "Aren't we filmed enough?"

"I don't know, I like the idea," Greg told her. "Renata, what do you say we head to town tomorrow and pick up some equipment to get right on that. If Clem wants to sabotage the show, hitting our energy systems is a good way to do it."

"Won't that be expensive?" Avery said.

"Not as expensive as losing a wind turbine or solar panels," Greg pointed out. "What do you say?" he added to Renata. "Should we catch us a troublemaker?"

Renata smiled for the first time since he'd caught up with her at the manor. "Sounds like fun."

It didn't take them long the next afternoon to find what they were looking for in an electronics store. Greg was enjoying the time alone with Renata, even if she still was a little stiff around him. The sun had come out, the temperature was above freezing for once. Spring didn't seem like such an impossibility, even though it was still far away.

"These are motion-activated," the clerk told them when they indicated some cameras they were interested in. He went into a long spiel about the small surveillance equipment's specifications. They bought a half dozen of the tiny cameras, with the intent to install them in several places around Base Camp.

"We could stop by Thayer's Jewelers," Greg joked when they exited the store, indicating the small jewelry shop down the street. "Pick up your engagement ring. You could have all of this"—he indicated himself—"right now!"

"Hmm…" Renata said. "Answer me this. If you didn't have to marry in forty days, would we be having this conversation?"

He hesitated only a moment, but that moment cost him dearly.

Renata ducked around him and climbed into the truck. He stopped her from shutting the door, however. One hand on the roof, the other on the doorframe, he leaned down to confront her. "I wouldn't be proposing this soon," he conceded, "but I'd be pursuing you—hard. Make no mistake about that." He shut the door and went to the other side of the vehicle.

Did she doubt that he cared for her? If so, he had some work to do.

Starting right now.

Back home, they fetched a ladder from the barn and set it up midway down the back of the bunkhouse. Greg figured no one trespassing would be dumb enough to pass by either the front or kitchen entrances they all used a dozen times a day. Someone trying to make his way unseen through camp might well go this way, though. Throughout the process, he made sure he touched Renata whenever he could. Grabbed a kiss or two when he could. He wanted her to think about him when she went to bed tonight, the way he was constantly thinking about her.

"Hold the ladder," he said and climbed up to install one of the security cameras in the eaves of the bunkhouse roof, but what he saw there stopped him short. "Hell, there's a camera here already. Renata—is this one of yours?"

RENATA PEERED UP at the eaves and made out a small, dark shape that had to be the camera Greg meant. "No, it's definitely not mine." It was well hidden but would track anything that went on behind the bunkhouse. Who had stuck it there? Clem?

"You sure?" Greg half climbed back down the ladder to face her. Renata's temper flared.

"Of course I'm sure. We thought about installing cameras like that back at the beginning of the show but decided against it because we knew you'd all figure it out after the first episode. I wanted to keep the immediacy of a handheld camera crew."

"Whose is it then?"

She shrugged, although the answer was obvious. "Clem's, maybe." She met Greg's gaze.

"I'm really starting to hate that guy," he admitted. "Least he could do was tell us we were being watched."

"That would defeat the whole purpose," she pointed out. "Probably wanted to catch you getting it on with some young thing back here."

"The only person I'd be getting it on with is you—" Greg bit off the rest of his sentence and climbed back up the ladder. A wave of heat crashed over Renata at the image his words conjured. She saw herself backed against the building, Greg's body pressed against hers, him lifting her up—pushing into her—

"Can you hand me that screwdriver? I'm going to take this down."

Renata blinked before getting a hold of herself and fetching the screwdriver. She didn't meet Greg's eyes as she handed it up, sure he knew exactly where her thoughts had drifted.

"If there's one, there's more. We have to find the rest of them." Greg tossed the camera down when he'd uninstalled it and came down the ladder again to get one of the ones they'd just bought.

"Clem will notice if his cameras are gone."

"Screw him." Greg was good and mad, and Renata didn't blame him.

No one liked being spied on.

"That's one of our cameras installed, five to go," he said a few minutes later. He looked around. "You know what? We're going to need a lot more of these things."

"GREG? THERE YOU are. We've got a problem," Boone said when he met them coming back to the bunkhouse an hour later. They'd found three more cameras and set up the rest of the ones they'd bought near the wind turbines, the root cellar and a couple of the solar panels, but Greg knew they had a lot more work to do. He was sure if they looked they'd find more cameras around, and the ones they'd installed barely covered any of the things Clem might decide to sabotage. It would be far too easy for whoever was causing trouble at Base Camp to simply evade them.

Greg sighed. "What now?"

"There's a problem with your backup brides."

"What backup brides?"

"You know I always line up backup brides," Boone said.

"What about them?" Renata asked.

"I put out an ad the day you drew the short straw," Boone said to Greg. "I went to check if there were any responses this morning, but there weren't."

"Good." Greg was relieved. He didn't want Renata thinking he was even entertaining the idea of marrying someone else.

"Not good," Boone told him. "You need a fallback plan. No offense, Renata."

"None taken. I agree with you. What do you think happened?" She was back in director mode. And speaking of directors, here came Clem.

"What's going on?" he demanded as a crew hurriedly set up to film.

"No one's answering Greg's backup bride ad," Renata explained, as if his impending marriage had nothing to do with her. Greg's frustration mounted. His body was still uncomfortably aware of her closeness. How could she turn off what had happened between them so easily?

"Maybe no one's interested in marrying him," Clem said.

"It's not Greg," Boone said. "It's that article you posted on the website. The one titled *Backup Brides Unite*. See? I didn't know it was there until this morning. I haven't been paying attention like I should." He showed them his phone. Greg leaned in to try to make it out, but the screen was too damn small to see it very well.

"I'll read it later on my own phone."

"Who told you to write an article?" Renata demanded.

"No one," Clem said. "I interviewed a bunch of the women who've answered backup bride ads and talked to Boone in the past. They're pissed that none of them ever make it on the show. They think it's a scam, and I think they're right. It's an article that needed to be written."

"Well, you've screwed up everything," Boone told him. "Now the women are forming a boycott, and no one's going to cross the proverbial picket line to marry Greg."

Renata laughed. "Sorry," she said when Boone—and Clem—glared at her. "You've got to admit it's funny. A backup bride boycott."

"Really funny," Greg told her. "You realize this means you'll have to marry me?"

FOR AN INSTANT, Renata pictured doing just that. Pledging her hand—and life—to the man standing beside her. The man who was half-relieved and half-pissed that his potential backup brides were boycotting him.

She smiled again. She couldn't help it. The *Base Camp* website was fantastic for riling up the fans—and the cast.

Her smile faded. She was part of the cast now. Who knew what Clem would post about her given the chance?

She vowed right there and then she'd never look at it again.

Instead a vision of married life with Greg flitted into her mind. Living in a tiny house. Waking up beside him—instead of across the bunkhouse floor, like she had this morning.

It had taken ages to fall asleep these past few nights. She'd listened to Angus snoring. Listened for any sign that Greg was awake, too.

What if she'd crept out of her sleeping bag, slipped into the kitchen—

And he'd come to join her?

What if they'd slipped away and spent a whole night together, not just a furtive quickie in a truck but a long, leisurely session of lovemaking that would go on and on—

Suddenly uncomfortable, Renata tried to focus on the conversation—

Then realized no conversation was happening. All three men were looking at her—

As if they'd read her mind.

Renata swallowed hard. "I'm not marrying anyone," she insisted weakly.

"Then you'd better find Greg a wife," Boone said, "because I don't know what to do. I tried some other dating forums, and the women are on there as well, warning everyone else away from him. It's a real problem."

"If you can't get it done, how do you expect me to?" She didn't want to find Greg a wife. She wanted to be his wife. Maybe she needed to start shaking down more of the inhabitants of Base Camp for money.

"However you can. I've got to get going." He moved to the entrance to pull on his outer gear. He was actually angry, Renata realized. Boone had put a lot into making this community a success, and they were standing on ground his wife, Riley, had once thought she'd inherit from her family. No wonder he was mad.

"Yeah, Renata," Clem echoed. "Find Greg a wife."

"You'd better not find me a wife," Greg warned her. "I won't marry her if you do."

"You'll do what you're told," she said primly.

"Like hell." Greg looped a hand around her waist. "I told you. I already know who I want to marry." His kiss was fast and hot, and the pressure of it left her clinging to him.

The bunkhouse door burst open. "Boone, Greg. Pasture." Jericho was gone as quickly as he'd come.

"What does that mean?" Renata asked.

"Something's up with the bison." Boone was halfway to the door. Greg steadied her, bent down to snatch a kiss. Renata lifted her chin to meet it before she remembered she needed to stop doing that.

"Be back as soon as I can," Greg said.

"SOMEONE CUT THE wires deliberately," Boone announced when Greg caught up with him, Walker, Avery and Jericho in the pasture. Walker and Avery were working to repair the fence, with Jericho's help. Boone came to meet Greg.

"Did we lose any bison?"

"No," Walker said shortly from where he was kneeling to unspool some wire.

"It must have just happened," Jericho added.

"We need cameras out here, too. Speaking of which," Greg added, "when Renata and I went to install ours, we found someone else had gotten there ahead of us." He explained what they'd found. As he did so, Renata approached. She'd stopped to pull on her spencer and boots, her old-fashioned gown hampering her progress through the snow.

"Cameras?" Avery repeated sharply.

"We found six of them altogether in various places, so far. Renata and I will drive into town when we can and pick up some more. We're taking down the other ones and putting up our own. We think we can catch whoever is slipping in and doing damage."

"Where exactly were these cameras?" Avery asked.

Greg tried to be patient as he explained again. He couldn't blame Avery for not liking being spied on, but he was a little surprised at the extent of her anger. After all, they were all on a reality television show.

"We need to be patrolling more," Boone said.

"There aren't enough of us." All of the men had been working on way too little sleep for months. They needed a break. Not that he was managing to get much sleep anyway these days, thanks to Renata's presence just feet away in the bunkhouse every night.

"Did you know about this?" Walker asked Renata.

"No," she said unequivocally. "Like I told Greg, we considered using cameras like these at the beginning of the show. At the time, Boone was pushing for almost no filming at all. We compromised on camera crews with handheld video cameras capturing what they can."

"Whose are they, then?" Jericho demanded.

"They have to be Clem's," Boone said.

Renata nodded. "That's my assumption. He's breaking rules left and right."

"Here he is," Jericho muttered.

Greg swung around to see Clem and a small crew making their way through the snowy pasture toward them. Boone went to meet the man, and Greg fell in behind him. "You put surveillance cameras up—without telling us?"

Greg thought Clem would deny it, but the other man must have realized it was useless. "So what? I've got every right to film every angle of what goes on here. That's the deal."

Renata swore as a new thought occurred to her. "I bet he's got them inside, too," she said to Greg. "We'd better sweep this whole place."

"Inside?" Jericho strode forward to confront Clem. "You put cameras in our houses?" His voice rose.

"No," Clem said, but Greg didn't believe him.

By the looks of it, neither did Boone, and after the fence had been repaired, he gathered everyone together in the bunkhouse to announce what they had learned. The result was pandemonium.

"There'd better not be a camera inside of my house," Clay threatened Clem.

"You've got that right," Curtis added.

As voices rose into an angry clamor, Greg muttered to Boone, "Better get this under control before there's a lynching."

"All right, everyone, sit down! Let's talk this over," Boone bellowed. With a lot of grumbling, they did. "We're going to work in pairs, combing every surface twice. We didn't sign up for this, obviously."

"This is ridiculous," Clem said from the back of the room. "I'm the director, and if I want cameras—"

"Pair up. One SEAL, one citizen," Boone went on, ignoring him. "Start with your houses. Examine every inch—inside and out. Then we'll split up to sweep the outbuildings."

It was a major undertaking, hampered wherever possible by Clem, who protested it every step of the way. He kept his phone clapped to his ear, trying to get through to Fulsom, who didn't seem to want to answer.

"I'm supposed to make this show interesting," he bellowed finally. He'd stomped a circle in the snow outside the bunkhouse door. "Why the hell can't any of you understand that?"

"He's losing it," Renata said dryly as she and Greg headed toward one of the unfinished tiny houses. "I'm not sure I've ever been inside your place."

"I'll be glad to show it to you." The building crew had hurried to frame in all the houses they'd need and get them weather-tight before the snow fell last fall. Now they were finishing the interiors in the order in which the men married. Since he was to wed next, they'd been concentrating on his. He checked in when he could, but it had been several days.

He opened the door and ushered in Renata, and when she sighed with appreciation for the sunny, beautiful interior, he smiled. "Clay, Curtis and Harris do good work, don't they?"

"These houses are one of my favorite things about Base Camp."

"Let me show you around." He guided her through the light-filled front living space with its floor-to-ceiling windows, to the kitchen and eating area. Upstairs was a loft that would hold a queen-size mattress. Every inch of space had been utilized for cupboards, shelves and storage spaces.

"They always feel so big for being so little," she said.

"I know what you mean. I was skeptical at first, but when I checked out Boone's house at the beginning of the show, I was hooked." Greg had shut the door when they entered. They were alone. He moved to kiss her.

"Don't you think we should check for cameras first?" Renata asked him.

"To hell with it. Let them watch if they want to."

GREG WAS KISSING her, and she wasn't stopping him, and she really ought to stop him because she still hadn't figured out a way to pay off the twenty-nine months' worth of payments still outstanding to Mayra and Gabriela.

Trouble was, Renata couldn't seem to remember why that was important.

If she did marry Greg, she'd live in this wonderful house, with this sexy, wonderful man…

Greg pulled back. "I guess you're right; let's make sure we're really alone before this gets out of hand."

They got to work, and to Renata's surprise, they didn't find any cameras in the little house's interior. They checked thoroughly, Greg looking in places she'd never have thought of.

Renata stored the information away for later. Who knew where her career might take her, after all?

Outside was a different story. They found not one but four different cameras there, two on either side of the house. Greg examined them.

"Why four? I can see installing one on either side, but why did Clem double up?" Each side had hosted a large camera and a much smaller, much cheaper one.

"Maybe he didn't." Renata pointed out that there were two different kinds. One set were larger and more expensive-looking. The other two were smaller, similar to the cheap ones she and Greg had bought earlier.

"You think someone else besides Clem is spying on

us? Who?"

She didn't answer that. Wouldn't until she got Avery alone and asked her a few questions. She'd caught Avery sneaking around more than once in the past, but until recently she'd been here to film the action, not shape the story.

Greg's expression darkened, and his brows drew together. "You know something." It wasn't a question.

"It's more of a guess."

"You've got a lot of secrets," he said when she didn't elaborate.

"Believe me, I wish I didn't."

CHAPTER ELEVEN

All in all, they found twenty-four large cameras and eighteen small ones. When they'd finished the sweep, everyone trooped up to the manor and started all over again, making sure Clem and all the camera crews stayed with them and didn't reinstall cameras back in the buildings they'd just swept.

It was a discouraged, disgruntled group that arrived at the bunkhouse for dinner that night.

Greg knew Boone had registered a protest with Fulsom, who'd promised to bar Clem from putting up new cameras, but when dinner was over, and Boone announced it was time to watch the week's episode, the atmosphere was mutinous. Clem was sulking. The camera crew seemed chastened, especially when Renata came near them.

"We didn't know anything about extra cameras," Greg heard William saying to her, but she just waved him off.

After the usual introduction, the episode began with a group of women Greg didn't recognize, seated around a table in a nondescript office.

A narrator's voice—Clem's voice—introduced them. "All of you sitting at this table have applied to be backup brides, am I right?"

"More than that," one woman said. "We were all informed by Boone Rudman that we'd passed the first clearance and our information would be given to the men in question."

"I think Boone was lying. I was told my information would be given to Clay. As far as I can tell from the show, Clay never even looked at any of our profiles," a frowning brunette said.

"That's right," a blonde to her left echoed. "I was told the same thing—my information would be passed to Clay. Why did I go through all that effort if he was going to marry Nora the whole time?"

"So you felt taken advantage of," Clem said. "As if you'd been used and discarded like an old condom."

The blonde blanched. "That's not quite—"

"How about you?" Clem asked a different woman. "Which Navy SEAL screwed you over?"

"Jericho. He never got in contact with me," she said. "I thought that was rude. I put myself out there applying to meet him and got nothing in return."

"Exactly," a fierce-looking woman to her right said. "I thought there'd be a chance to meet Jericho. Talk to him. No one even called me back to tell me it wasn't going to happen."

"So the show preyed on your gullibility," Clem said. "You really thought you stood a chance." He turned to the camera and made a face, showing just how unlikely he thought that was.

"It's like, did those men just take one look at our photos and refuse to even meet us?" a redhead asked from in back.

Clem turned on her. "Don't you think appearances are important?"

"Maybe," the woman retorted. "But I'm more than just tits and an ass."

The interview went down from there when Clem introduced three new women.

"You're here to talk about Greg Devon, am I right?" Clem asked them.

"That's right. I'm Monica Halton," a pleasant-looking brunette stated. "I saw the ad, and I went online to *Base Camp*'s website and saw how the other backup brides had been treated, and I thought it was wrong for them to keep getting women's hopes up when the men never picked one."

"That's not entirely true," Clem pointed out. "Samantha Smith married Harris Wentworth."

"After she was led to believe she'd be marrying Clay Pickett—and after Curtis Lloyd, the next man she was matched with, refused to even pick her up from the airport!" another woman interrupted. "I think the whole thing is meant to humiliate women. I was going to apply to be a backup bride, too, but I changed my mind when I saw what was really going on."

"I think Greg Devon should explain himself. Does he really mean to pick a bride this time?" the third woman demanded.

"Here's some video that might interest you," Clem said.

On the episode, the women turned to a video screen. Footage came up of Greg's encounter with Fulsom, Clem and Renata at the hospital the day after he'd drawn the short straw. Greg wanted to cover his face with his hands, but he forced himself to watch. When onscreen version of himself pointed to Renata and said, "She's the one. She's the woman I'm going to marry. She has to stay because she's going to be my wife!" the group of women shrieked with outrage.

"It's happening again!" Monica said. "Women are being lured to beg to be considered as wives when there's obviously no chance they'll make it on the show. *Base Camp* is all about denigrating women!"

The show cut away to what seemed to Greg like an hour of footage—just of him and Renata. Where was everyone else?

Pretty soon he saw a pattern. A pattern he knew would infuriate Renata, just as Clem had intended. The footage wasn't even real. It consisted of short cuts spliced together in ways that created a story line that didn't exist. Some of the footage had been mixed up to look like all Greg did was order Renata around while she followed him like a docile slave.

Other sequences featured Greg talking, interspersed with close-ups of Renata listening with all her being, as if she was held in thrall by every word Greg said. Clem was trying to make her feel small. Greg hoped it wouldn't work.

"Renata wasn't even there for that conversation," he spluttered a few minutes later. "I was talking to Boone!"

"The camera doesn't lie," Clem said.

Renata didn't say a thing, but her lips were pressed together in a thin, angry line. Clem had taken every opportunity to showcase her cleavage in his shots. The way he was slicing and dicing the footage made her out to be a simpering fool.

Meanwhile, he'd portrayed Greg as if he barely could be bothered to give Renata the time of day. There were so many shots of him walking away and Renata staring after him, Greg lost count. In some of them, Clem had barely attempted to make the backgrounds or the angle of the sun match up from one frame to the next.

"No one's going to fall for this," Greg told him. "It looks like a kindergartener edited it."

"You're overestimating your audience's smarts," Clem retorted.

The bunkhouse fell silent as the episode went on and on. When it was finally over, Boone shut it off. Renata stood up, crossed the room, grabbed her spencer and walked out the door.

"Boo-hoo, Renata. Better toughen up if you want to make it in this busin—"

The door slammed shut before Clem finished his sentence. Greg lunged from his seat, but Boone and Jericho jumped in to stop him.

"Not like that," Boone muttered. "We've got to get

him in a way that will end this once and for all."

For a second Greg thought he meant a more permanent solution than he'd ever even considered, but then he realized Boone was talking about getting Clem off the show.

He followed Boone out of the bunkhouse, Clem's continued taunts ringing in Greg's ears.

"We've got to get that guy," he said when they made it outside.

"We will," Boone promised him. "Avery, could you and Eve get us some damaging footage of Clem? Now that we've taken his hidden cameras down, you know he'll get up to trouble."

"With or without him knowing?" Eve asked.

"Without, preferably."

"Just to be clear," Avery said. "You want us to *spy* on Clem?"

"That's right. Get us some dirt on him."

"O-kay. Will do, boss," Avery said. She turned to Eve. "Let's go make a plan."

Boone waited until they were gone. "Can you hold tight a couple of days? I have a feeling it won't take long to capture something unflattering."

"I guess so," Greg muttered, but if Clem pushed him much harder, he couldn't predict what he'd do.

BY THE FOLLOWING afternoon, Renata felt like the tension in the air was palpable. Everyone was cranky, worried about whether they were being filmed in private moments or if they had been in the past. Eve and Avery were doing their best to keep tabs on Clem, who spent his time keeping tabs on her. She thought she'd scream if she didn't get some time alone soon.

"Gather around, people," Boone called out, entering the bunkhouse as the afternoon faded to darkness. "I've got an announcement." He waited for everyone to get settled.

"We're going to DelMonaco's for dinner. I checked the rules, and there's nothing that says that we can't treat ourselves to a meal out."

"Baloney," Clem called out. "You're supposed to grow all your own food."

"Which we are, and we're using it for every meal we serve here, but we can still go to a restaurant."

"Prove it. Call Fulsom."

Boone did better than that. He set up a video call so Fulsom could see everyone gathered. He explained the situation, and Fulsom nodded. "Sure. Why not? But no more than one meal out per month—and you pay for yourselves. This isn't in the budget."

"Will do," Boone assured him. When he'd cut the call, he told Clem, "See? What'd I tell you? Let's get going, folks. Clean yourselves up and meet back here in an hour."

There was a scraping of chairs as everyone stood up.

"What do you think?" Boone asked Greg after making his way over to him. "Will it cheer people up?"

"I think it's the best idea anyone's had in ages."

Renata had to agree.

As they congregated again in the bunkhouse an hour

later, everyone seemed more cheerful already, and the conversations buzzing along were far livelier than they'd been in days. The women had changed to their nicest dresses. Then men had put on their good jeans and boots.

They split up into several truckloads, and Renata wasn't surprised when Greg managed to position himself beside her. As usual, his solid presence was hard to ignore, and she found herself wishing she could lean into him, but there were too many other people around for that.

"Dinner out is exactly what I needed," Avery remarked as they drew near to town. She was sitting on the other side of Greg.

"I'm ordering a big juicy steak," Jericho said from the front passenger's seat.

I'm getting a pizza. Does DelMonaco's have pizza?" Renata asked.

"What on earth is that?" Boone asked. He'd commandeered the driver's seat, and no one had fought him for it.

Along with everyone else in the vehicle, Renata craned her neck to see what he was pointing at. Her mouth dropped open as they passed a large billboard attached to the side of a barn that read, "Don't Date This Man," next to a huge photograph of Greg's face.

"What the hell?" Greg asked as Boone swerved over to park the truck on the side of the road. The other two vehicles carrying the members of Base Camp followed suit, and they all trouped back to look at the billboard again.

Don't Date This Man.

"It's the backup brides," Renata groaned. "It has to be."

"You mean it's Clem," Clay said.

Boone swore. "There goes any chance we might have had to find Greg a wife in town. Everyone in Chance Creek will be talking about this."

"That picture doesn't even look like me," Greg said.

"Yes, it does," Renata told him. It was a good likeness, actually, and she had a hunch a woman or two might just get in touch despite the backup brides' message.

"Why are they picking on me? I'm not the one who—" Greg spotted the camera crew setting up to film. "Hell. Now the whole world will know about this."

"Come on, let's go eat," Boone said. "Standing around complaining won't change the fact it's here."

They left the film crew to follow when they were ready and kept going, but it was a somber group who sat down at three large tables at DelMonaco's.

"Hey, I know you. You're the guy I'm not supposed to date," their waitress announced cheerfully when she got to Greg.

"I'm not a bad guy—"

"Yeah, yeah, everyone's innocent," she cracked. "You must have done something pretty awful to get a billboard about it."

Renata couldn't help feeling sorry for Greg, and to distract him, she regaled him with stories of famous people who'd been brought down to earth publicly over the years.

"Think of it as a badge of honor," she told him when the waitress came back to take everyone's drink orders.

"I already have a few of those, thank you very much."

"Really? You don't talk much about your time in the service." Maybe he'd talk now. Renata was ready to listen.

"It's not my favorite topic. I learned a lot. Saw a lot. Saw some things I wish I could unsee." He made a face. Renata considered, not for the first time, that all the men around this table had lived lives far more dangerous than most people could imagine. Greg hid the parts of himself that had probably served him well during his time with the Navy SEALs, but once in a while she got a glimpse of the warrior.

"What made you leave the service?" she asked.

"Same as everyone else here, I think. People think guys who serve don't believe in global warming. They couldn't be more wrong. We're on the ground, seeing its effects all over the world. The military takes climate change more seriously than just about anyone else. We have to. It effects everything we do."

"Everything from how our equipment functions, to what equipment we need, to the dangers we face, the ways we react to them—you name it," Curtis added. He'd obviously been listening in to their conversation.

"I wanted to find a way to make people more resilient. Look how many people have been displaced by conflicts and climate change already," Greg said. "We've got waves of immigrants we're struggling to contend with. What happens when Central America heats up another few degrees? People down there are already suffering climate change's effects. I got to thinking: What if we could stop it, or what if we could make it easier for people to remain in place, even if conditions worsened? What if there were ways for them to mitigate climate change in their own locales?" He grinned suddenly. "Sorry, I'm lecturing."

"You're answering my question," Renata told him. She looked up, caught a glimpse of the crew filming them. They'd arrived in the last few minutes and quickly set up. Hell, she was doing Clem's job for him, interviewing Greg like this.

"Anyway, I wanted to help."

"We all do," Curtis said.

"That makes sense," Renata said. She thought about the mudslide in Colina Blanca. Knew conditions in many countries were growing more and more difficult as climate change led to unpredictable storm patterns, heat waves and crop failures. Several of the girls she was sponsoring had decided to study environmental science, hoping they could figure out ways to help their people, too.

After dinner, Greg took her aside as everyone pulled on their jackets and got ready to leave. Dinner had mellowed her out, and she thought everyone was in a better mood.

"Can we talk later? Alone?"

"How are we going to manage that?" They moved toward the door, lagging behind the others.

"After Byron is asleep we can slip out through the kitchen door."

"We can try, I guess."

Hours later, long past when the crew had left and everyone settled down for the night, Renata was sure their plan would never work, but one by one, Walker, Angus, Avery—and Byron seemed to fall asleep. Greg got up first, moving so quietly she wouldn't have known he was doing so if her eyes were closed. They'd been open all this time, however, and when she saw his shape against the lighter squares of the bunkhouse windows, she got up, too. They collected their boots, coats, hats and gloves as silently as they could, tiptoed into the kitchen, got into their outer gear and Greg quietly opened the side door.

Outside, a crescent moon lit a clear sky, stars twinkling in the frigid air.

"Now what?" Renata asked in a whisper when he'd shut the door again.

"Now we walk."

He took her arm and led the way down the snowy track toward Pittance Creek, ducking into his tiny house and reappearing with a substantial backpack. "This is a Base Camp insider's trick."

"Oh, yeah?"

"That's right." He leaned over and kissed her cheek. "You're going to love it."

By the time they reached the banks of Pittance Creek, Renata was shivering. She stood back and watched Greg spread a tarp on the ground and then zipped together two sleeping bags and lay them out on top.

"Climb in. You probably won't need your coat once you're in there."

"I never said I'd get naked with you." This wasn't a good idea, although she had to admit slipping into that sleeping bag with Greg sounded pretty wonderful right now. For one thing, it was cold out here, a thousand stars twinkling overhead.

For another, Greg was… Greg. She wanted to be close to him again.

"I didn't ask you to get naked with me. We're just going to talk." He ditched his own coat, slipped out of his boots and climbed into the sleeping bag, still wearing the sweats he slept in. "It's too cold to spend time out here without being bundled up. In here we'll keep warm."

Knowing she was making a mistake, Renata followed suit. She wasn't nearly innocent enough to think Greg only wanted to talk.

The thing was, she wanted more than talking, too.

Folding her coat and setting it on top of her boots, she crawled in and sighed as she lay on her back and looked up at the stars. Greg put an arm out, and she snuggled into him, resting her head on his bicep.

"There's the big dipper," he said unnecessarily.

"I noticed that one."

Greg pointed out a few more constellations. "There's Orion's belt," he finished.

"I know my constellations. Stop showing off."

"What else can I do? I've got my favorite girl in a sleeping bag. I have to impress her."

"It's going to take more than that. Didn't you bring me here for something specific?"

"Yep. This." Greg turned her toward him, gathered her close and kissed her, taking his time, exploring her mouth, finally slipping his tongue in between her lips to taste her.

Renata found herself melting into him, meeting him on his terms.

Melting was right. As they clung to each other, the temperature in the sleeping bag was rising fast.

Greg groaned, pulled back and tugged his shirt over his head. He tossed it on top of his other things.

"That's better. I was overheating."

She knew what he meant. She was pretty warm, too. What the hell, she thought. You only live once. She pulled her shirt up and over her head, too, tossed it aside and turned back to find Greg watching her, a smile tugging at his mouth.

"Come here," he growled.

She did so, gasping as her breasts brushed his chest. She wrapped her arms around his neck and savored the feeling of her nipples against his hard muscles. He was warm, and as he circled her in his arms, she knew there was nowhere she'd rather be.

Greg's kisses slid down her throat, behind her ear

and down to the hollow in her neck before he dipped lower, brushed his lips over her breasts and wriggled down to get better access to them.

"Renata, you are stunning." His voice was husky. All she could do was arch back and let him do what he wanted. Every move he made felt wonderful. She closed her eyes and reveled in it.

Greg took his time exploring all her curves, kissing and caressing her all over. When he tugged her close and reclaimed her mouth, she could feel his hardness, evidence of his desire, and she couldn't wait for him to slip inside her. She had no doubt he wanted that, too, and—

Oh, when he did, she could only moan.

Greg filled her perfectly, sliding in and out again so slowly she had to fight to keep herself from forcing him to speed up. She wanted to enjoy every moment of this, and so she let him set the pace, closing her eyes and riding every thrust with unbridled enjoyment.

"We were meant to be together," he whispered in her ear.

"Mmm" was all she could think to answer. He was right; their bodies fit together perfectly. His touch woke every sense within her. There was no awkwardness with Greg. No pauses or fumbling motions. Just—

"Renata, I want to be with you forever. You know that, right?"

"I know."

He kept moving inside her, making it hard to think.

"Say yes to me."

"I can't. Not yet."

"But you're thinking about it?"

She was definitely thinking about it.

"What do I have to do to convince you?" He picked up the pace, and another moan escaped her. If he kept this up, all her defenses would shatter. She'd find herself agreeing to anything he asked, and she couldn't. Not until—

Renata let herself go, crying out as Greg brought her over the brink. He joined her, gasping out his release along with her, both of them crashing into each other, rushing to a conclusion they could no longer stop.

When it was over, and she'd caught her breath, rolling onto her back and staring up at the stars, Renata chuckled.

"What's so funny?" Greg asked her, propping himself up on one elbow.

"You have no idea how strange it is to end up here—with you. I'm supposed to be directing this show. Instead, it's all happening to me."

"Thank goodness no one's filming us now."

"Let's hope," she agreed.

"I want to hope," he told her, brushing a strand of her hair out of her eyes. "Am I a fool to do that?"

"No," she said. "You're not a fool. I just don't know how…"

"I wish you would let me help you solve whatever problem you're trying to solve by yourself."

Should she tell him about her promise to her students? Name the sum she still owed? What would Greg do about it? Would he try to pay it off himself?

Everything within Renata rebelled against that idea. This was her obligation. She was the one who had to figure it out. She'd made a promise to the girls she'd left in Peru, and unlike all the different people whose homes she'd drifted in and out of as a child, she meant to fulfill it. Besides, what if she told him—

And he backed away?

"I'm taking care of it," she told him finally.

Greg sighed. "I'm here if you ever need a hand."

CHAPTER TWELVE

SEVERAL DAYS LATER, Greg woke early with the sense that something had changed.

The weather.

After the brief thaw, a harsh wind had whipped through Base Camp for the past forty-eight hours, making every outside job miserable. He'd stood watch for the first half of the night and had been grateful when Walker relieved him. He'd kept a close eye on the settlement and had driven out with Clay a couple of times to check on the herd. He figured no one would be out causing mischief on a night like that, but on the other hand, it was the kind of cover a person could use to his advantage if he wanted to get away with something.

He slipped out of his bedroll and tidied it as Walker was entering the bunkhouse. Greg went into the kitchen to search out a cup of coffee, and Walker joined him there.

"Any trouble?" Greg asked.

"No." Walker leaned against the kitchen counter.

"Did you ever find your ceremonial fan?"

"Nope." Always a man of few words, Walker was more taciturn than ever. The loss of the ancient object had affected him deeply.

"You let your grandmother know?"

Walker sighed. "Not yet. Putting it off as long as I can. Hoping it will turn up."

"It's got to be Clem."

"Maybe."

Renata slipped into the room, followed by Avery.

"Walker is still looking for his ceremonial fan," Greg told them.

Renata lifted an eyebrow. Turned to Avery. "Have you seen that around?"

An expression crossed Avery's face that Greg couldn't quite pin down. Surprise? Anger?

"You should be asking Clem."

Kai entered the kitchen. "Uh oh, everyone's up early today. And probably hungry. Good thing I prepped a lot of the food last night." He crossed to the refrigerator, opened it and stopped. When he turned around, he wasn't smiling anymore. "Okay, very funny. Where is it?"

"Where's what?" Greg asked.

"Breakfast? All the chopped vegetables. The bison sausage. The eggs! We're having omelets today. We *were* having omelets," he corrected himself. "We won't be having breakfast at all unless someone brings back that food!"

Avery turned to Renata. "Have you seen *that*

around?"

Renata frowned, but before she could speak, Kai stepped toward her. "I heard it was you who robbed the root cellar last fall. Did you take our breakfast, too? What else have you done?"

"It wasn't me," Renata said. "I'm not the director anymore, remember? I'm on the show."

"You still work for Fulsom—"

"All of us work for Fulsom," Greg reminded him, "and if Renata says she didn't do it, then she didn't do it."

"Someone did."

Angus poked his head in the door. "When's breakfast?"

"Whenever the person who stole the food brings it back!" Kai snapped.

Addison slipped under Angus's arm and joined her husband. "What's going on?"

Kai ran a hand through his hair. "Someone stole breakfast." He opened the refrigerator door to show her. Addison began a search of the room.

Where would someone take enough food to feed a small army? With a sinking feeling, Greg crossed to the kitchen door and opened it.

It was still dark, stars twinkling overhead in a blessedly clear sky, giving off enough light that after his eyes adjusted, he could see footsteps through the snow. He went back in, shoved his feet into boots, shrugged his jacket on, grabbed a flashlight and headed out again to follow the tracks, Kai, Walker, Angus and Renata close behind.

"They're heading toward the barn," Kai said a few moments later.

"Not the barn," Greg said with a sinking heart.

They followed the tracks another dozen yards and stood in front of the chicken house.

"Wasn't that locked up last night?" Angus asked. They always shut the chickens in at night to keep them warm and safe from predators.

"It was locked up an hour ago," Walker said. "I checked."

Their breakfast—what was left of it—was spread on the snowy ground in the chicken run. Although the door was open, it didn't look like any of the chickens had escaped. They'd made short work of the bison sausage and chopped vegetables, though. Chickens ate just about anything, in Greg's experience. A pile of eggs lay smashed in one corner. The chickens would even eat some of the shells, he knew. They craved the calcium.

"You must know something about this." Kai turned on Renata.

"I don't. I swear." She lifted her hands in appeasement.

"Well, everyone better get to work. We're not eating until lunchtime." Kai stalked off, and the rest followed him back to the kitchen, where they found Addison had taken the helm, reheating a large container of soup she must have found in the freezer.

Kai shook his head when he saw her. "We need to save our food."

"We've got a whole herd of bison out there," she told him practically. "I know you're mad. I am, too. We still have to feed people. Breakfast will be in ten minutes," she told the rest of them, and they took the hint, heading into the main room.

"Why the long faces?" Clem crowed when he and the crew burst in the front door.

"You know why." Greg confronted him.

"I'm not a mind-reader." Clem skirted around him and waved a hand to the crew to set up. When they did, he repeated his question. "What happened?"

No one answered for a long time, until Avery tiredly said, "Someone stole our breakfast."

Clem immediately turned on Renata. "Still trying to direct the show, huh? Trying to stir up controversy? I know you loved to pit everyone against each other when you were running things."

Renata flushed. "I—"

"But you still don't know how to set up a scene, for all that," he went on. "Watch and learn." He strutted across the room, waving a cameraman to follow him. "Angus! You know you need to marry in the next few months, and yet all you're doing is mooning around like a little boy who broke his yo-yo. Are you going to be a man and find a girl or what?"

Angus, who'd grabbed one of the folding chairs and taken a seat, surged out of it again and advanced on the director, who quickly retreated. "When I draw the short straw, I'll marry. Until then, bugger off!"

"Let's go catch the action in the kitchen," Clem said

to the crew.

"Why the hell did I ever come here?" Angus said bitterly when they were gone. "Why am I still here?"

"Because you made a promise," Renata snapped. "And you don't break promises to people you care about."

Greg wasn't the only one surprised by her retort. After a moment, Angus nodded and sat down again. Avery took a chair on the far side of the room. Walker paced restlessly, something Greg didn't think he'd ever seen the man do before.

As other couples filed in, looking for breakfast, the dour mood spread.

It was going to be a long day.

NO ONE WANTED her here. Kai had made it clear what he thought of her, and while Greg had leaped to her defense, no one else had. Why should they? She'd spent her first seven months here grilling them in front of the cameras, setting up awkward situations and, yes—helping to steal their food. At Fulsom's behest. One of his first attempts to liven up the show.

Back then she'd viewed the job as a job, done what she needed to do to keep getting paid. Like Addison had pointed out, no one at Base Camp would have starved with all the bison around, but she'd helped make their lives harder, every step of the way. Of course they didn't want her here.

After a silent breakfast, Greg asked her to accompany him on his rounds of the energy systems in the settlement, but Renata begged off. "I need to talk to Boone."

"About what?"

"It's personal."

Greg didn't protest, but his shoulders hunched as he went outside, and she knew she was letting him down. He must be struggling to figure her out. Every time they were close it felt like heaven, but things between them couldn't work out. Not now.

If only they'd met somewhere else.

Something tickled at her mind—a memory that simply wouldn't come clear—and Renata shook her head to drive it away. She needed to focus on the problem at hand. She squared her shoulders and went in search of Boone, finding him outside talking to Riley.

"Boone? Got a minute?" she asked.

"Sure."

"I'm off to the manor," Riley said, giving her husband a peck on the cheek and heading off.

"What can I do for you?" Boone asked when they were alone.

Renata tugged her jacket closer around her, grateful for the sturdy boots she'd bought in town when the weather had turned. Overhead a blue sky held a bright sun that gave little warmth. Still, it was better than the wind.

"About the backup bride. What are you doing to find one for Greg?"

"Didn't we agree that's your job?" Boone countered. When she didn't take the bait, he shrugged. "What can I do? Between putting the angry past backup brides on the show and plastering up that billboard near town, Clem's made sure no woman is going to step forward now."

"Greg needs a bride."

"Greg doesn't want anyone but you, so why even bother?"

"Greg can't have me," she snapped. "Oh, forget it. I'll take care of this."

She stomped off toward the manor, changed her mind and headed down to Pittance Creek instead, hoping her cell phone coverage would work out there. She found a log to sit on near the frozen-over creek. Underneath its skim of ice, water was still running. It was quiet out here.

A good place to think.

She didn't want to think, though. Imagining Greg with another woman made her skin itch. Greg was meant for her. She was meant for him.

Should she just tell him about the money she owed?

No.

She simply… couldn't.

Renata stared at the ice-covered creek, letting her thoughts run their course. She wasn't going to choose her own happiness over the promise she'd made to those girls, and she wasn't going to make Greg pay off her debts, either. Being dependent on someone else made you vulnerable. She had to pay her own way. Take care of her own obligations. That's what had gotten her this far.

Renata pulled out her phone, ready to look through her contacts, but continued to gaze at the icy surface of the creek instead. Surely some woman she'd met over the years needed a husband. What kind of a woman would Greg want?

Strong. Smart. Sexy. Renata squirmed a little. Not too sexy.

She dropped the phone in her lap.

What would she do when Greg was married, the show over? What if Fulsom didn't need her anymore? Where would she go? How would she earn the rest of the money she needed?

What about later—when all her girls had graduated and needed nothing from her except her continued friendship?

It would be too late to be with Greg.

Too late to stay at Base Camp.

"There you are."

Renata straightened. Quickly wiped tears from her face she hadn't known had fallen. It was Clem, followed by a film crew.

"Plotting your next breakfast theft?"

"Don't be ridiculous."

He peered closer. "Have you been crying? What's wrong? Trouble in paradise?"

Renata stood up. "You want to pretend you're a man, Bailey? Ten thousand dollars. That's the bet."

"What's the contest? Can't play nickels out here." He made a show of looking around the forest.

"Let's see who can make it over the creek without

getting wet." She gestured at a line of steppingstones jutting just through the ice that covered the creek.

"Child's play. We'll both cross over. Then what?"

"Then we cross back." She wasn't surprised it looked easy to him. After all the cold weather he'd think the ice was so thick he couldn't fall through no matter if his foot slipped off the rocks. Renata knew different. She'd been watching the creek while she sat here. Saw the flash of water in the small spaces surrounding the stones. Just days ago there'd been a thaw, so she hadn't been surprised to notice gaps between the ice and the rocks. Clem was a big guy. If his foot slipped, he'd get wet.

She stood up. "Ladies first, right?"

Once again she was thankful for the good boots she'd splurged on when the snow began to fall a few months back. They looked attractive, but their grip was strong, and they fit her well. After staring at the creek and the steppingstones for the past half hour, she had their layout in her mind. She had to make it look easy, though.

Renata took a breath and stepped lightly and quickly across from rock to rock, hopping up onto the far, snowy bank with a little flourish. "You're right; it's totally easy!"

"Told you." Without a second's hesitation, Clem launched himself out to the first rock, nearly overbalanced, caught himself and hopped to the next. He made the third and fourth—

And then slipped right off the fifth.

Crack! His boot went straight through the ice and he stood calf-deep in the icy flow of the creek.

"Fucking hell!" Clem lunged for the next stepping-stone, missed that one, too, and brought his other boot down into the water.

Renata bit back a laugh, not wanting to incense Clem further. He already looked like thunder. He lurched and blundered his way to meet her.

"That was a trick!" He climbed out on the bank and faced her.

"How was that a trick? You're the one who didn't look where he was going. Ten thousand dollars." When it looked like he'd argue, Renata called back to the camera crew, "You heard us, right? Ten thousand? I won fair and square!"

"That's right," William hollered back. "We got it all." He patted his video camera.

"Fuck," Clem said again, but he pulled out his phone and tapped it. When Renata's phone buzzed with the notification of an e-transfer, she accepted it gratefully. That ought to finish taking care of the school bus, at least, and go a little way toward the boiler.

"You're going to pay for this," Clem told her.

"First you'll have to catch me." She skipped lightly over the stones again and ran all the way back to the bunkhouse, where she caught her breath and transferred her winnings so far to the school's account. She got a text from Mayra almost immediately.

Thank you.

More is coming, Renata texted back. She'd have to let

Clem simmer down a little, but she couldn't wait long. How much would he be willing to bet next time?

Enough that she could marry Greg?

That would be an enormous bet.

Renata crashed back to earth, her ebullience gone in a flash. She tapped on her phone again, brought up her contacts and began to make a list of likely women.

She couldn't fool herself. Couldn't ruin things for everyone else, either.

Greg needed a bride, and it wasn't going to be her.

CHAPTER THIRTEEN

"WHY WAS CLEM all wet earlier?" Greg asked Renata late that night. The married couples had retreated to their tiny homes. The camera crews had left for town, including a very snappish, Clem who'd been in a sour mood ever since he stomped into the bunkhouse earlier and kicked off his soaking wet boots.

"He fell into Pittance Creek."

"I know that much. Now I'd like to hear the rest of the story."

"He lost a bet."

A bet. How many of them would there be between the two directors? Greg didn't like the way Clem targeted Renata with his spiteful remarks, but he didn't like the way she challenged him to so many contests, either. There was an ugly dynamic between those two, and Greg was afraid it was going to end up with someone getting hurt.

Or all of them.

"What kind of a bet?"

"Who could stay dry while crossing the creek." Renata fetched her sleepwear and headed for the bathroom to change. Avery, spotting her, followed.

"Did you push him in?" Greg asked, coming after her.

"Didn't need to," she said with a quick grin. "He's a clumsy oaf."

"Or he's letting you think he is," Greg countered. "Don't underestimate him."

"He's a fool."

"He's a fool who's stolen your job—and who's got a thing for you, too."

"Clem doesn't have a thing for me." But the way Renata looked away confirmed that she knew it, too.

Avery met Greg's glance behind Renata's back and nodded. Greg felt vindicated; he wasn't the only one who'd noticed.

"You push him too far, and there's going to be trouble."

"Whatever."

Renata and Avery disappeared into the bathroom, where Greg knew they'd help each other with their old-fashioned gowns. He wished he was the one in there helping Renata, but they weren't going to get any time alone tonight.

Unless he did something drastic.

"Let's go look at the stars," he said to Renata when she came back out dressed in sweatpants and an oversized shirt.

"Too late." She gestured to her clothes. "I'm not changing again."

"You don't have to. Pull on a coat and boots. We'll sit in one of the trucks."

"Everyone's going to sleep." But Renata went to the door, where the jackets hung on pegs, and pulled on hers.

Outside, it was cold, clear and crisp. So quiet that Greg relaxed for the first time in ages.

"Much better," he said.

"I agree."

It was cold in the truck, but they were warmly dressed, and Greg knew they wouldn't be out here long. Like Renata had said, everyone was heading to bed. They wouldn't want to wake them again coming back inside.

"I want to ask you something serious," Greg said, reaching out and taking her hand. He felt Renata tense and knew it was best to simply get it over with. "Do you have a gambling problem?"

"A gambling… No!" Renata snapped. "I do not have a gambling problem." She tried to pull her hand away, but Greg kept hold of it.

"I'll help you, if you do. Go to counseling with you—whatever it takes."

"I do not have a gambling problem."

"Then what's going on between you and Clem?"

"Nothing!" She must have sensed her too-quick reply only made her seem guiltier. "He drives me crazy. Someone needs to put him in his place."

"By risking a lot of money?" He was sure Fulsom paid her well, but he doubted it was so much that she could afford to gamble large sums.

"It isn't a risk. I can beat almost anyone at nickels, and I've seen Clem trip over his own feet on flat ground. I knew he wasn't going to be able to cross a creek on slippery stones."

"Sooner or later you'll overestimate your abilities."

"You're forgetting I've been watching out for myself since I was six. I know exactly what my abilities are."

He was angering her, and that was the last thing he meant to do. "What I'm trying to say is that I'm on your side and I want to help you, no matter what you need. Look, Renata." He turned to face her and covered her hand in both of his. "I want to marry you. Provide for you. Give you a home. Babies."

"Babies?"

"I've watched you every time one of the other women announces she's pregnant. You want a family. I want one, too."

Renata stared up at the sky through the truck's windshield. "I don't know how you can know what I want when I don't even know it," she said.

"I think you do know it. You just don't want to admit it. Something's holding you back. What is it?" He held his breath, hoping she would trust him.

When she shrugged, he knew she didn't.

That was a problem he needed to fix.

RENATA WOKE TO the same question she'd gone to sleep pondering. Did Greg know her better than she knew herself? Did she want a baby? Or more than one?

He was right that each time one of the other women announced her pregnancy, a longing overcame her. She wanted life to feel easy. Not that a baby simplified things, but she would be able to care for and protect her own child in a way she hadn't been able to do with all the girls from Peru.

Knowing Greg wanted a family, too, made the situation even more difficult. Every time she pictured him cradling their baby in his arms, she couldn't help imagine the act that would make that possible.

What would it be like to wake up in a tiny house with Greg each morning for the rest of her life? Could she stay here long term? Become true friends with the people she used to boss around all day?

She was already on her way with Avery and Eve.

What would she do if she wasn't directing films? Greg had suggested opening a film studio, but that hardly seemed likely.

The truth was she didn't have any idea what she wanted to do next. She wanted life to be far less complicated than it had been so far, though. Was that possible?

Not until she paid the rest of what she'd promised.

She'd never bet ten thousand dollars before, but that was a drop in the bucket of what she still needed to give to Mayra and Gabriela to finish providing for the girls' care. Where could she get more cash?

The door opened quietly, and to Renata's surprise Savannah slipped in. Walker sat up in his sleeping bag across the room. Greg, who'd had second-shift guard duty, wasn't back yet. Avery stirred but turned over.

Angus was still snoring.

Savannah tiptoed to the kitchen, a bundle in her arms Renata realized was Jacob. Renata slipped out of her sleeping bag and crossed the floor after her, joining her in the kitchen a moment later.

"Shouldn't you be resting?" she whispered.

"I'm sick of resting," Savannah whispered back. "I'm fine. Just starving. Think Kai has something I can eat?"

"Let's look."

Renata rummaged around until she found some eggs. She showed them to Savannah, who nodded. "That will work."

It had been ages since Renata had done any cooking, but it was hard to mess up eggs, and soon she had several frying merrily in a pan on the big stove.

When the food was ready, she served up a plateful for Savannah and held her hands out for the baby. "I can hold him if you like."

"Thank you." Savannah handed him over, and Renata took the little bundle in her arms, her whole body softening at the sweetness of his tiny face and hands.

"He's so delicious," she crooned.

"He is," Savannah agreed. "Best baby ever."

"Of course you are," Renata cooed at the little boy. She couldn't help herself. She bent down and kissed Jacob's forehead.

"What did I tell you?" Greg said, entering the kitchen. He came to stand close to Renata and get a good look at Jacob. "Renata wants babies," he informed

Savannah.

"Of course she does. Everyone wants babies." Savannah scooped a forkful of eggs into her mouth.

"Not yet," Renata managed to say.

"I don't see why not," Greg said.

"Neither do I," Savannah said.

"I have… things to do." Heck, she'd almost come out and spilled the beans about the girls in Peru. Jacob was too darn cute. He was distracting her.

"Anything you can do without a baby you can do with a baby, too," Savannah pointed out.

"I want my children to have all of my attention," Renata said. She felt Greg's gaze on her.

"Like I said, when we have kids, you don't have to do anything else if you don't want to. We've got everything we need here. I've got money in the bank. We'd be fine."

"I think you should take Greg up on that." Savannah finished her eggs, put the plate in the sink and came back for Jacob. Renata hated to let him go, but of course she did. "Don't overcomplicate things," she advised. "Greg's a keeper, and you seem like you're at a crossroads with your career. Would a break be so bad?"

"Hear that?" Greg said when she was gone, taking Jacob with her. "I'm a keeper."

"Let's get some sleep."

Back in the main room, Walker had lain back down again. Avery was still sleeping. So was Byron apparently.

Greg left her with a kiss to return to his sleeping bag. She climbed into hers. It took a long time for the thoughts racing through her mind to settle down enough for her to drift off again, though. She had barely woken up a few hours later, when people began to pile into the bunkhouse.

"What's going on?" she asked Avery, who was sitting in her sleeping bag, yawning and looking as perplexed as she felt.

Hope and Curtis came in last, urging the stragglers in before them. "Gather round, everyone," Curtis said.

"Now what?" Renata sighed. She hoped there hadn't been more mischief committed around the community.

"What's all the commotion?" Clem burst in, cameramen in tow. Renata caught Hope giving Curtis an amused look.

"We almost pulled it off," she told her husband.

"Almost but not quite. Some people took too long to get in here." His gaze singled out Angus, who, unlike most of the others who had dressed before arriving at the bunkhouse, still wore sweatpants and a ragged T-shirt, his feet jammed into his boots.

"Well? What's happening? Why is everyone standing around? Where's breakfast?" Clem demanded.

"I haven't even made it into the kitchen yet," Kai said.

"We have an announcement," Curtis said. "Hope? Take it away."

"I'm pregnant!" Hope cried.

Congratulations, clapping and laughter filled the room. The camera crews documented it all. Renata felt rather than saw Greg move to her side and put an arm around her waist. "You all right?"

"Of course I am." But she wasn't. A feeling she could hardly name filled her, a sense of being left behind. All the women of Base Camp were getting pregnant.

"We can slip away right now and give it a go."

The offer was more tempting than she wanted to admit. Marrying Greg, having a child, taking a break from her career, such as it was—*belonging here*—

It sounded like heaven.

She wanted a family. Wanted to settle down. Wanted to try something new.

Remember the money, she told herself. *Remember your promise.* She wouldn't walk away from those girls.

If only she'd worked harder. Saved more. Taken a second job or something—

"What do you say?"

Renata shook off his arm and walked away, grabbing her clothes and heading for the bathroom, where she locked herself in. She couldn't be with Greg.

But, oh, she wanted him.

CHAPTER FOURTEEN

SEVERAL DAYS LATER it was time for another episode. Gathering in the bunkhouse with the others, Greg noticed more than one person turning to look at him. He knew why. He was running out of time to get Renata to the altar, and there wasn't a backup bride in sight. He needed to fix things.

It hadn't helped that he'd come across Renata and Clem betting again, this time pitching snowballs at a low-hanging branch of an apple tree. He wondered where it would all end.

The episode started normally enough, but he braced himself all the same, knowing what was to come. There was plenty of footage of the billboard on the way to town in all its incarnations. Local kids apparently were having a field day with the thing, adding a mustache, horns, steam coming out of his ears.

There were several interviews with angry backup brides, who now were calling for a boycott of the show's advertisers. Beside him, Renata groaned.

"That's going to get Fulsom's panties in a twist," she

said. "I'm surprised he hasn't put a stop to this."

Greg didn't think things could get worse, but Clem was grinning in a particularly gleeful way. When someone gasped, he turned his gaze back to the screen and saw why everyone else in the room was riveted to it.

This footage was different from the rest. Grainier. He realized it must come from one of the old surveillance cameras they'd found and removed. One that had been set up somewhere inside the bunkhouse with a view of the main room they all sat in. The footage showed Avery slipping in, looking around, then slipping across the room to rummage in one of the big duffel bags where the men who stayed in the bunkhouse stored their stuff. The footage must have been taken earlier in the year when there were more unmarried people in Base Camp. Avery pulled out a pair of men's dress shoes.

"Hey, those are mine," Clay protested. "I've been looking for them for ages."

Avery slid down in her seat a little, as if that could hide her.

The footage continued. This time the camera was outside. The pasture fence was in the foreground, the bison and several riders far away. As they watched, Avery stole into the scene, took hold of the jacket that was hanging from the nearest fence post and slipped away with it.

"My coat," Boone said, turning to look at her.

On screen, the camera angle changed. Now it showed the kitchen. Kai leaned forward. There were the neat shelves lined with dishes and the tools he and Addison used to make their meals. And there was Avery again, slipping into the room, looking around, crossing to the counter by the sink where Kai always left his recipe book. When she picked it up, slipped it under her jacket and left, Riley gasped. Everyone knew how much Kai prized that book.

Greg frowned. He was pretty sure they would have heard if the book was still missing. In fact, he seemed to remember Kai had a second copy of it now. He wondered what that meant.

He had no time to think about it. On screen the grainy footage showed the bunkhouse room again. This time when Avery stole inside, she made a beeline for the ragged old duffel bag where Walker stored his things. Greg glanced over to where Walker sat near her. The large man had his arms crossed, and his face was as impassive as a block of granite. Beside him, Avery's was twisted with worry. As well it might be.

None of this looked good.

When the Avery on screen pulled out an old, ceremonial flat feather fan, Greg could swear every person in the room held his breath. The camera cut to her zipping up the bag and slipping out of the bunkhouse again.

Riley put a hand over her mouth. Savannah looked like she might cry. Everyone knew Walker had been looking all over for that fan.

But the show wasn't over yet.

Next came scene after scene of the damage that had

been done around the place over the months since they all moved in. The broken equipment. The greenhouse door left open and the dead plants inside. The pasture fence cut. The solar array packed with snow.

The implication was clear; Avery had done that, too. The show ended with a close-up of Clem, just like *Tracking the Stars* used to do at the end of its episodes. "That's what happens when you let a fox into the henhouse, folks," he intoned. "It doesn't end well for the chickens."

And the episode was over.

"It's not like that." Avery got to her feet unsteadily, gripping the back of her folding chair for support. "I swear there's a good reason—"

"I don't want to hear about reasons." Riley stood up and faced her. "I invited you here because I thought you were my friend. I trusted you. I loved you like a sister! You know what will happen if we don't win this—I'll lose my home! The property that's been in my family for over a hundred years! All this time you were working against us?"

Avery's face crumpled. "Just listen—"

Boone stepped in between them.

"Avery, I think you'd better spend the night at the manor. We'll figure out what to do with you tomorrow."

"But—I swear—it wasn't like that at all! Walker!" Avery turned to him, but he remained impassive, studying her as if he'd never quite seen her clearly before. Avery blinked back tears. "You know I wouldn't—"

"Avery—manor. Now," Boone snapped. "And maybe when you come to breakfast tomorrow, think about bringing Walker's fan with you. The rest of you get to bed. We'll deal with all this in the morning."

BASE CAMP HAD never been so quiet, Renata thought when she took her things to the bathroom to get ready for bed.

"Need help?" Greg asked her. "Avery's not here," he explained.

She nodded, and he followed her into the bathroom.

"I can't believe Avery stole all that stuff," he said.

"I can," Renata said. She met his gaze in the mirror as he worked on the fastenings of her gown.

"What do you mean?" His hands stilled on her back.

"I mean I saw her stealing things before. I can't believe the rest of you didn't. But I guess I was keeping a pretty close eye on things."

"Why didn't you say anything?" Greg demanded.

"It wasn't my job to say anything. It was my job to document what happened, not to take part. You see how well that went."

"But—"

"It was harmless. Petty theft."

Greg stopped again. He turned her around, his hands on her waist. "Petty theft? What about major destruction? She was trying to shut down Base Camp."

"No, she wasn't," Renata said. "Come on, Greg, think. There was no footage of her messing with any equipment, or cutting the pasture fence, or leaving the greenhouse door open. If there was, Clem would've used it. So what does that say to you?"

"Someone else did that," Greg said finally. "And he used Avery as a scapegoat. Sorry. I Let my temper get the best of me."

"I'd say everyone did. Clem put the footage together in exactly the right way to make things look as bad as possible." She shrugged. "Which is how we've put together all the episodes."

Greg chuckled. "Yep. One thing I don't get is how Clem installed all those security cameras back at the beginning of the show when he's only been here a couple of months."

Renata stiffened. Bit her lip. Shook her head at her own stupidity. "Those weren't Clem's cameras—those were Avery's."

"That doesn't make sense—why would Avery film herself stealing stuff?"

"Because she's an actress. She's always working away on short films." She waited for him to get it. "When Clem went to install his cameras, he must have found hers. Then gone looking for the footage she'd gotten."

"How would he have found her footage?" Greg challenged her. "I bet it's Fulsom who's been filming us all this time. He probably gave the footage to Clem."

"I know Avery, and I'm pretty sure I'm right. All Clem had to do was wait for a chance to get a hold of her laptop. She leaves it lying around all the time at the manor when she's working up there."

"How would he know her password?"

"He wouldn't need to." She searched for a way to explain. "She goes there with the other women almost every day. Sets up at the kitchen table to work, but she's up and down all the time. She'll clean a bathroom, run back to make notes about an idea, get back to cleaning and so on. It's just sitting there. She trusts her friends; she doesn't shut it down every time."

"He'd have to have been sneaky."

"Clem's whole career is about being sneaky."

"I guess it doesn't matter," he said. "What can we do about it, either way, if Clem is the one who's got the footage?"

Renata smiled. She reached into her pocket and pulled out a card key.

"This is for the motel room where we do all the editing. Fulsom took away my personal room there, but he didn't take my key to the common one. Bet your bottom dollar the footage is on a laptop there, both Avery's and his."

"No more betting." But Greg looked thoughtful. "We need to go there. Tonight."

"We'll have to work fast—and be very quiet."

"No one sleeps in that room?"

She shook her head. "We had the hotel remove the beds and put in extra tables to work at. We'll have to make sure no one else is pulling an all-nighter, though."

"Everyone should be asleep by one-thirty or so," Greg said. He passed her a set of keys. "Those are for the trucks. You slip out first. I'll follow. If Byron wakes up, I'll keep him from calling Clem while you high-tail it to town."

"Got it."

In the end, it was simple to slip out. Greg had alerted the men on patrol so they wouldn't be startled by them driving away. They waited until it was clear Byron was fast asleep, crept past him and through the kitchen, then hurried to the truck parked farthest away. Renata knew no one in the bunkhouse would be able to hear the engine starting. She only hoped Byron didn't wake up until they were back again.

When they reached town, the room Renata led Greg to was dark. She used the card key to open the motel room door carefully.

"No lights," she warned and moved to check that all the curtains were tightly closed, so the blue screens wouldn't catch anyone's attention outside.

Greg bolted the door behind him. "Where do we start?"

"Here. Clem will have uploaded everything to the main system for the crew to work on." She sat in front of one of the laptops and began to type. "Here's the last episode." She hit a few more keys, scanned a file directory and nodded. "I bet this is Avery's footage." She pointed to a file, and Greg laughed at the name. "Yeah, I bet you're right."

Greg was no slouch once Renata showed him how to call up the video footage and run through it at high speed, looking for something interesting to happen. As the hours ticked past, they worked furiously, saying little except to point out what they found. Once they'd pulled together the most interesting bits, Renata took over and edited it into complete file. Greg pitched in on the narrations, his warm, low voice making him perfect for the job. Near dawn they made their way back to Base Camp.

"Do you think this will work?" Renata asked as they pulled in. Base Camp was still quiet. Greg had dimmed the truck's lights as they edged down the lane and rolled it silently to a stop in its normal parking place. Now all they had to do was sneak inside without waking Byron.

"God, I hope so," Greg said. He lifted her hand and kissed it. "You're a hell of a woman, Renata."

"You're a hell of a man."

CHAPTER FIFTEEN

IT WAS HARD to keep it a secret that they were up to something. Byron had woken up just as Greg and Renata were sliding into their sleeping bags. Renata covered up the disturbance by getting up again and going to use the washroom. Byron had rolled over and fallen back to sleep until it was really time to get up.

Greg knew the sleepless night would catch up to them at some point, but he was buzzing with adrenaline and couldn't wait to show everyone else what they'd found. He and Renata got up with the others, did their chores and ate breakfast as if nothing was different, but as soon as the meal was over, Greg strode to the front of the room.

"Don't tell me you two are pregnant already!" Curtis called out.

"No," Greg said. "Not yet. But we have something we'd like to show everyone if you don't mind."

Boone sighed. "Is it going to take long?"

"You got somewhere to be?"

"We need to talk about Avery."

The door opened as he said this, and Avery, who so far had remained absent, slunk in, looking miserable. Her hair hung limp around her shoulders. It looked as if she'd done up her gown wrong. Her arms were empty, something Boone took in immediately, and Greg thought Walker did, as well.

"I don't have the fan," Avery said stubbornly, heading off Boone's question.

"Then I don't know what we can do," Boone began.

"Before this goes any further," Greg said loudly, "you need to let us show you something."

"Greg—"

"I wouldn't ask if it wasn't important." Greg met Boone's gaze and held it. Maybe he wasn't one of the original four men who'd founded Base Camp, but that didn't mean Boone shouldn't trust him as much as he trusted Clay, Jericho or Walker.

"All right. Fine. Let's see what you've got." Boone lifted his hands like he couldn't be held responsible for anything that happened around here anymore.

Renata took that as her cue to set up the laptop and screen they normally used to watch the show's episodes.

"What's going on?" Clem called from the back of the room as the crew tromped in and set up to film them. "I need something good for the show, and you're planning to sit around and watch TV?"

"This will be good," Greg promised him. Clem's brows lowered, but Renata hit a few keys on the laptop, and the movie they'd made together began.

It began much like an episode of *Base Camp* with the

regular intro, but they'd sped it up so much that it flashed by in only a matter of seconds. Greg caught one or two smiles around the room before everyone became serious again. Good, that had cut the tension a little. Avery slouched into the chair closest to the door and clasped her hands in her lap. Her face was drawn, and Greg doubted she'd gotten much sleep last night, either.

"Once upon a time there was a community called Base Camp," Greg intoned on screen. He and Renata had decided to launch right into the theme they wanted to focus on: that Base Camp was a success as a sustainable community and that everyone involved had worked hard to make it that way. Instead of the tense, malicious and outrageous footage Clem had concentrated on these past few weeks, the scenes they'd chosen for the first part of their show illustrated how tirelessly everyone was working around the community. There were images of Boone, Samantha and the rest of the gardening crew working hard in the greenhouses to replace the food they lost during the theft. Scenes of Addison and Kai working morning, noon and night to provide delicious meals for everyone else, even when their supplies had been diminished. Footage of the women running the bed-and-breakfast at the Manor, trying to make people's vacations effortless and fun. Walker and Avery horsing around near the bison out in the pastures, their love for the animals and each other plain for all to see.

Greg glanced Avery's way and found she had her face in her hands. Walker, across the room, sat as stoically as ever.

The footage changed, and now they saw Clem climbing up a ladder behind the bunkhouse, his face coming closer and closer to the screen as he ascended it. It was easy to see when he noticed he was being filmed—and just as easy to see he had climbed the ladder to install his own camera there. He shook his head and sneered. "So you're not the goody-goody you claim to be, are you, Renata?" he asked the camera.

It had been a surprise to find out Clem thought the earliest set of surveillance cameras had been Renata's—and had left them there on purpose. "They're not mine," Renata said. "None of the cameras we took down were mine."

"Whose were they?" Angus asked.

"Hold on—you'll see," Greg said.

The scene changed. A new theme song boomed out of the speakers, and Avery straightened in her seat, her mouth dropping open.

"Where'd you—" She closed her mouth with a snap. Greg knew why; she'd figured it out. The folder of Avery's material they'd found on Clem's computer had contained a lot of different footage but also several full episodes of a show she'd created herself along the way.

She must've had some grand plan about when she would air it. They were ruining that plan, but there wasn't anything for it. Avery twisted her hands in her lap, biting her lip. Greg pitied her, but airing this footage was the only way he knew how to help. He wasn't sure why she hadn't thought to air it herself.

The cheerful theme ended with Avery bursting into

the frame yelling, "Stealing from SEALs!" Those same words popped on screen over her head in a cheesy '80s title font.

Everyone in the room glanced around and straightened in their chairs. They hadn't expected this. Greg savored their surprise. This was only the start.

Avery's show was far more jumpy than *Base Camp* usually was. It reminded him of the kind of thing you found on channels aimed at young people. The camera angles constantly changed. The action was nonstop. He wondered how she'd done it, because Avery herself was always the star of the film. There she was stealing Boone's jacket, stealing Clay's shoes, stealing Kai's book. That time she ran right up to the camera and waved the book around with a triumphant grin before disappearing again. Finally, the camera stayed still. Avery popped up again. "Hi, I'm Avery Lightfoot, and I live with ten Navy SEALs. You would think Navy SEALs would be a sneaky bunch, but what I've discovered is that none of them are as sneaky as I am. In fact, I found there's nothing as fun as *stealing from SEALs*!" The title appeared in all its cheesy '80s-style glory again.

Boone sat back in his chair. Riley was smiling. Greg held his breath, knowing what was coming.

The footage went back to its jumpy, crazy, zany style. Avery stealing food from the kitchen just seconds before Kai walked in. Avery stealing clothes from the wash line when Riley turned her back. Avery pilfering silverware out of Maud and James Russell's kitchen. Greg hoped she'd returned that.

There was a scene he loved, in which Addison asked Avery to steal Kai's cookbook so she could make a copy of it, explaining what a tragedy it would be if the original was ever lost or damaged. That explained the footage of Avery sneaking into the kitchen and pilfering it late at night. She explained to the camera that she had spent five hours scanning it page by page before slipping it back into the kitchen the next morning.

Last, but not least, came the theft of Walker's fan. The room quieted again as the familiar footage rolled by. Avery sneaking into the room, checking to make sure no one was around, unzipping Walker's bag and pulling out the beautiful old fan.

What Clem's footage hadn't shown was Avery sitting on the floor, touching the fan reverently, cradling it as if it were a newborn baby for a moment, lost in thought, obviously thinking about a future with Walker. Then came the footage that had made Greg's heart twist in his chest. Avery unzipping the bag again and slipping the fan reverently back inside, making sure everything was in its rightful place before she darted out of the room again.

"But—" Savannah began and then subsided as the show continued. Renata had spliced this next footage into Avery's film. They'd found it among Clem's footage, as if he couldn't resist filming himself pulling off such an evil stunt. It began where Avery's did but from a slightly different angle, showing Avery sneaking in and rummaging in Walker's bag. It filmed her cradling the fan, then putting it back and leaving—but then it showed Clem himself sneaking into the bunkhouse after Avery had gone, opening the bag and pulling the fan out again. Silence reigned as he zipped the bag closed, put it back into place and left, the fan in his arms.

When a sob sounded, Greg turned to Avery, but it was Riley who was crying. She wasn't the only one. Savannah was wiping her eyes, and Addison was fishing in her pockets for tissue. Walker stood slowly, turned to Avery and held out his hand, his face a mask of anguished regret.

She stood, too, and warded him off.

"No." Her voice cracked on the word. "Don't say a thing. Not one single thing. I waited eight months for you, eight months while one after another of my friends married *your* friends, with no indication that you would ever ask me to be your wife. I waited. I was patient because you said there was something you needed to do. But you never did it. *Stealing from SEALs* was a game, something to pass the time. Something to make me feel like I wasn't a complete chump. Because that's what I feel like. I feel like an idiot for ever believing in you. And now I feel like an idiot for ever believing in any of this. You all talk about community, you talk about knowing each other, working together, living together, how special that is. But when a stranger made it look like I did something wrong, you didn't even give me a chance to explain. You know what I think? None of you have ever *seen* me. None of you know *me*. Certainly not you," she flung at Walker. "Well, I'm done. I don't want your forgiveness. I don't want your friendship. And I don't want your love. I wouldn't marry you if you were the last man on earth."

Avery turned on her heel and walked out the door.

GREG DIDN'T THINK he'd ever spent a more excruciating week than the one that had just passed. The temperature outside had dipped, and winter was back with a vengeance. More snow had fallen. The unrelenting gray sky was making him restless, but there was no way to accomplish anything much outside. He wanted to make improvements to all his energy systems, but all he could do was think and plan rather than getting anything done.

He'd finished his model of Base Camp, but when he sat down to look it over and try to think of ways to improve upon it, all he could see was Avery's face when Walker had reached for her.

Renata seemed just as dismayed their plan hadn't worked. Clem was furious with them, and he'd had the motel reprogram the card keys for the workroom so that Renata no longer had access to it. He kept a crew following her every minute of the day, which meant all the time they had together was filmed.

Which meant Greg was frustrated as hell.

Renata would let him steal a kiss or two if the crews were around, but that was it, and their presence made her snappish. She had a very different personality when she was being the show's director than she did when they were alone, and it was clear she was back to trying to figure out how to wrest her job away from Clem. He wondered how hard it had been to put on that mask every day of the more than ten years she'd worked for Fulsom. Had it ever felt like second nature, or had it always been a strain?

Her bets with Clem were piling up, too, the sums they wrangled over getting larger and larger. Clem kept losing. Kept bitching about the money he had to pay out but kept coming back for more.

Greg had the feeling everyone was watching Avery and Walker, although they were all trying to be inconspicuous while doing it. Avery kept close to Eve, apparently the only person she trusted at this point, although Greg thought that was unfair. He and Renata had cleared her name, after all.

As far as he could see, Walker spent all his time lurking in the barns and outbuildings or riding out among the bison herd. Under duress, Clem had returned the fan, claiming that a crew member had found it. Walker had simply taken it and turned his back on Clem. Since then, he'd ignored the director completely. Greg had caught him arguing with his grandmother, Sue, once, but as soon as Sue had spotted him, she'd gotten in her car and driven away.

He'd approached Walker to ask him what was going on, but Walker had turned on his heel and stalked off. Greg hadn't bothered to follow.

He caught up with Harris one morning at the makeshift forge the man had set up recently behind the barn. Harris planned to make a more permanent structure in the spring, but like everyone else, he'd gotten too restless to wait. He'd been working with Roy Egan, who'd been a blacksmith all his life, and had taken Harris on as an apprentice some months ago, but Harris wanted his own forge to practice in while he was home.

"I'm not here for any good reason," Greg told him when he approached.

Harris lowered the hammer he'd been wielding and plunged the metal he'd been working into a barrel of cold water. It hissed and steamed. "I think everyone's got spring fever."

"You got that right. A few months early by the look of things." He squinted at the lowering skies. There'd be more snow soon if he wasn't mistaken. "Maybe we need another trip to DelMonaco's."

"Something like that."

Greg followed Harris's gaze and spotted Avery leaning against the rail fence that enclosed the bison pasture. "I'm kind of surprised she didn't leave the show."

Harris thought about that. "She's not a quitter." He nodded in a different direction, and Greg saw Walker riding in on his horse. He slowed for a moment when he spotted Avery, then kept going toward the stable. "She was here at the ranch before Walker."

"I guess so. I hope she makes it up with Riley, Savannah and Nora. Those four used to be inseparable." He remembered when he'd first arrived at Base Camp. How all the new men had viewed the four women living at the manor with interest until Boone, Clay, Jericho and Walker had made their intentions known. In the early days, Avery and her friends had done everything together, fierce in their intentions to have their arts-driven lives, even as Fulsom kept making rules that made it impossible for them to stick to their guns.

"Remember how they had everything set up in the beginning?" he asked. "They all spent so much time painting and playing piano, writing and stuff. They hardly do any of that anymore."

"Savannah plays for us sometimes," Harris said. "I think Riley still paints now and then, and isn't Nora working with Walker's grandma on that curriculum stuff?" He shrugged. "Avery was making *Stealing from SEALs*."

"I don't think an hour here and there was what they had in mind," Greg said.

"They're running the B and B," Harris pointed out, "but I take your point. Base Camp has changed because of the show. Which will be over soon."

"Will we survive it, though?"

"Hope so."

"I'm going to go talk to her," Greg decided.

"Avery?" Harris paused. "Want me to come, too?"

"Maybe she'd think we were ganging up on her."

Harris nodded and went back to work. Greg checked to make sure Walker wasn't in sight and trudged through the snow to the pasture fence.

"All the bison present and accounted for?" he asked when he drew near.

"Far as I can tell." Avery shrugged. "I haven't really counted them."

"I figured you had a lot on your mind." When Avery didn't answer, he went on. "I think you should give Walker another chance." Might as well get to the heart of it. "That fan obviously means a lot to him and his family, and he saw you steal it on screen. What was he supposed to think? Walker cares about you, but his feelings got hurt. He thought you set out to mock him deliberately."

"That's not good enough," Avery said determinedly. "He should've known I would never do that. I know how important his heritage is to him."

"Maybe Walker's been hurt before like that," Greg pointed out. "Maybe kids at school made fun of him. We all carry wounds that make us judge each other more harshly than we should."

"It's more than that," Avery said. "I'm sick of being played for a fool. Months ago, Walker said he has a prior engagement. He's never cleared that up, and he's never done anything to get out of it. And I've just stood here and taken it. I've played second fiddle to a ghost. I'm done with that. I'm moving on. Maybe I'll ask Boone to find me a backup bride." She waved a hand. "Backup husband, whatever."

Greg was heartened by her small attempt at a joke. Avery was a fighter. She might look sweet, and she might be silly sometimes, but she was determined, too. Harris was right; she wouldn't quit Base Camp even if her heart was breaking. If Walker let her go, he was the fool.

"What about Riley and Savannah? What about

Nora, for that matter?" he asked Avery. "I think it's sad to let those friendships fade away over a misunderstanding."

Avery shook her head. "I'm not ready to talk about this," she said.

"Do you plan to stay?" Greg asked her.

"Yes," Avery said firmly. "I made a commitment to Base Camp, and I'm going to see it through no matter how awful everyone else is to me."

"Then you'll have to face them someday," Greg pointed out.

"Someday I will," Avery said. "But not today. I think for now I'm going to let the future alone. Let it take care of itself for a change, without me worrying about it."

"I'm glad you're going to stay. Base Camp wouldn't be the same without you."

For a moment Avery's determined veneer cracked, and true anguish shone through. He wished there was more he could do to help.

"Thanks" was all she said, her voice thick with unshed tears. She turned back to the bison, her eyes brimming, and he left her there reluctantly. Maybe he needed to talk to Walker next.

He didn't see the man that afternoon, however. At dinner there were too many people—and film crew members—around to get him alone. Greg supposed he shouldn't have been surprised when after dinner Boone and Riley moved to the front of the room. Riley was beaming, and he had a feeling he knew what they were about to say.

Renata was sitting with Avery and Eve across the room, in solidarity with her heartbroken friend. She folded her arms over her chest as she waited for Boone and Riley's announcement.

"Thanks for giving us a minute of your time," Boone said. He kept an arm around Riley's waist, as if he never wanted to let her go. "Riley, take it away."

"You all know I miscarried last year, so I didn't want to say anything, but I just can't wait anymore. I'm pregnant! I'm eight weeks along!"

Everyone leaped up at once to gather around the happy couple. Renata, too, although she stayed on the outskirts of the group. Greg moved to her side.

"Boone and Riley deserve this, don't you think?"

Renata nodded. "Absolutely. I've been hoping this would happen."

They offered Boone and Riley their congratulations, and everyone lingered in the bunkhouse. Savannah played a bit at the old upright piano, and conversation buzzed around the room.

"That's six of us pregnant now!" he heard Addison say. "And Savannah already had Jacob. Fulsom will have to agree we've met that requirement, at least."

"We've nearly met them all," Eve said. "We've got this in the bag."

"Don't get ahead of yourself," Curtis warned her. "We've still got a few dyed-in-the-wool bachelors to marry off." Greg could tell he'd meant it as a joke, but the mood of the room instantly dimmed. Who would

Walker marry if Avery wouldn't have him? His mystery woman?

That would make things awkward around here.

A minute later, Angus came to find Greg. "Guard duty. We might as well head out now."

"Sure thing."

They were silent as they pulled on their outdoor gear and made their way out of the bunkhouse, but as they tramped down the track toward the barn and stables, Angus peered at him curiously.

"Renata seems… different… lately. Preoccupied. And I don't mean about Avery."

"She's obsessed with money," Greg said. A light wind brushed his face. Overhead, clouds still covered the sky. The quiet, cold landscape had a stark beauty all its own, but Greg was more than ready for spring. Someday this TV show would be over and they could all get back to living their lives. They'd be able to stop worrying about how the cameras would document their decisions.

If Base Camp was still standing.

Back in June the whole thing had seemed like a fun adventure, a chance to reconnect with Renata and see if he still felt the same way about her after all the years that had passed since they'd met before. Now it felt like one of the endless, slogging marches through the rain he'd taken when he was in boot camp.

"What makes you say that?" Angus asked. He seemed to be struggling with his own thoughts, and Greg couldn't remember the last time he'd cracked a joke or put on a strong accent.

"Every time I turn around she's in some contest or other with Clem. Betting money—big money."

"Maybe she's bored." Angus seemed to realize what he'd said. "Not that you're boring. She's used to being in charge, though. Directing things. How's she spending her days?"

"Helping Avery," Greg admitted.

"Why aren't you spending them with her?"

It was a damn good question. "I keep trying. She keeps keeping me at a distance. Most of the time."

"Try harder. Surprise her a little. Keep her on her toes."

Greg imagined surprising Renata. Imagined ducking when she gave him a strong right hook.

"Not sure that's the best idea." But at least he could see the humor in it. That was something.

"Get her away from Base Camp," Angus suggested.

Greg remembered the fun they'd had in the truck, and his smile grew. "That's a better idea." He'd love to be alone with Renata again. "What about you? How are you doing these days?"

Angus shrugged. "How do you think?"

"No word from Win?"

"No word," Angus confirmed. "She made it clear we were over."

Greg remembered the day Win had left. He'd never seen a man so heartbroken. Hoped that wouldn't be him in a few weeks.

His fingers clenched in his gloves, and he determined to not let Renata slip away from him. He was going to spend each and every day of the next two or so weeks with her and convince her they were meant to be together. He didn't see why she needed convincing after their encounter in the truck, but he'd do it anyway. He loved every little thing about Renata—

Except her need to goad Clem and bet large sums of money in contests with him.

"She underestimates Clem."

"Is that possible? The guy's an idiot."

"He is, but idiots like to go for the jugular when they're pushed. Besides, he wants to stay director of *Base Camp*."

"Then give her a better alternative," Angus said. "Renata doesn't want to direct TV shows."

Greg met his gaze, surprised. "How do you know that?"

"Because Renata's one of the most ruthlessly ambitious women I've ever met. TV isn't big enough for her."

Was that true? Greg wasn't sure. She'd talked about Hollywood but also about starting over and doing something entirely different. He hadn't been lying when he said he knew she wanted a family. She'd already done so much in her career, and she was in her thirties. Lots of women he knew chose that time of life to start their families. What did Renata really want?

She'd mentioned wanting to change everything. Did that mean she wanted to direct something new—or stop directing altogether? Did she simply want out of

Montana?

Or would she be happy to marry and settle down?

What did she have to accomplish before she could be with him?

"Why does she need more money?" Greg asked out loud. "Fulsom's got to be paying her well. She doesn't have any family. She doesn't have a mortgage, that I know about. No expenses the show doesn't cover. Why gamble?"

"Most people do it for the thrill."

They reached the barn, and Angus opened the door. Inside, all was quiet. They did a thorough check and met outside again, heading for the stables.

"Maybe she's just trying to get back at Clem," Angus went on. "Trying to humiliate him by taking his money."

"When she loses, she'll be the one humiliated." And that would make her even pricklier than she was already. More committed to taking Clem down.

"*If* she loses." When Greg turned to him, he added. "Renata's a smart cookie. I doubt she makes bets she doesn't intend to win."

"We all intend to win our bets."

They checked out the stables and the chicken coop, then headed for the pasture where the herd was.

"Renata's no fool," Angus said again as they walked on together.

"But Clem's bad to the core," Greg countered. "I wouldn't put it past him to hurt her. Really hurt her."

"There's too many of us around for him to get away

with hurting her," Angus pointed out. They reached the split rail fence that defined the bison herd's pasture. Greg scanned the snowy landscape, looking for the large, shaggy beasts.

"That's what people always think," he said. "Safety in numbers. It never occurs to them that the numbers make the predator safe, too."

Angus didn't answer. Greg realized his attention was on the pasture. He scanned it again, looking for the—

"Greg, where are the bison?" Angus asked.

"Oh, hell."

"THEY'RE GONE?" BOONE asked when Angus came rushing back into the bunkhouse with his news. "All of them?"

Renata moved closer to better hear the answer.

"All of them," Angus confirmed. "We need everyone. They're heading for the highway near as we can tell, and someone's going to get killed if they come zooming around a corner and run into one on the road. Greg's still out there tracking them."

"Why are they heading for the highway?" Savannah spoke up, baby Jacob in her arms. She'd been nursing him when Angus burst in. Renata had been chatting with her.

"Don't know," Angus said shortly. "Maybe they were being herded. We saw tracks—tire tracks—and followed them far enough to spot the herd in the distance. Didn't see any vehicles, though. Whoever it was got the bison running and took off."

"They could still be around somewhere," Renata said. "Greg's out there alone."

"Which is why we need to get out there, too. Kai, Anders, Curtis, take the trucks and head out toward the highway. We can use them to turn the bison around. The rest of you men get on a horse. Avery, you and the others call for backup. Get every rancher you can think of. We'll need everyone to help when we get those bison back here."

Avery already had her phone out. "I'll call the Mathesons. They have experience with bison."

"I'll call the Halls," Savannah said. "Nora, call Two Willows."

"Will do!"

"We need to film this," William said as the men rushed for the door. Riley looked like she'd follow, but Boone said something to her and laid a hand on her belly momentarily. Riley huffed out a frustrated breath but stayed put. Renata knew she was an excellent horsewoman; she must have wanted to ride out, too.

"Obviously," Clem snapped. "Get in the SUV."

"SUV?" Renata said. "All the action will be on horseback before the bison get to the road."

"I'm sure as hell not riding out on some horse in the dark with a bunch of overgrown hell-creatures running around," Clem said. He strode off with William and Ed, leaving the rest of them behind.

Renata turned to Byron. "Any chance you know how to ride a horse?"

He nodded. "Been riding since I was five."

"Seriously? And you never thought to mention that until—" She broke off. "Never mind. Let's go."

Fifteen minutes later they were trailing the men of Base Camp, riding cautiously over the snowy landscape. Byron hadn't been kidding that he knew his way around a horse, and Renata was grateful he'd been there to help her saddle up the mare assigned to her and mount it. She'd taken riding lessons briefly as a child, at one of the better foster situations she'd found herself in, and had other chances over the years to ride but was far from expert at it. Byron stuck close, one hand on the reins, the other on a small video camera, filming when he could.

The young cameraman had grown more confident in the months he'd been working at Base Camp, and Renata was struck by how he was establishing the setting for this segment without having to be told. Looking back, she realized he'd grown used to her way of doing things and often got started filming before she even had to tell him what to do. His dislike of Clem was easy to see, but he'd been as professional as possible around the man.

"You're a credit to the team," she told him now.

Byron lowered the camera and turned to her in surprise.

"I'll be sure to pass that on to Fulsom," she went on. "You're doing a good job."

"Thanks," he said. After a moment, he raised the camera again. Thank goodness; she didn't know what else she'd say to him. She wasn't used to handing out compliments in her role as director.

A shout ahead of them signaled that someone had seen the bison. The group picked up its pace, Renata doing her best to keep up with them, Byron riding by her side. Peering through the darkness, she spotted a dark shape far in front of them, and then another.

Walker slowed his horse until they caught up to him.

"Herd's unpredictable. We'll have to swing them around, urge them back the way they've come." He pointed to a rise of ground covered with short wiry shrubs. "There. Keep out of the way."

"Got it," Byron said before she could. He swerved off in the direction of the mound, and Renata followed him, exasperated. It was one thing to anticipate her orders, another to think he could read her mind.

"It's a good spot," she said grudgingly a few minutes later, however.

"Should we dismount?" Byron asked. "I could get a steadier shot."

"I don't think so. We might need to move fast." She could imagine the bison would want to skirt this impediment in the landscape if they came back this way, but they might not, too.

Byron nodded, fiddled with the camera and hunched his shoulders against the cold breeze. It frustrated Renata to watch the rest of the men peel off after the bison, the thuds of their horses' hooves fading into the distance. What if they ended up going in a completely different direction? They could wait out here for ages and never get a shot.

"I bet you've been on lots of interesting locations," Byron said.

"Some," she admitted. "There's always a lot of waiting when there's something good to film. Doesn't always pan out, though."

"I suppose not. Thanks," he added. "For what you said earlier. And for hiring me in the first place."

"Ed recommended you."

"But you didn't have to say yes. You took a chance on me. I appreciate it."

Renata thought back to those early days when she'd assembled the team for *Base Camp*. Byron was right; when she'd first seen his résumé she'd shaken her head and determined to tell Ed to find someone else to round out his crew, but then she'd taken a second look, noticed all the extracurricular activities Byron had participated in at college. He'd come from a modest Midwestern background and gone to school at a little-known liberal arts school in Illinois, where it looked like he'd availed himself of every opportunity offered to him.

He was a go-getter, just like she'd been.

"You were a good bet," she said. "I thought—"

Byron pointed. "There. They're coming!" He lifted his camera and focused on a shadow sweeping toward them that soon developed into a thundering herd. A tremor under her feet grew into full-out shaking of the ground as the massive beasts hurtled toward her.

"Byron—"

"Hell."

Byron swiveled on his saddle, but it was clear there was nowhere for them to go.

"Hold tight," she said. She hoped like heck her horse didn't bolt. Hoped Byron's didn't either.

Byron whooped as the first of the bison sped past, and then another and then another, the herd parting around the rise of ground like the sea around a boulder near shore. Exhilaration soon replaced terror in her heart, and Renata whooped, too, watching the beasts flow around them and stream back toward Base Camp and their home territory.

"Do you think they'll stop when they get there?" Byron called over the din, still filming.

"God, I hope so!" Otherwise Base Camp was lost.

A rider flashed by in the midst of the herd. Walker, if she wasn't mistaken. There was Jericho. Boone. Clay.

"It's the Four Horsemen of the Apocalypse!" Byron shouted. "That's what Riley calls them."

Renata remembered that from the early days of the show. She couldn't believe she'd forgotten, but so much had changed since then.

Suddenly Greg was with them, his horse galloping up the rise of ground through the scrubby bushes to join them. "You all right?" Greg called, leaning from his saddle to snatch a kiss. His gelding circled around, snorting and huffing in the cold air, eager to get back to the chase.

"We're fine," Renata called back.

"See you at the bunkhouse!" And he was off again, urging his horse on, at home in the saddle.

She hadn't seen this side of Greg before.

"You love him, don't you?" Byron asked, still filming.

Renata didn't answer, and he turned the camera to her. He wasn't going to let her hide. She wouldn't either, if their positions were reversed. She nodded. "Yes, I love him."

"Then don't let Fulsom—or Clem—get in your way."

AS HIS HORSE flew over the snowy ground, Greg thought he'd never felt so much alive. The adrenaline coursing through his veins was pure and heady, the night air cool against his flushed skin, the bison thundering past him all muscle and motivation, racing just to race at this point, he thought. All of them acting on instinct alone.

"Think they'll stop when we reach the pasture?" Jericho called, angling near him. His mount's sides were heaving, but none of their horses were slowing down.

"I don't know. I guess we'll find out," Greg called back.

It was coming up fast.

"What if they go right past?"

"We'll have to round them up all over again."

Greg kept his wits about him, but something caught his eye in the distance. Figures milling around by the pasture gate. "Someone's there!" He pointed.

"They'd better be careful!" Jericho veered off. Ahead of them, Walker was urging his horse forward, trying to get to the head of the herd.

"They're not going to turn," Greg shouted even though no one was near enough to hear him, but just as he'd given up all hope and resigned himself to a night of chasing after bison, wheeling them around again and again until they somehow got them into the pasture, a set of powerful lights flicked on, and then another and another—more and more until a whole row of headlights lit up the night.

Boone and Clay, urging their horses on the far side of the herd, whooped and hollered, and the bison, caught between them and the vehicles, began to swerve.

Greg shouted and rode on, corralling the giant beasts from his side, along with Jericho and Walker.

"They're going in!"

Greg wasn't sure who shouted the words, but they were right; the bison were racing for the gate of the pasture, siphoning in between riders and the line of trucks. Once inside, they raced in a wide arc within the confines of the pasture, their pace slowing, some animals breaking off, turning against the tide, slowing all of them down.

When three or four neighbor men shut the gate behind the last animal, a whoop went up from all sides.

"We did it!" Greg high-fived Jericho, riding past. Clay tossed his hat in the air. Men and women climbed out of the line of trucks, shouting greetings and expressions of relief.

"When they started coming straight for us, I thought we were done for," a woman called.

"Me, too," someone answered.

"Everybody come up to the bunkhouse," Boone shouted. "We've got something hot for everyone, at the very least, right, Kai?"

"You got it," Kai shouted.

"There's more reinforcements coming," Ethan Cruz called out. "Autumn will be here any minute with some food."

"So will Fila and Camila," Ned Matheson added. "They're bringing stuff from the restaurant."

Greg hung back with some of the others to ride the perimeter of the pasture fence line and make sure there were no breaks. Some of their visitors arranged to take short guard shifts while everyone else celebrated so no one would have to miss out completely.

By the time he reached the bunkhouse, a stream of people were walking up the hill toward the manor.

"Too many to fit here," Boone called out to them. "Grab something from the kitchen and come, too. Renata's already at the manor," he added as if he'd read Greg's mind.

"There's nothing left to bring," Kai said, appearing in the bunkhouse's doorway, lugging a bowl of something. "I've sent everything I have with the others. Can you close the door behind me, though?"

"Sure."

At the manor, it looked like the whole town had turned up for the impromptu celebration. Someone had lugged out the folding tables they used for their weddings, and the large ballroom was filled with people. A stream of women carried covered dishes and set them on the tables. Others brought out plates, cups and cutlery.

"How'd everyone cook so fast?" Greg asked Austin Hall, who was just walking past with his wife, Ella. He'd met the man at other gatherings in town.

"Are you kidding? Chance Creek women have casseroles on hand for just such occasions," Austin joked.

"This is our dinner for tomorrow," Ella said, setting a serving dish on the table with the others. "I heated it up while you men were saving the day."

"Should have let you round up the bison. She's a crack rider," Austin told Greg proudly.

"I'll bet." Greg knew about her equine therapy program.

He caught sight of Renata and Byron filming the proceedings on the other side of the room. "Catch up with you later," he told Ella and Austin and made his way to them.

"You both look none the worse for wear," he said, giving Renata a frank look up and down.

"Nothing touched us," Renata said. "It was a perfect position to film the proceedings. We got great footage."

"I'm the one who got great footage." Clem sidled up to them.

William, who was standing nearby, shook his head. "We got footage of some bison that broke away from the herd and galloped around in circles for a little bit. We were much too far away to get anything interesting."

"We got interesting stuff," Clem contradicted.

"Like hell we did." William didn't seem willing to put up with Clem's games tonight. He leaned forward to catch Byron's eye. "I hope you got something as good as Renata's saying, or we missed a bonanza."

"We were right in the middle of the herd and filmed everything! I'll tell Fulsom it was you who got it," Renata told Byron. "Maybe he'll give you a raise."

"It doesn't matter what happened tonight. In every way that matters, I'm the better director than you," Clem said.

"You aren't better than me at anything," Renata retorted.

"I know how to rile people up and get a great story. I know how to film people when they don't suspect a thing. I know how to dig up dirt and release it at exactly the right moment." Clem ticked the items off on his fingers.

"But you're weak," Renata said. "You always fall short. You don't command any respect. You don't have any sense of theme or purpose. You can't keep an audience interested." She ticked her statements off her fingers, too.

"I don't fall short." Clem stepped close to her. "When I set a goal, I win it."

Renata made a derisive sound. "Prove it."

"I'll prove it. I'll beat you at your favorite game. What's more, I'll make it worth your while. One hundred thousand."

"One hundred thousand what?" Renata snapped.

"Dollars. What else?" Clem asked. "You're all about

the Benjamins, right? I'll give you a stack of them. If you can beat me."

"That's ridiculous. Renata's not going to risk losing money like that," Greg said, but when Clem smiled triumphantly, he realized he'd walked right into the man's trap. "I mean—"

"That's right," Clem said over him. "Renata's a loser. She's the one who falls short, and she knows it."

"Renata never falls short," Avery stated.

"Admit it," Clem demanded of Renata. "You're nothing. Ten years working for a billionaire, and you're still living hand to mouth. How much gambling do you do in your spare time?"

"Renata doesn't live hand to mouth," Eve said.

"Say it." Clem moved even closer. Greg stepped forward to get between them, but Renata put up a hand.

"I'm not a loser," she said tightly.

"But you don't have a penny to your name, do you? You've got no family. No one to bail you out. No one to tell you you're an addict and you need help," Clem said. "Come on, addict. One last game. For one hundred grand."

"I don't have a hundred grand," she spat. "And neither do you."

"I've got a hell of a lot more than that." Clem's grin mocked her. "Here's what we'll do. You win, you get the money. I win, you leave Base Camp and Chance Creek for good."

"No!" Greg blurted, stepping between them. "Renata, don't listen to him. You don't have to prove anything—"

She ignored him. "One hundred thousand dollars?" she repeated.

Clem nodded.

She put out her hand. He shook it.

"Renata—" Greg tried again.

"Deal," she said.

THIS WAS A bad idea. A really bad idea. She had no doubt she could beat Clem on any normal day, but he'd just made the stakes so high her hands were shaking. On the other hand, if she won, she might get everything she wanted.

"You've got to be kidding me," Greg said.

She was knocked off-guard by his anger, but then she looked at it through his eyes. He thought she was risking her future with him. Didn't he see this was the only way they had a chance to have a future together?

She couldn't tell him that until she'd won the game, though. If Clem got any indication of how devastated she'd be if she lost, he'd press that advantage hard.

"Trust me" was all she said. Greg rolled his eyes.

"Trust you? When you trust no one? That's rich." He strode away to the far side of the room, leaving Renata to wonder what he meant.

"Let's get this game going," Clem said. He pulled out two nickels. "Same rules as before."

"Same rules," she agreed and shook herself free from the thoughts tangling in her mind. She'd sort things out with Greg in a minute—

Or she wouldn't, depending on how this game went.

The truth of what she'd done hit her like an eighteen-wheeler, leaving her shaken, struggling to control her breath. If she lost this game—

If she lost—

She might never see Greg again.

"Ready to get your ass kicked?" Clem asked.

Renata swallowed hard. Took a deep breath. She could do this.

She had to.

Her first toss landed close to the wall, no thanks to her shaking hands or skipping heart. Lucky. A lucky shot. She couldn't depend on those to win this contest.

Clem tossed and landed just a little farther from the wall than she had.

Renata went to fetch the coins, calming down a little. She'd beat Clem handily before.

"Don't get cocky," he warned her.

"Whatever." She tossed her coin again and swore when it bounced off the wall farther away than she'd like it to land. *Screw up*, she willed at Clem, but he didn't. His coin landed within a half inch from the wall.

"That's how a pro plays the game," he said.

"Right. You're definitely a pro," Renata sneered. Taunting him made her more comfortable now. This felt familiar.

Clem chuckled. "Don't say I didn't warn you." He tossed his coin, and it landed within a hairbreadth of the wall. Renata's stomach sank. It was hard to beat lucky breaks like that. She tossed, too, but was a half inch off the mark.

"Two–one," Avery said.

Renata won the next round, and the next. Her confidence came back. A glance told her Greg was watching from across the room. He wouldn't be able to see the coins from there, but Avery tallied the score loudly each round so that everyone could hear.

When Renata won the next round, she sighed in relief. This was more like it. She won another round, and hope blossomed inside her. A hundred grand would get her so close to paying off her promise she could easily marry Greg, stay at Base Camp and find some way to pay the rest—

"Four to two, Renata winning," Avery said.

"Let's do this," Renata said to Clem.

"Don't get ahead of yourself," he warned her.

"I'm winning."

"Maybe it's time to put a stop to that."

She didn't think he'd unnerved her again, but her next shot wasn't stellar. Clem won the round and fetched the coins. "Watch this."

He won the next round, and the next, and the next and the next.

"Seven–four, Clem's winning," Avery said worriedly.

She wasn't the only one worrying. Renata's hands had started shaking again. Clem was tossing the coins differently—as if he knew what he was doing. He'd never done that before.

"Think you're the only one who grew up in foster

care?" Clem sneered as he handed her a coin. "Think you're the only one who was ever bored shitless day after day? The only one no one bothered to feed sometimes?"

He tossed his coin, and it landed so close to the wall they both had to go and inspect it to make sure it wasn't touching.

"The trick to playing someone is to make sure they're not playing *you*," Clem said. "And to be clear—I've been playing you since the moment I got here, Ludlow."

Renata ignored him. Tossed her nickel.

Lost.

Greg had drifted closer. "You don't have to do this, Renata. You can stop right now."

"No, she can't," Clem retorted. "She made the bet. She shook on it. She was all ready to take my money. All of you were willing to let her." He turned to Avery. "Say the score. Eight–four."

"Eight–four," Avery whispered. "Come on, Renata, you can do this."

Renata swallowed hard. She wasn't at all sure she could.

CHAPTER SIXTEEN

"HELP HER," ANGUS growled in Greg's ear when he wheeled around to walk away again.

Help her? Renata had taken this stupid bet without thinking twice about the repercussions if she lost. She was so money-hungry, so determined to prove herself against Clem, she didn't care that if she tossed her nickels wrong, she'd be gone, and he'd have to marry someone else.

"Don't blow this," Angus said.

"I'm not the one who's blowing this," Greg returned in a furious whisper. "She's the one who's putting money ahead of everything else."

"Did you ever think to ask why?"

"She won't tell me."

"Nine–four," Avery said. "Renata, take a break. Clem, leave her alone. You don't get to bully her into losing."

Angus jabbed Greg in the shoulder. "You keep saying you love her. That you want to marry her. And yet, the first time the chips are down, she's over there and you're over here. Maybe she's got a reason for needing that money. Maybe if she hasn't told you what it is, it's because she doesn't trust you to understand and be there for her. You're about to lose the woman you love. Get over there and fight!"

"How?" Angus's accusations stung.

"Stand by her side. Tell her she can do it." Angus shoved him in the right direction. "Hurry."

Greg hesitated until Renata turned, searching the room for him. She held a glass of water in her hand that Avery had put there, but she wasn't drinking it.

When their gazes met, he read the desperation in hers, and something shuddered through his whole body—the need to protect her from Clem.

That's what he had been put on this earth to do. He'd told her that once, hadn't he?

Angus was right; he was blowing this. Renata needed him.

What the hell was he doing over here?

He crossed the room in several long strides, lifted the glass in her hand higher. "Take a drink. Settle down. You've got this. You've beaten this clown a half-dozen times."

"He was playing me. He knew how to win all the time," she whispered shakily. "Greg, I don't want to leave."

His heart nearly missed a beat, but then it caught up, pounding hard to match the ache in his throat. "I don't want you to leave. I love you. You know that, right?"

She nodded.

"I want you to stay, and I want you to win that money, whatever you need it for. I'm right here, okay? Clem can't touch you when I'm right here."

"But if I lose—"

"You're not going to lose." Greg gripped both her shoulders. "Hear me? You're going to win because you need to stay right here, get your job back if that's what you want and marry me. Because I want to spend the rest of my life being right here for you no matter what you do."

Renata's lips parted. After a moment, she nodded.

"Don't go getting all sappy on me, Ludlow," he whispered in her ear, pulling her into a fierce hug. "You've spent months cutting every last one of us men down to size. You know what you're doing with a lightweight like Clem."

She laughed, blinked back the tears gathering in her eyes and nodded again.

"You can do this," Greg assured her. "Win this game, and I'll take you out for another spin in my truck," he added.

Her smile broadened. "You really think you're something, don't you?"

"I know *you* are."

RENATA WIPED HER eyes on her sleeves, took another gulp of water, set the glass down on a nearby table and returned to face Clem.

"Done with your pity party?" he sneered. "You won't miss that overgrown ape."

"You're right, I won't." She took the coin he handed her, waited for him to toss and then took aim.

Clem's coin was close to the wall, but hers was closer.

"Nine–five," Avery said.

"I won't miss him because I'm not leaving."

"Getting cocky tripped you up before," Clem pointed out, snatching his nickel from her angrily when she scooped up the coins and handed one to him.

"I'm not cocky. I just know my capabilities." She tossed first this time and felt a surge of satisfaction when her coin slid close to the wall again. "And I know your lack of them."

Clem frowned, tossed and swore. Renata went to fetch the coins.

"Nine–six. Clem is still in the lead," Avery said.

"You got this, Renata," Greg said quietly.

Renata tossed. Waited for Clem's throw and went to fetch them again.

"Nine–seven," Avery said.

"Keep your eyes on the prize," Greg coached from beside. Renata tossed again.

Won.

"Don't think you've got this," Clem said. "You're going to choke. You know you are. No woman beats a man when it counts."

She nearly laughed but instead thanked Clem for the most energizing thing he could have said to her. She'd faced this girl-boy stuff all her life.

She won the next round, too.

"Nine–nine," Avery said. "Come on, Renata!"

"You win, and I'll make you pay," Clem growled. "You'll regret it for the rest of your life."

"Focus," Greg said calmly behind her. "Take your time."

It was as if Greg's love was surrounding her, steadying her, holding her in its arms and guiding her shot. She raised the nickel. Tossed it—

And knew there was no way Clem could win.

With a growl he threw his nickel so hard at the wall it bounced back almost to his feet.

"You're a bitch, you know that, Ludlow? A goddamn bitch."

He stormed out before she could answer, slamming the door so hard the entire building shuddered.

"Better catch him before he runs off without paying," Angus said.

"I got it all on film," Byron said. "You were awesome, Renata."

"Yes, you were." Greg enveloped her in an embrace. "Jesus, I was afraid I'd lost you for good. Don't ever scare me like that again, you hear me?"

"What do you need all that money for, anyway?" Avery demanded. "Is Clem right? Do you have gambling debts all over Montana?"

Renata shook her head. "Of course not. It's just—I made a promise a long time ago, and I have to pay it off before I—well, before I can marry anyone."

"Who did you promise money to?" Byron asked.

She could tell Greg wanted to know, too, but didn't

want to push her. She supposed it was time to come clean. These people were on her side. They'd understand.

"A long time ago, when I was just out of school, I was doing a documentary on a girls' school in Peru." She saw recognition dawn on Greg's face. He'd seen the movie, after all. "A mudslide happened while I was on a field trip with them. It took out their village. Left all twenty-three girls orphaned."

"Oh, my God," Avery said. "What happened to them?"

"Their teachers found them a new school building and kept them as boarders until they were grown enough to be on their own. I wanted… to stay," she admitted. "To help raise them. You have no idea how much I wanted that." She got her voice under control again. "But that wasn't what they needed."

"They needed money," Angus said quietly, meeting Greg's gaze. He raised his eyebrows as if to say, "See?"

"That's right. They needed money. Those first years were especially tough. Every bit I sent to them meant so much. I pledged I would pay the way of the girls until they had graduated. And now they almost all have. There's just a handful of them left, but their bus broke down, and so did the boiler in their school, and there's always something—" Her voice wobbled. The shock of nearly losing everything important had finally hit her.

"Why didn't you ask?" Greg was staring at her like he couldn't believe his ears.

"Ask what?" Renata had expected Greg to be as jubilant as she was, but he looked—angry. A trickle of dread threaded through her.

"Ask for help."

"Why would I ask for help?" She didn't know what he was talking about. The girls were her responsibility. The only reason she was at Base Camp was to raise money for them. It had nothing to do with anyone else.

"Because we're your friends," Avery said in astonishment.

"Because we're supposed to get married," Greg said. "I'm going to be your husband. Why wouldn't you ask me to help you with something so big?"

Renata opened her mouth, but she didn't know what to say. "I didn't think you'd…" She trailed off.

"You didn't think what? That I'd say yes? That I'd care?" Greg's disbelief was clear.

"It had nothing to do with you," Renata tried to explain. "It happened way before you met me. It was my responsibility."

"Nothing to do—" Greg broke off, stuffed his hands in his pockets and walked in a circle. "How can you say that? I was there—"

Renata had no idea what he meant. They stared at each other.

"I was there," Greg said again more distinctly. "Right behind you that whole first night. I searched the camp with you for those girls' parents. I gave you blankets, food and water to give to them. I helped translate for you. Kept you upright when you nearly collapsed from exhaustion and shock—" He pulled his hands out of his pockets. Lifted them toward the ceiling. "You never even saw me, did you? I might as well not have been there. Or here, evidently."

"But—" Renata struggled to find words. Greg had been there? Those had been his hands holding her up? His arms holding her when it got too much? "I didn't—"

"No, I know you didn't. Because you were too damn busy trying to save the world all on your own. Which is really freaking admirable, don't get me wrong, except look around you, Renata. We're all here, too. We're all trying to save the world, too!"

"I would have donated money," Avery said softly. "I still will, if they need more."

"Me, too," Byron said.

"Me, as well," Angus said. "That's what it means to be part of something, lass. It means you're not on your own. You don't have to do it all by yourself."

"I would have loved to lighten your burden," Greg said. "I was looking for ways to connect with you. Trying everything I could think of. And you bet our future on the toss of a coin. Did you secretly hope you'd lose?"

"No! Of course not." To Renata's horror, tears stung her eyes. She wasn't going to cry in front of everyone. Not while Byron was still filming. Didn't Greg know how hard it had been to hold back from him all this time?

He probably didn't.

She'd left him in the dark about her motivations from the start.

"I thought you had some horrible past you had to deal with. An ex-husband, or bad debts, or I don't know—a criminal record." He flung his arms wide. "But this is why you kept pushing me away? You just couldn't bear not to do everything yourself? We could have solved this in a minute if you'd trusted me enough to tell me." When she didn't answer, he stepped closer. "Why didn't you tell me? You must have had a good reason."

How could she explain the rules that had kept her going this far? They didn't make sense unless you'd had a childhood like hers. "People… leave," she finally burst out helplessly. "When you need them, they disappear. So I don't need anyone."

Greg let out a ragged breath. "That's the thing, Renata. I won't disappear. That's what I've been trying to tell you."

They stared at each other.

"Well?" he asked.

"Well, what?"

"You've got your money. Are you going to marry me at least?"

She blinked. This wasn't the proposal she'd hoped for, but it was her own damn fault. She'd been so sure no one would ever want to help her she'd never once even asked. And all this time, Greg had been waiting for her to notice him. To remember when he'd been there for her before. To see that he was trying to be there for her now.

She'd always thought her single-mindedness was her

best trait. Maybe it was her worst, too.

"Yes," she said in a small voice. "I'll marry you."

"Good. I… God, I love you, Renata, but I…" Greg wheeled around and followed the same path Clem had just taken out the door. He didn't slam it quite so hard, but he didn't close it softly, either.

Everyone watched him go.

"Congratulations?" Avery ventured after a long moment.

Renata laughed. And started to sob.

Now what was she supposed to do?

CHAPTER SEVENTEEN

"I THINK THAT'S the least romantic proposal I've ever heard," Boone said an hour later when he caught up to Greg outside where he was splitting a pile of logs left over from summertime. Wood, while a renewable resource, wasn't what Greg would call green energy, but it was nice to have a bonfire now and then, and he figured it was a better idea to throw himself into a helpful exercise rather than vent his frustration some other, far more destructive, way.

"Well, it was a proposal," Greg growled. "And she said yes, so you should be happy."

"Don't you mean *you* should be happy?"

Greg didn't know what he was. He couldn't get that last game with Clem out of his head. The way she'd said yes to the possibility of losing him just for the chance of winning all that money. Every time he thought about what could have happened, his chest hurt so bad he thought it would split in two.

He understood she thought she owed it to the girls in Peru, and he supposed he couldn't blame her for not remembering he'd been there, too. Still, he couldn't seem to suppress the sense of panic that kept closing his throat.

"What if some other disaster comes along that's more important than I am?"

Boone's eyebrows shot up. "Is that what this is about?"

Greg wasn't sure. Ever since he met Renata he thought he'd been put here in order to help her—protect her—whatever she needed. He'd tried to do that in Peru, and he'd tried to do it again here during her struggle against Clem.

She hadn't wanted his help, though. She'd wanted to fight him on her own. She hadn't even told him about the money she wanted to provide to the school in Peru.

"She doesn't trust me. She doesn't depend on me," he said.

"Those are two very different things. Modern women don't want to depend on men. They want to do things on their own, like we do."

"But—"

"The trick is to be there. To be ready in case they do need you—or want you."

"I can't be ready if she won't even tell me what's going on," Greg complained.

"I think that changes over time, though, don't you?" Boone asked, picking up some of the split logs and beginning to pile them up. "The longer you know Renata, the more unspoken clues you'll pick up on, and the more she'll learn about you, too. Once she sees you're able to listen without taking over for her—that you can back her up—she'll tell you more about what's bothering her."

"How do you know all this?" Greg demanded, resting on his ax.

"You think Riley simply opened up and let me into her life? She's a modern woman, too, and a long time ago I hurt her—bad. That kind of thing doesn't heal over in an instant."

Greg considered this. Why had he ever expected love would come easy? People were always complicated. Life had so many twists and turns.

"I heard Renata mention foster care. Can you imagine losing your parents and then being passed from family to family? In the best of circumstances that would be heartbreaking. I bet she learned a long time ago it was safest to depend on only herself."

Greg didn't even want to think about Renata's past. When he tried to picture her losing her parents so young, it made him want to cradle her in his arms forever. He wanted to protect her. Was that so bad? It galled him she wanted to protect herself.

As soon as he had the thought he had to shake his head at his own stupidity. He couldn't fault her for not wanting to depend on a man to fight her battles for her—or pay her bills. Boone was right; that probably hadn't worked out so well for her in the past.

"Guess I should go back in there and apologize."

"Damn straight you should. Go find your fiancée," Boone urged. "Celebrate. The worst is over."

Was it?

God, he hoped so.

"SO I'LL BE able to pay off everything I've promised within a few days," Renata said, clutching her phone to her cheek. To her surprise, Clem's payment had already gone through. She'd expected him to balk and make her hound him to come through on his promised bet, but the money was in her account plain as day, and she wanted to move it over to the school's account before that somehow changed.

There was silence on the other end of the line as Mayra took this in. "I'm not sure I understand," she said. "It almost sounds as if you thought you might *not* be able to come through with the money over the next few years."

"Well… I mean, of course I would, no matter what. I said so," Renata stammered. "It's just… now I can pay early and be done—" She bit off the end of the sentence. "It hasn't always been easy," she added lamely, wishing she could take the words back the minute she'd said them. Mayra hadn't known it wasn't easy, and she'd never wanted her to know. Now it was as if she was asking for some kind of pat on the head. That had never been her intent.

Another silence. "Renata," Mayra began and then stopped. "We thought… You always made it sound… If we'd known it was a hardship for you to support the girls, we never would have asked."

A twinge of anger twisted through Renata. Mayra

and Gabriela had to have known it was a hardship, at least at first. "I was twenty-six when the mudslide happened," she pointed out.

"Yes, twenty-six. A rich girl from a foreign country come to see how the rest of the world lived," Mayra said flatly. "With your fancy video cameras and entourage."

Renata bit back a disbelieving laugh. "Fancy cameras? Those were provided by the grant I'd won. And my entourage was another film student. You know that. I paid his way."

"You studied at a famous university," Mayra pointed out.

"With scholarships and money I saved! I told you I grew up in foster care. Anything the school didn't cover, I did."

"But… all this time, you sent money every month. You never missed once. We thought—"

"What? That I'd married some rich man and was siphoning funds off from his bank account?" Renata's voice rose even as she knew she had only herself to blame.

"No. You never mentioned a man," Mayra said. "We assumed it was some family connection."

"Well, it wasn't! It was me. I took a job the minute I got back from Peru and kept it all this time. I've sent you every penny I didn't need to survive myself, and I was glad to do it!"

"You don't sound glad."

Mayra's words brought her up short. "I am glad," Renata reiterated. "I'd do exactly the same thing again.

It's just—I've been so worried all this time. So scared I'd let you all down. My job—I nearly lost it, and I didn't know what I was going to do—"

When Mayra spoke again, she'd softened. "I wish you'd told us. We never meant to put a burden on you like this." She let out a breath. "This is my fault. I never asked questions because I didn't want to know the answers. You've been a godsend all these years. What a fool I was to assume some man or family was behind you. You always took on so much responsibility even when you were here. You had to give every girl in the school a chance to say good-night every night, remember? Every one her fair share. And all this time you were working yourself to the bone for them! And us. Gabriela will be heartbroken when she knows what we've done."

"You don't have to tell her," Renata said. "I was happy to. It made me feel useful to help the girls."

"But what about you? Your life. Your family? You've never married, or—"

"I'm getting married," Renata said. At least, she thought she was. Greg's proposal hadn't exactly been confidence-inspiring.

"Really? To whom?" Mayra asked.

"His name is Greg. He was actually there, the day of the mudslide."

"Greg Devon!" Mayra exclaimed. "That useful young man. The one who helped you all day and night! I didn't know you'd kept in touch."

Renata held the phone away from her face, then

brought it back. "Yes, that's the one," she said slowly. Mayra had remembered him when she hadn't. What was wrong with her?

It had been the shock, she decided. The quick flip of her life from worrying about only herself to worrying about a busload of girls. "Mayra," she said. "I'm so embarrassed." She related the truth of it.

Mayra laughed. "I believe it," she said. "Gabriela and I had already seen our share of life's ups and downs, but that was the first time you'd seen such a disaster. There's no shame in the fact that you focused on the one thing you could do. You helped us so much that day. All the girls remember the way you hunted for their parents. It's part of what makes you so special to us."

"You really remember Greg?" Renata asked. "You think he'll make a good husband?"

"He'll make a fine husband. He knows how to help," Mayra said firmly.

"I wish you could come to the wedding," Renata said softly.

"Me, too. We'll all be there in our hearts," Mayra promised.

"Renata?"

She turned to find Greg had entered the manor's kitchen, where she'd gone to find a little peace and quiet.

"Mayra, I've got to go. Thank you for everything."

"Thank *you*," Mayra said meaningfully, and Renata's heart warmed. Despite all the difficulty of the last ten years, she knew she'd done something significant. The girls who'd lost their families the day of the mudslide had gained a new family with Mayra and Gabriela, and she'd helped make that possible. If she had to do it all over again, she'd make the same choice.

When she'd hung up, Renata faced Greg. "Did you come here to call off the wedding?"

One corner of his mouth tipped up. "No. Sorry about that proposal."

"I suppose I deserved it."

"No. You didn't. You deserve the best of everything." To her surprise Greg sank down on one knee. "Renata Ludlow, I've loved you since the moment I laid eyes on you in the middle of a disaster in Peru. The woman I met there was strong, fierce, determined to help everyone and tireless in her desire to bring comfort to twenty-three girls and their teachers. I can't tell you how much you inspired me that day. Even if we'd never met again, you would have changed my life."

Renata squirmed, uncomfortable with his praise, but Greg went on. "I haven't been my best self these past few months. I should have told you immediately we'd met before, but my pride kept me silent. I should have told you why I came to Base Camp, but I was worried you'd think I was a fool—or worse—for following you. When I met you all those years ago, I saw everything I'd ever wanted in a woman, all in one wonderful package. I think I lost my mind that night, and I haven't fully recovered since."

"But—"

"Hang on," he said quietly. "I came to Base Camp

because I was looking for something important to do and because I saw your name as the director of the show. I wanted to see if you were really the woman I'd thought you were or if I'd dreamed up some fantasy that was making it hard to settle for less. The first day I got here I realized you were exactly the woman I'd fallen for so many years before."

"The day you got here I was bossing you all around, trying to make you uncomfortable in front of the cameras so you'd inadvertently spill your innermost secrets," she pointed out tartly.

"And you also rescued a half-grown chicken that had wormed its way out of its coop and put it back without anyone else noticing. And went and found some extra feed and made sure it got some because you thought the other chicks were crowding it out."

"How—how did you know that?" Renata sputtered. No one had been there to see that—she'd made sure. She'd needed all the men of Base Camp to think she was a hard-ass so they'd be afraid of her.

"I saw you," he said gently, pulling a little velvet-covered box out of his pocket, "And I immediately knew you were exactly who I thought you were. You go looking for people—and chickens—to save, regardless of what you want everyone to think. You pretend to be heartless when the truth is you have a heart a mile wide." He opened the box and showed her the ring inside. "Which is just one of the hundreds of reasons I want to spend the rest of my life with you. What do you say? Will you marry me, Renata?"

"I—" Her words stuck in her throat. She felt exposed and cared for all at once. Greg knew her in a way she didn't think anyone ever had—or would. Was that worth taking a chance on? Maybe loving him would leave her open to heartache. Maybe some unthinkable disaster would take him away, too, just like it had her parents and her first foster family.

Did she want a life so safe it meant she let no one else in?

Everything inside her rejected that idea. She wanted people to love who would love her back, even if there was a chance they'd leave her. She wanted Greg. "Yes," she said. "Yes, I will marry you."

Greg surged to his feet, scooped her into a bear hug and whirled her around. "I'll never get in your way if you've got big plans," he promised her. "I'll always be right here, though. If you need me." He set her back down, pulled the ring out of the box and slid it on her finger. "Do you like it?"

Renata held up her hand to see the ring better, a beautiful, swooping thing with a cluster of diamonds that winked in the light. "It's wonderful." Far more than a circle of silver and a few precious stones, it meant she was being given the chance to start a new family. One she hoped would last.

He pulled her close again and kissed her. "Not half as wonderful as you. Let's go tell everyone you said yes."

She didn't point out that half of Base Camp had been there when she said yes last time. She understood why he needed to make a far more official announcement, and so would everyone else.

A half hour later, everyone was assembled in the bunkhouse.

"I want you all to know that I asked Renata to marry me for real, and she's accepted me," Greg said. Renata lifted her left hand and waved it like the queen of England in a parade, having trouble holding back a smile as the diamonds on her finger glinted. After all the long months of stress, and especially the last few weeks with Clem here, her relief was overwhelming, and she found it possible to smile for real.

"You're never going to get rid of me now," she called out.

Riley approached the front of the room as the rest of Base Camp's participants clapped and cheered, and the camera crews filmed it all. "That's okay—we need all the extra hands we can get here. We've got a lot of babies coming!" She gave Renata a big hug.

Groans and laughter greeted this. "That's for sure!" Clay shouted from the audience.

"Speaking of babies," Avery said, pushing forward to the front of the room, too. "I have an announcement to make." She paused for silence.

Riley broke away from Renata and turned to look at her, openmouthed. The camera crews fairly bristled with interest. Walker, lounging against the far wall between the windows, straightened.

Avery scanned the room. Made sure all of them were facing her. "I'm pregnant!" she cried.

Renata turned to Walker, like everyone else in the room. The man stood as still as stone. Renata didn't think she'd ever seen him so stricken.

"Psych!" Avery shouted. "I'm just joking. For now. But just because I'm still here doesn't mean I'm not going to create the life that I want."

"Avery, we want you to have—" Boone began.

"I want a husband. I want a family. I want a tiny house." She met Boone's gaze, and Renata could see Avery had changed. There was steel in the line of her jaw. She wouldn't be put off with empty promises. "I'll take his. Now." She pointed to Walker, who was breathing hard, his hands shoved in his pockets.

"But—" Boone said.

"He owes me that much. You all can build him another one come spring. I know his isn't finished, but it's close enough. I'll move in tonight. I'm not sleeping in here anymore."

"Avery—"

"Give it to her," Walker growled.

"Where are you and your bride supposed to sleep?" Boone asked him.

The look Walker gave him should have felled him where he stood. Renata held her breath, then tried to break the tension.

"You're not alone," she said. "I'm not pregnant, either," she added lamely when Avery turned her way.

"Yet," Greg said.

"I'm not pregnant," Angus said darkly.

Avery shook her head at him. "You're not even a woman." She turned to Clay. "You're in charge of the tiny houses. Get theirs done." She pointed to Renata and Greg. "And then finish mine. I'll camp in there until you've managed it." She crossed the room to where she and the other singletons stored their gear, pulled out a large duffel bag and headed for the door. Walker tracked her with a gaze so bleak it squeezed Renata's chest. When the door shut behind Avery, it was quiet in the bunkhouse for a long moment.

"Well, we have an engagement to celebrate," Riley said shakily. "Savannah, would you play us something?"

"Of course." Savannah handed Jacob to Jericho and made her way to the upright piano. Soon her fingers tripped across the keys, and a lively melody filled the room.

Around them, conversations sprung up, low at first but soon gathering steam. Renata let out a gusty sigh. "Walker needs to get it together."

"I bet he knows that now if he didn't before," Greg said dryly. "What about you and me?"

"What about us?"

"Do we have it together?"

She had to laugh at that. "You know what? I think we finally do."

"Good. Any time you're ready to try for that baby," Greg murmured to Renata as conversations buzzed around them, "just let me know. I'm your man."

"You are my man."

"Soon there'll be paperwork to prove it," he agreed. "Want to check out my tiny house?"

"I thought you'd never ask."

CHAPTER EIGHTEEN

"I THOUGHT YOU were never going to live in a commune again," Greg's mother, Phoebe, said on the day of his wedding, when Greg was on his way to change into the Revolutionary War uniform all the Base Camp men wore on these occasions. It was strange how a community that hadn't even existed for a year could have so many traditions already, he'd mused earlier. It seemed like a good sign, somehow. Traditions stood for continuity, after all.

"Please, it's a sustainable community," he said, giving her a peck on the cheek. He was glad his parents had made it to the wedding.

"Whatever helps you sleep at night," Phoebe said dryly.

"Renata and I would like to come visit Greenside when the show is over. Maybe this summer?"

"Can't wait. Eileen has settled in well."

Greg thought of the home his parents had built from scratch when they were in their twenties. The farmland they'd worked jointly with the other members of the commune all those years. For the first time he really understood what Greenside meant to his parents.

"I'm sorry I've been an ass and not come home much," he said. "That changes as of now."

"Good." His mother hugged him. "Where's your sister? Wasn't she supposed to be here by now?"

"I'm right here," Eileen said, coming down the hall toward them. "I wouldn't miss this wedding for the world."

Greg met her embrace and held on a little too long, grateful beyond words to see her again. It had been several years. He swore that length of time would never pass without a visit again.

"You look good," he told her. Something had changed, he thought. She seemed happier than he remembered. Lighter—like a burden had been lifted.

"You know what? I think settling down in one place for a while might suit me."

"Me, too."

"My babies are all grown up," their mother deadpanned. "My work here is done."

"No, it's not," Greg told her. "Pretty soon there will be grandkids. You're just getting started."

"WELL, WELL, LOOK at the blushing bride."

Renata stiffened and turned to see Clem lounging in the door of one of the guest rooms at the manor where she'd come to prepare for her wedding day.

"What are you doing here?" Avery and Eve, her bridesmaids, had gone downstairs to get tea and give her a moment to her herself before the wedding. Evidently, she wasn't going to get that.

"Fulsom asked me to come."

"Why would he do that?"

"So he could congratulate me, I guess."

"Clem—"

"There you are." Fulsom pushed past Clem into the room and looked her up and down. "Renata, you look radiant," he said. "You're going to make Greg a happy man."

"Just because I'm getting married doesn't mean I can't finish doing my job," Renata hastened to tell him as Eve and Avery returned, too. She'd been directing the show ever since Clem disappeared after their last game of nickels. It had been a little awkward, since she needed to be on camera a lot, but her crew were professionals, and they knew what she wanted for the most part. She huddled with them several times a day to talk strategy and then left them to it.

"I know that. I'd hate to lose you before the show ends, but after that the future is open," Fulsom said. "I've gotten a feeling from the last couple of episodes that you're thinking about making a change."

"When the show is over, I want to take a break and decide for myself what to do next. It's been a long time since it's been my decision to make." Now that she'd paid off most of what she'd pledged to Mayra and Gabriela, and Greg and the others had already said they'd make up the rest, she could do whatever she wanted.

"Maybe we should open a film school right here," Avery said. "We could build a dormitory somewhere on the ranch. Classrooms. Have people come to study."

"I think it's an interesting idea," Eve said.

"Maybe," Renata said, but her mind was already whirling with possibilities.

"Time enough to figure it out later," Fulsom said. "You have a wedding to get to." He took out his phone, messed with it for a moment and nodded at Clem. "That's your final payment. You were right—you pulled it off."

"Of course I pulled it off." Clem winked at Renata. "She never suspected a thing."

"What are you talking about?" He was trying to rile her up again, and this was her wedding day.

Fulsom tsked at her. "It was clear the first time I came here that Greg Devon had fallen for you—hard. It was also clear you were going to be so damn professional you'd never even look at him. I could see where things were headed. As long as you were directing *Base Camp*, you'd refuse to see the good thing standing right in front of you. I hoped I was wrong," he added, "so I let things play out for a few months until it became clear you were as stubborn as I thought you were. When it came down to just a few men left and I knew Greg would draw the short straw soon, I sent in the big guns." He pointed to Clem, whose smug grin widened.

"You thought I'd fall for Clem?" she asked in disbelief.

"I thought you'd quit in a huff, and go for it with

Greg," Fulsom said. "But you didn't quit. You kept hanging on by your toenails."

"Which is where *I* came in. I'm the one who realized you needed cash," Clem said. "I could smell your desperation from across the room."

"Eww," Avery said.

"Clem hatched a plan," Fulsom said. "A good one. He'd let you win until you got as much as you needed, I'd foot the bill and—voilà!" He gestured to her wedding gown. "You'd say yes to Greg."

"You realize that's insane!" Avery told him. "You were playing with Renata's life!"

"I'm playing with all of your lives," Fulsom said bluntly.

"You didn't let me win!" Renata turned on Clem. "Not once. I beat you fair and square." She turned back to Fulsom. "I did!"

"I believe it." Fulsom put out his hands as if to ward her off. Clem was shaking his head, his smug satisfaction enough to drive a woman to drink.

"I beat him," Renata said again to Avery.

"I know you did," Avery said. "But I guess it doesn't really matter, does it? The important thing is you and Greg found each other."

"The important thing is that I get to get the hell out of this godforsaken place," Clem said. He patted his pocket. "Now that I've got some extra cash and you all have rehabilitated my reputation, I'm hitting the beach."

When he was gone, Renata shook her head at Fulsom. "You really think you made me marry Greg?"

"I know I didn't want to see you lose your chance," Fulsom said. "Kiddo, you've been with me a long time. You've been incredibly loyal. Worked your ass off. Put up with all my shit—and I know I dish out a lot of it. I want you to be happy."

"Even though I'm quitting on June first?"

He clapped a hand to his chest as if she'd shot him. "Ugh. Yes, even though you're quitting. I have no idea where I'll find someone to replace you."

"Not Clem," Avery said.

"No, not Clem. I only used him for a particular purpose, and between you and me," Fulsom grinned, "I don't think his reputation is as rehabilitated as he thinks."

"Start with Byron. He's going to go far," Renata suggested.

Fulsom nodded thoughtfully. "Byron. Interesting." He straightened again. "It's just about time to walk you down the aisle. How do I look?" He joined her by the mirror, and Renata gave herself a once-over.

"You look fine," she said.

"So do you. I hope you'll be very happy in your new life."

"I think I will."

IT HAD SEEMED right to choose the last two unmarried men at Base Camp to stand up with him at the altar on his wedding day, especially since he'd learned that whoever picked the short straw would face an additional challenge. The backup brides had confronted Fulsom with an ultimatum, and he'd gone along with it. They'd demanded that one of their number be allowed on the show for a thirty-day period during which they'd date the next man to marry. The man who drew the short straw wasn't required to marry her, but Greg could tell there would be a lot of pressure to do so.

Greg was more relieved than he could say that he wasn't letting down the rest of the inhabitants of Base Camp or being forced to date a woman he didn't love. He hoped Angus and Walker could find their way to happiness, too.

All those years ago in Peru he'd felt a visceral connection to Renata, but he hadn't dared to hope that it would turn into something real. Now here he was, getting everything he'd ever wanted.

"Almost time," Angus said as they checked their old-fashioned uniforms in the mirror.

"That's right, and you know what that means." Boone came into the room, holding up a fist with two straws poking out of it.

"Hell, I'd hoped you'd forgotten," Angus said. "It had better be your turn," he told Walker.

Walker just grunted, strode over to Boone's side and yanked a straw from his fist.

Held it up. It was definitely long.

"Come on," Angus growled. "Are you serious?"

"Walker's always serious," Boone said, nudging his friend. "You're up, Angus. Sorry, but you're going to have to get over Win and move on."

"Easy for you to say."

"I'm not just saying it." Boone looked uneasy. "Your backup bride will arrive tomorrow, and she'll stay here for the next thirty days. You're going to need to pull it together."

"What if I don't like her?"

"It's just thirty days," Boone reiterated. "Give her a fighting chance, that's all they're asking for. You going to be able to handle this?" he asked with concern.

"Guess I have to be," Angus said stiffly.

Boone clapped him on the back and moved away. "All right, people. It's wedding time."

"Maybe she'll be the woman of your dreams," Greg said when Angus came to take one last look in the mirror.

"The woman of my dreams is in California," Angus retorted.

There was going to have to be another Base Camp miracle, Greg thought. He checked himself over one last time. "I'm ready," he declared.

"Me, too." Angus led the way out of the front parlor, across the hall and into the ballroom, which had been set up with folding chairs and an altar. Walker joined them.

The chairs were filled, his father, mother and sister sitting up front. He took his place near the altar. Reverend Halpern, who'd presided over almost all the Base Camp weddings, took his place nearby.

The men and women he'd worked hard with to build Base Camp arranged themselves in the first few rows. Behind them sat other people from Chance Creek who they'd gotten to know over the past year.

Satisfaction filled him at how far they'd come. This was home now.

The music changed. Angus nudged him. He seemed to have regained a little of his sense of humor. "Last chance to make a run for it," he muttered, but Greg didn't want to run. He wanted to plant his feet right here where he belonged. Where Renata belonged, too.

Avery appeared in the doorway in a deep-blue gown, her hair piled on top of her head with tiny white flowers tucked into it. Eve followed in a matching outfit. Greg took a deep breath, and when Renata stepped into the room, he swallowed.

She was beautiful in a deceptively simple white, Regency-era gown that even he with his untrained eye could tell was crafted with the utmost skill. It set off her dark hair, her angular features and shining eyes. When her gaze sought his, he held steady, wanting her to know he would always be here for her, ready to help no matter what challenge she decided to take on.

The women made their way down the aisle, Fulsom, serious for once, walking alongside Renata. He gave her away with a quick nod to Greg, but no other comment, surprising Greg. He hadn't known Fulsom was capable of being in front of a crowd without trying to steal the show.

The man valued Renata, Greg realized. Perhaps even saw her as the daughter he'd never had. Maybe there was more to the billionaire than he'd realized.

Hell, there was more to everyone than he'd realized,

wasn't there?

That was life, he decided. Complicated when it should be simple. And simple even when you made it complicated.

Because at the end of the day what mattered was the people you gathered around you, and he'd lucked out in that respect. The people of Base Camp were the kind you could depend on no matter what happened.

Greg took Renata's hand and squeezed it. She squeezed his back, and they turned to face the reverend.

"Dearly Beloved," Halpern began. "We are gathered here today…"

Greg listened to every word, wanting to remind himself of every part of the vow he was about to take. This was the one and only time he'd stand up in front of a congregation and make a pledge like this.

When Halpern turned to Renata to start their vows, Greg did, too.

"Renata Celia Ludlow, will you have this man to be your husband, to live together with him in the covenant of marriage? Will you love him, comfort him, honor and keep him, in sickness and in health, and, forsaking all others, be faithful unto him as long as you both shall live?" Halpern asked.

Renata was shaking, but she lifted her chin and nodded. "I will," she stated clearly. Greg's heart squeezed, but now it was his turn.

"Greg Andrew Devon, will you have this woman to be your wife, to live together with her in the covenant of marriage? Will you love her, comfort her, honor and keep her, in sickness and in health, and, forsaking all others, be faithful unto her as long as you both shall live?" Halpern asked him.

"I will." He hoped Renata knew how deeply he meant it. He'd never felt so dedicated to anything as he did to being her husband.

"The rings," Halpern said.

Angus stepped forward and handed them to the reverend, who distributed them to Greg and Renata.

They took turns slipping the wedding bands onto each other's fingers.

Now the events of the day seemed real to Greg. He'd done it. He'd married Renata.

He thought his heart might burst with joy.

RENATA COULD HARDLY breathe during the ceremony, her hands shaking so hard she was afraid she might drop the ring before she got it on Greg's finger. He was so handsome in his uniform, his face shining with love for her, his touch so gentle but so strong, too. She had never been with a man who was so thoroughly present. It was addictive.

Halpern joined her hand with Greg's, and he squeezed hers again. They turned toward the congregation full of their friends, and Renata took in the pleasure radiating back at her from so many faces.

She had finally found a place where she belonged as much as anyone else. This was her home—her forever home.

No more searching. No more moving.

No more lonely days—or nights.

"Now that Renata and Greg have given themselves to each other by solemn vows, with the joining of hands and the giving and receiving of rings, I pronounce that they are husband and wife," Halpern went on.

When the ceremony was over, Halpern smiled. "Well? What are you waiting for? Kiss the bride already!"

Greg swept her into his arms and did just that, kissing her long and hard and happily until all Renata could do was cling to him and kiss him back.

"I love you," he whispered into her ear when they parted, their friends' cheers loud around them.

"I love you, too," she said.

"Forever?"

"Forever."

"Then kiss me again."

SEVERAL HOURS LATER, after dinner and dancing, drinks and toasts, the reception began to wind down, and Angus, visiting the dessert table, met up with Avery. Walker was nearby, but the two hadn't been talking. The tension between them was still thick enough to cut with a knife. He supposed it was probably better for everyone he was the next to marry, even if he didn't have the slightest desire to do so. He'd hoped he would have gotten over some of the pain Win had caused him, but it was still fresh in his heart.

"Try the cheesecake," Avery told him flatly. "Kai really outdid himself."

"Don't mind if I do," Angus said with another surreptitious glance at Walker. It occurred to him how awkward it would have been in the bunkhouse tonight with just the three of them if Avery hadn't demanded her own tiny house.

He had picked up a plate holding a slice of cheesecake when Avery gasped. He turned to see Walker stiffen, shock slackening the features of his face.

"What?" He followed their gazes toward the front hall, where a number of guests had gathered to say their goodbyes, and nearly dropped his dessert.

Win Lisle entered the large ballroom and scanned it as she shrugged out of the heavy jacket she'd worn over her emerald green dress.

"Oh, my God," Avery breathed. "She's pregnant."

Angus's heart was thundering in his chest. The periphery of his vision went dark. He set the plate on the table with the thump, then grabbed the table itself to stay upright.

Win's eyes met Angus's across the room. She placed a hand deliberately on her belly and nodded.

Angus couldn't move. Couldn't breathe.

Win was here.

Win was pregnant.

And the baby was his.

To find out more about Greg, Renata, Boone, Clay, Jericho, Walker and the other inhabitants of Base Camp, look for *A SEAL's Struggle*, Volume 9 in the *SEALs of Chance Creek* series.

Be the first to know about Cora Seton's new releases! Sign up for her newsletter here!
www.coraseton.com/sign-up-for-my-newsletter

Other books in the SEALs of Chance Creek Series:

A SEAL's Oath

A SEAL's Vow

A SEAL's Pledge

A SEAL's Consent

A SEAL's Purpose

A SEAL's Resolve

A SEAL's Devotion

A SEAL's Struggle

A SEAL's Triumph

Read on for an excerpt of
A SEAL's Struggle.

WIN LISLE STARED at the white and pink plastic wand she held in her hand.

Pregnant. She was pregnant.

How the hell had that happened?

She leaned against the metal partition of the bathroom stall in Linda's Diner where she'd come to take the test away from all the prying eyes—and cameras—back at Base Camp, and counted backward, then quickly straightened, remembering where she was. She had to hold it together.

Her life had changed so much since she'd come to

Montana and decided to stay at the sustainable community funded by billionaire Martin Fulsom. At first, she'd been a guest at the manor, the Jane-Austen inspired bed and breakfast run by some of the women here. Her friend, Andrea, had made her come on a bachelorette weekend leading up to her wedding. Win had thought she'd hate the ranch; miserable in her own life, she'd hated everything back then. Instead, she'd been mesmerized by the manor, the tiny houses, the gardens and greenhouses, the renewable energy systems, the al fresco meals around a campfire—and Angus McBride, the man who'd stolen her heart and had never given it back.

Now she was carrying his child.

Which meant she'd never go back to San Mateo.

Win took a steadying breath. Why did that thought leave her so unsettled? She'd already made up her mind to stay. All the men of Base Camp had to marry before June rolled around again, including Angus. She'd hoped to marry him, help him and his friends keep their home and build a life here.

Uneasiness settled in her stomach as she looked at the plastic test stick again, though. It had all seemed so simple just a day or two ago—before she'd looked at a calendar and realized she was late. Now her heart was racing. Her parents had been calling for weeks telling her to get off the show and come back home. Her father, congressman Julian Lisle, was up for re-election, and it seemed some of his financial backers didn't like the spectacle of his daughter on a pro-environment television show.

"I have to represent everyone," her father had said just a few days ago. "I can't have my daughter looking like she's a radical."

"Since when is sustainability radical?" Win had asked.

"Since some of my biggest donors represent fossil fuel interests."

Win had gotten off the phone, but she knew that wouldn't be the last call her parents made. Her father planned to run for Governor in two years. He was a shoe-in to win his congressional battle—he'd already served two terms and won handily in the last election—but he had to get his ducks in a row now if he expected to move up to the big leagues in a couple of years.

What would her parents think when they found out she was pregnant and realized she was serious about marrying Angus?

"Go ahead, slum around and get it out of your system," her mother, Vienna, had said the last time they talked. "We both know very well you're a princess. You won't be happy without a palace. Leif Dunlevy could have gotten you a doozy of one if you hadn't blown things with him."

"I didn't blow things with him," Win had said. "I broke our engagement. I don't love Leif."

"You've been friends all your life. Are you saying you hated him all this time?"

"Of course not." Win had wanted to hang up. "I'll always love Leif as a friend, but not as a husband. I couldn't go through with it."

"Darling, marriages between families like ours are business transactions. You can find love anywhere you want after you marry. Just be discreet. Did no one ever tell you that?"

Win wiped a hand over her brow, coming back to the present. That conversation had upset her more than she cared to admit. She had a memory from when she was five or six, running to her parents' bedroom, Maria, her nanny chasing after her. Win had burst in through the door to find her mother, naked, not with her father but with another man Win had never seen before.

Maria had snatched her up, murmured an apology, rushed back into the hall and slammed the door shut. "Mommy was just… resting with a friend," she'd said and then whispered a prayer to the Madonna in rapid Spanish.

There had been no explanations. The incident had never been spoken of again, leaving a young Win to wonder whether it had really happened or if she had dreamed it all.

Her gaze fell on the test stick in her hand again.

She knew she'd forgotten a pill or two over the last month, but she'd caught up again as soon as she'd noticed. Could those small mistakes add up to a pregnancy—even if she and Angus McBride had been together almost every night since they'd met? She shook her head at the number of inventive ways they'd found to be together, despite the close quarters and how difficult it was to be alone here. They'd never actually done it in a bed. Their moments together were short and stolen, so they'd made use of sheds, barns, and spare rooms at the bed and breakfast up at the manor. In the back seats of trucks tucked away in turnouts by the side of the road. In the woods down by Pittance Creek.

Angus was insatiable, and with him, so was she. She'd never experienced anything like it before.

And now she was pregnant.

There was no denying the results of this test stick. It was one of the modern ones that clearly stated "pregnant" or "not pregnant" in its little plastic-coated window. And it said "pregnant" clear as day.

What was she going to do?

Win closed her eyes, imagined taking Angus somewhere private and telling him about the baby, imagined the way he'd kiss her. The way he'd slowly undress her in that way he had. The way he'd make love to her tenderly, careful because of her pregnancy, until she urged him to take her the way she liked. Angus' passion—his pure enjoyment of the sexual act—was one of the things she loved about him. Things between her and Leif had been… well… tepid.

When her phone rang, Win nearly dropped the test stick into the toilet. She hurried to collect her purse, exited the stall, rushed to wash her hands—and the stick—at the sink, quickly dried them and answered just before the call went to voicemail.

"Hello?" She hadn't even checked the name of the caller.

"Win? It's Dad."

"Dad?" Not again. Not now. He'd berate her about turning down Leif again, most likely. Once she told her parents about the baby, those suggestions would have to end.

First she needed to tell Angus, though.

"You need to come home. Now."

End of Excerpt

The Cowboys of Chance Creek Series:

The Cowboy Inherits a Bride (Volume 0)
The Cowboy's E-Mail Order Bride (Volume 1)
The Cowboy Wins a Bride (Volume 2)
The Cowboy Imports a Bride (Volume 3)
The Cowgirl Ropes a Billionaire (Volume 4)
The Sheriff Catches a Bride (Volume 5)
The Cowboy Lassos a Bride (Volume 6)
The Cowboy Rescues a Bride (Volume 7)
The Cowboy Earns a Bride (Volume 8)
The Cowboy's Christmas Bride (Volume 9)

The Heroes of Chance Creek Series:

The Navy SEAL's E-Mail Order Bride (Volume 1)
The Soldier's E-Mail Order Bride (Volume 2)
The Marine's E-Mail Order Bride (Volume 3)
The Navy SEAL's Christmas Bride (Volume 4)
The Airman's E-Mail Order Bride (Volume 5)

The SEALs of Chance Creek Series:

A SEAL's Oath

A SEAL's Vow

A SEAL's Pledge

A SEAL's Consent

A SEAL's Purpose

A SEAL's Resolve

A SEAL's Devotion

A SEAL's Desire

A SEAL's Struggle

A SEAL's Triumph

The Brides of Chance Creek Series:

Issued to the Bride One Navy SEAL

Issued to the Bride One Airman

Issued to the Bride One Sniper

Issued to the Bride One Marine

Issued to the Bride One Soldier

The Turners v. Coopers Series:

The Cowboy's Secret Bride (Volume 1)

The Cowboy's Outlaw Bride (Volume 2)

The Cowboy's Hidden Bride (Volume 3)

The Cowboy's Stolen Bride (Volume 4)

The Cowboy's Forbidden Bride (Volume 5)

About the Author

With over one million books sold, NYT and USA Today bestselling author Cora Seton has created a world readers love in Chance Creek, Montana. She has twenty-eight novels and novellas currently set in her fictional town, with many more in the works. Like her characters, Cora loves cowboys, military heroes, country life, gardening, bike-riding, binge-watching Jane Austen movies, keeping up with the latest technology and indulging in old-fashioned pursuits. Visit **www.coraseton.com** to read about new releases, contests and other cool events!

Blog:

www.coraseton.com

Facebook:

facebook.com/coraseton

Twitter:

twitter.com/coraseton

Newsletter:

www.coraseton.com/sign-up-for-my-newsletter

www.ingramcontent.com/pod-product-compliance
Lightning Source LLC
Chambersburg PA
CBHW031659170626
46808CB00005B/1529

9781988896250